Copyright © 2022 by Zachary Ashford
First published in 2022 by DarkLit Press
Cover Art © 2023 by Jota Cravo
Illustrations © 2023 by Greg Chapman

ISBN 978-1-7387054-7-4 (Paperback)
ISBN 978-1-7387054-8-1 (Ebook)

PRAISE FOR
POLYPHEMUS

"This book is one hell of a ride. Ashford writes as easily about friendship, jamming, and obsession as he does about Faustian deals gone wrong and gore. His voice is assured and accessible, drawing you in; before you know it, you're three hours past midnight and two hundred pages in. *Polyphemus* is tragic, compulsive, and wonderfully laced with allusions to Greek myth and death metal. I swear you can hear the screaming vocals and thudding bass while you read. Highly recommended."

-Geneve Flynn, Bram Stoker and Shirley Jackson Award-winning author, editor, and poet

"A dark foray into a blackened world where Ashford drags the reader in one direction, fully knowing the horrors that await in all directions. *Polyphemus* is uncomfortable, compelling and perfectly depraved."

-Steve Stred, Splatterpunk-Nominated author of *Sacrament* and *Mastodon*

"This book is a swirling maelstrom of culty, cosmic darkness, wrapped in a smokey haze of crushing death metal and I loved every bloody second of it."

-Kev Harrison, author of *The Balance* and *Below*

"*Polyphemus* is a robust tale of addiction, masculinity, demons, and heavy metal. A big and brutal horror novel. Read it."

-Mike Thorn, author of *Shelter for the Damned* and *Darkest Hours*

"I devoured this book in a matter of hours. I was hooked by the depiction of death metal so authentic that I could HEAR the riffs! The deeply psychological and unflinchingly bleak portrayal of demonic influence and avarice was a wonderful train wreck to behold. One of the best books of the year!"

-Valkyrie Loughcrewe, author of *Crom Cruach*

"An unflinching odyssey into the abyss, where the seasons change but the ambitions, vices, and weaknesses of doomed humans don't. Zachary steps up his damnation game and impales decorum on the twinned horns of hallucinatory horror and heavy metal with the demented glee of a diehard fan. Crank *Polyphemus* to eleven and count yourself lucky if you make it out of the pit in one piece."

– Matthew R. Davis, Shirley Jackson Award-nominated author of *Midnight in the Chapel of Love* and *The Dark Matter of Natasha*

"A blood-soaked tale of compulsion and agony."

-Aron Beauregard, Splatterpunk Award-winning author of *Beyond Reform* and *Playground*

"*Polyphemus* is a dark deliverance into a world of death metal, Faustian deals and the cost of fame."

-Leanbh Pearson author of *Bluebells*

"Aggressive. Throaty. Distorted. Let the screaming begin.
Zachary Ashford's *Polyphemus* employs metal music as the very blood running through these pages. From the opening riffs to the twisted fade out on the last page. Every chapter hits harder than the last, the rhythm pounding in our ears, as we watch old friends come back together; some fighting their demons, while others embrace them. Ashford's mastery of language rivals great lyrical composers while creating characters that will live on with us long after they leave the stage.
I sorely need an encore."

-James Sabata, award-winning screenwriter, podcaster, and author of *Fat Camp*.

"A darkly realized heavy metal nightmare that takes an unflinching look at the cost of fame and the lengths the worst- and best- among us will go to achieve and maintain it. For anyone who's spent time in 'the scene,' the real horror may not come from the Mephisophelean elements but how well Ashford has captured the psychology of the banality of a very particular type of evil endemic to the entertainment world."

-Preston Fassel, IPPY Award Winning Author of *Our Lady of the Inferno* and *Beasts of 42nd Street*

BOOKS BY
ZACHARY ASHFORD

When the Cicadas Stop Singing

Sole Survivor

Sole Survivor 2

Autotomy Cocktail

The Encampment by the Gorge &
Blood Memory

ZACHARY ASHFORD

Polyphemus

DARKLIT
PRESS

CONTENT WARNING

The story that follows may contain graphic violence and gore.

Please go to the very back of the book for more detailed content warnings.

Beware of spoilers.

DEDICATION

If you know me, you'll know I dedicate to lots of people. I don't know if that flies in the face of the word, but I feel like it does. Either way, here we are.

So, first and foremost, just like I did with Sole Survivor, I have to start with Mum. Mum, you've been gone since 2014, and a LOT has changed since then. That said, your Stephen King books are still on my shelf. Your love of horror is still with me. The first time I saw those lurid horror paperback covers was when we were coming home from a trip to the library and I was inspecting your book-pile. I'll always have you to thank for this and for encouraging me to write. I miss you every day.

By the same token, my Uncle John, Mum's brother. The McGowans have been hit hard over the last few years, and stuck on the other side of the world, it feels like I'm just watching and not there participating in the support and love we all need. We lost John this year, and for me, John was as pivotal a figure in my reading as Mum. Yeah, the books were on her shelf, but he was the one who handed me Needful Things and told me I'd love it. John was a champion of a man. He was happy, funny, and lover of life. To you, Uncle John. See you at the big standing stones in the sky!

Next, my wonderful wife Ramona. Sasquatch, you're the best. Yeah, I'm punching in the looks department, but the way our minds work together, even when our opinions differ...just WOW! That's what life—and love—is all about. Thank you for helping me be a better person every day, for your tireless support of my writing, and for your patience when I start to burrow down into a project. I love you.

Finally, this may seem weird or contrived, but I really want to dedicate this to Trevor Strnad, the late front man of The Black Dahlia Murder. I know I included the band in the dedication of *Cicadas*, and those in the know will know I was watching TBDM at Soundwave when I got the news about Mum. As you can imagine, the band meant a lot to me.

Fast forward a few years...when I was writing this tome, it was not long after Trev had the good grace to accept a copy of Sole Survivor from me. I don't know if he ever read it. I hope so, but who knows? Of course, I wrote this with his band as my major soundtrack, and in the final days of finishing it, news about his passing came through. While I doubt he could identify me in a line-up, or even remember me, I first spoke to Trev as part of an interview for Tsunami Magazine in 2005. We spoke several times after that. In person at gigs, we shared drinks, and there were also a few more interviews. He was a true legend of the genre, and you've only got to check in with the Blast Fiends—and cover artist Jota Cravo—to know how loved he was. In a weird way, his death hit me hard.

So, Trev, this book, I really want to dedicate it to your memory. If you'll let me. You were a real one. Rest in power, legend!

CONTENTS

CHAPTER ONE
OF ROT AND RUIN

Nathan March's fingers danced across the fretboard like quicksilver spiders. His head bobbed in time to the rhythm he'd programmed into his metronome and he palm-muted the following riff as he changed the chord progression. He was halfway through it when the D string, dropped to a C to make it lower and fatter, snapped with a plink. He polished off the warm beer resting on his amplifier, drew a colder one from the small cooler beside his chair and cracked it open, enjoying the satisfying sound of air escaping the can.

He was restringing the guitar when someone knocked at the door. "Yo, hold up," he said. He spun the tuning peg to about the right position, snatched up a second brewski and walked to the door. "That you, Oaks?"

"Yeah, man. I made it."

The responding voice was quieter, meeker than he remembered. Shame could do that to a person, but he figured it would pass. It would take time, but he intended to start that journey tonight. "Get the fuck in here." He took Oaks's bag off him, thrust the beer into his hand, and wrapped him in a bro-hug. "I can't tell you how good it is to see you, dude." He pounded a fist on his childhood friend's shoulder and met his eyes. "It's all gonna be sweet, brother. It's all gonna be sweet."

"Come on; don't look at me like that. I'm clean. You think I'd have left the clinic otherwise?" Stephen Oaks, just

Oaks to most who knew him, embraced Nathan this time. "You've always been there for me, man. I wanna thank you for that."

Oaks appeared to be a million times healthier than when Nathan had last seen him. He'd cut his hair short; scraped a razor over it. The half-wasted corpse-look that plagued so many junkies had certainly gone out the window. Nathan waved the gratitude away. "Then come in. It's cold out there."

Nathan closed the door behind Oaks and showed him around the apartment. The short hallway led to a bachelor's lounge-room. The furniture: a couple of recliners, an old coffee table, and a futon, had come from separate garage sales, but the television was brand new. There were several Marshall amps stacked haphazardly around the place, and the bar fridge had a Marshall amp decal on it too. Despite that, walls adorned in tour posters pilfered from dozens of live gigs told the real story.

Nathan grinned when Stephen noticed the poster from their first ever show, a twenty-five-minute stint playing live before four other bands. Nathan, who always saw himself as a fan first and foremost, had been young and naïve enough to have the band that'd headlined sign it, and it was one of the only framed posters on the wall. There were horror movie posters and a few reprints of famous artworks there too. Above the television, a series of postcard-sized prints featuring Delacroix's images from Goethe's *Faust* had been pinned to the wall in a scattered mosaic. Opposite them, the first t-shirt design they'd ever sold at a live show had been framed as wall art. Their name, Polyphemus, lettered in a barely legible scrawl akin to a spider's web hovered over a giant Cyclops clutching a spear rammed through his eye. "What you reckon?" he asked his old friend.

"I used to love that fucking shirt. I think I gave it to some groupie chick like a total dumbass. Never treasured things like that, you know," Oaks said.

"It's nostalgia. I'm sure we could find you one." Nathan swigged a large gulp of beer then reached over and opened Oaks's can for him. "Here's to good friends and good health." He raised the can to his lips and waited for Oaks to do the same.

"Part of the whole deal is staying away from intoxicants. I shouldn't."

"Dude, how long have we known each other? Aren't I the straightest dude you know?"

"It's not the point."

"Did you bring drugs?" He didn't mean to use the tone he did, but it naturally came out that way.

Oaks sighed. "Jesus Christ, I haven't sat down yet. You know damn well I didn't."

"Then what harm can a couple of beers do? You're out, you're clean, and I haven't seen you in months. Drink the fucking beer." He held Oaks's sad gaze. "Brewski with a broski, man, just like the old days. Say cheers, you motherfucker."

"Cheers, you motherfucker." It sounded weak, but Oaks clinked his can against Nathan's and sipped lightly.

Nathan finished his long, deep swigs and wiped his mouth. He gestured to one of the recliners. "Now, you gonna tell me all about the nurses at the clinic or am I gonna have to keep using my imagination?"

Oaks picked up the acoustic guitar resting on a stand near his couch and gave it a peremptory strum. He twisted a tuning peg. Played a few chords. Moved through an old blues scale.

"Hey. Play that again."

"Play what?"

"Riff you just played."

"This one?" He played the chords he started with.

"No, man, the other one." Nathan picked up the electric he'd been playing earlier. "This one." He played something similar to the blues riff Oaks had busted out. It was familiar, not in the way that all old blues riffs are familiar, but in a more precise way that an exact riff from an established song is.

"This one?" Oaks played it. "Crossroads. Everyone knows it. Pretty much a standard."

Nathan flicked on his little 40-watt amp and switched off the distortion. Played the opening notes with Oaks. Cringed. Tuned to standard. Played it again and kept it going.

Oaks's eyes settled on the *Faust* postcards, then, once the riff had played through a couple of times he sang. "I went to the clinic, fell down on the stage." He grinned a big goofy grin at Nathan, a semblance of his old self in there.

Maybe, Nathan thought, *maybe everything's fine and he's been fixed.*

"I went to the clinic, nearly died, heroin. But there weren't no damn fine nurses. Only Mrs Palmer for meeeeeee."

Laughter consumed them. Beers, a mildly crude joke and a friend you haven't seen in a while had that effect. After a full belly-laugh, Nathan pulled a bag of weed out of a drawer in the coffee table. Oaks pointedly didn't pay attention. If this was the old Stephen Oaks, he'd be on that mull like a fly on shit. Nathan picked out a fine bud and dropped it into a bowl. He went to work with the scissors. "You still smoke?"

"I told you. It's the program. There's a whole bunch of faith-in-Christ, clean-living shit in it. I'm pretty sure it's helped."

"We got plenty of that at school. It didn't help then. I don't see why we can't smoke a spliff. It doesn't mean…"

"You don't have to say it. I know I fucked up, all right." He set the guitar down and sat on the couch. "I don't expect you to understand what it's like, and beers are one thing, but for you weed's nothing. For me, it was always part of the whole thing. It'd always start by getting ripped off my face with a good joint, then a couple of hours later I'd be on the nod floating away." He wiped his face with his hands. "You read Slash's book, right? You know how he talks about getting so fucked up he saw demons and shit. That never happened to me. What happened to me was worse. I fucked shit up for people I loved."

"Dude."

"No, not 'dude,' it's true. We were about to tour the world with the Violent Dead. That's the kind of tour that gives you some pull when the big festivals start making calls and that's where the respect and the kudos come from. All I had to do was stay straight and I was so fucked up it wasn't an option. You remember how hard you worked trying to keep me away from it?"

"It's the past. You're fine."

"Yeah, I'm fine, but you know how many people in that clinic were repeat visitors. Some of them, I don't know why they bother packing and unpacking. They should set up a room there."

"I had no idea."

"I don't want that to be me. I don't want to let you guys down again."

Nathan placed the bowl of weed into the drawer. He stood, stretched his arms and cracked his knuckles. "How about another beer?" He pulled Oaks into a headlock. "I've got you, man. Always have." He picked up the little cooler he kept by the couch and made his way to the fridge. He filled it with another six-pack and grabbed two extra beers out. "We've got the label breathing down our necks, though, man. They want us to find another vocalist pronto. They've given us three months before they sue us for breach of contract, and you know they've got technicalities for addiction and arrest in the fine print."

Oaks was rustling in his bag when Nathan offered the beer to him. "I need to show you these," he said, holding out a couple of small Moleskine notebooks. "Loads of time in there to write. I want to be the vocalist for Polyphemus again, man. I've been in since high school; you know it makes sense."

Nathan took a deep breath. He cracked his beer and took a big swig. "If it's entirely up to me, you know it's a done deal…"

"But it's not."

Oaks squeezed the books so tightly, Nathan was surprised they didn't crumble under the pressure. "You know full well that me and Spiros always talk about it. This has been our life – your life. But this is a career and there's a lot of trust that's not there anymore. We've got to rebuild all the momentum. We've got to convince promoters and producers and label reps that we've moved past what happened and that we're not…you know?"

"Not junkies? You can say it. You're not going to hurt my feelings." He took the beer and passed the notebooks to Nathan. "I've been beating myself up since it happened. You wake up from that spray they blast up your nose, that Narcan, and you know how badly you've let everyone down. If I could take it back…" He drank. "Let me show you some of the lyrics. I know you've been working on riffs and shit. You always do. Just talk to the boys. See if they're open to me coming to a jam sesh. I know everything's on me, but I can do that this week. It'll give the label something good to see too. I promise I won't let you down."

Nathan weighed the notebooks in his hands. Everyone made mistakes, and everyone had to live with the outcome of those mistakes, but while it was obvious Oaks needed something with some meaning in his life, he wasn't sure the touring circuit and all its temptations were the best option. "I'll do what I can."

Spiros Coumantouros tossed the tomato in the air and caught

it behind his back. He flicked it over his head, caught it in front of him this time, positioned it neatly on the cutting board and planted a kiss on his baby girl Calliope's forehead. "You see that, darling? All the years in your Pop's grocery store have prepared me for this day with you." Calliope giggled as he balanced a carrot on his nose.

For Spiros, time away from the band hadn't been a bad thing. Sure, he was aching to play music again, but spending weeks riding in a shitty rented van while your daughter grew up rapidly in your absence could be a downer. He flicked the carrot into the air, clapped twice, and caught it on the way down. "Now that, my sweet, is not something any grocer can do."

He knew she couldn't understand him yet, but that didn't make her laughter any less heart-warming. Thanks to their time in the storeroom of their father's grocery store, he and his brother could juggle anything: lettuces, carrots, cucumbers, pineapples, oranges, apples, and onions. You name it, they could have it wheeling and rolling through the air in pirouettes and tumbles before stacking it calmly on display without a blemish.

Funnily enough, it had only been a little while ago that his father had told him he'd known all along. "You always got the work done," his father had said. "With that in mind, I chose to let you play. You were happy and productive." Unfortunately, he hadn't been able to replicate that in his relationship with Calliope and Pandora. His dedication to the band was at odds with his family life. As a result, his wishes were often at odds with Pandora's expectations of a husband. He diced the carrot into soldiers, tipped it into the bowl with the spine of the knife and positioned it on the tray of the highchair. He lifted Calliope into place, buckled her in, tickled her nose and let her eat her lunch.

Pandora, Dora to those who knew her best, arrived home soon after, beeping the horn as she pulled into the driveway. Spiros met her in the garage, squatting on one knee so she would find him flexing and kissing his biceps like the proverbial Adonis when the roller-door opened. She pulled a face at him. He made a love-heart shape with his fingers then pinched his nipples and winked at her.

"The only thing that turns me on more than a man who doesn't take himself seriously is one who can carry all the shopping bags in one trip," she said, leaning her head out of the driver's window. "Do you think you're up to the challenge?"

"My love, God gave me these arms to carry things for you." He wrapped his arms around her and pretended not to know that he was squeezing her butt.

"First, you grab the bags, then you get to objectify me."

"Well that's not fair. You were objectifying me as you drove into this garage. I saw it in your eyes."

"What can I say? You are irresistible." She patted his ass. "How is Calliope?"

"As cute as a button." Spiros watched his wife kick off her shoes and hang her handbag on the rack inside the internal door. He followed her in with the shopping and together they unpacked the bags.

"Did you check your Facebook today?" she asked, tipping sugar into a jar. "Stephen is at Nathan's apartment. Why didn't you tell me he was out of rehab?"

Spiros dumped a bag of peas in the freezer and closed the door. "I didn't know. This is great news. Is he healthy?" He flicked his phone open. He had a couple of text messages from Nathan, a missed call, and a Facebook notification. In that time, he'd been so engrossed in hanging out with his family and having fun, he hadn't checked his phone. The notification led to a photo-post of Oaks and Nathan. Arms around each other's shoulders, they were clinking beers. Nathan had captioned the photo by tagging Spiros. *The boy is back in town! Just need Spiros to complete the triumvirate!*

Spiros responded to Nathan's last message, telling him he'd call later and asking how long Oaks was around. "His color is back," he said to Pandora. Spiros had spent weeks trying to convince the others that Oaks' overall pallor had been beyond sick in the weeks before the overdose. Oaks had gone missing for long stints, often turning up at their hotels in the early hours of the morning after disappearing with strange 'fans' the rest of them had never been introduced to. He'd become gaunt. His hair had thinned. His nails and teeth had browned to the color of old paperbacks. Spiros had thought Oaks had been *dusty* somehow. When he'd mentioned this to the others, only Nathan had seemed genuinely worried. Chops had been more easy-going about it. Despite Nathan's concern, he was worried about confronting Oaks and the effect it would have on the band right when they seemed to be gaining traction. His only proffered solution was to be there for Oaks when they were needed.

Pandora, having finished packing the groceries away, leaned on the kitchen bench and eyeballed her husband. "Do not tell me this means you are going to drop everything and run over there. Things have been so good here lately."

"Dora, come on, he nearly died. We've been friends since we were kids." He stepped closer. Reached out a hand. Calliope banged her bowl on the table and called for her mum.

Pandora went to her. "You have a family now. You will go see them and you will drink beer and you'll talk about making that album the label is hassling you for and from there...well, you know what happens from there." She unbuckled the baby from the highchair, lifted her to the ground and passed him the empty bowl. "Besides, if you were all such inseparable friends, why didn't they tell you this catch up was happening first?"

"They go way back. Also, they know I have a family." He stuck the bowl in the dishwasher. "Besides, I missed calls from Nathan." He showed her his phone. "Maybe I would have been there if I wasn't so caught up here."

He saw from her eyes that he had worded it wrong. The flare of her nostrils, the furrowing of her brow, the tightness of her lip; she was on the verge of tearing him a new asshole.

"Baby…"

"Don't you 'baby' me after that. It has been said. You were 'caught up' here. Caught. Up." She jabbed him in the chest. "You would always rather be playing guitar with your stupid friends."

"Baby, I didn't mean it like that."

"That's how you said it." She snatched a cloth from the sink, wiped down the highchair with rapid jerky movements, slammed it into its closed position and jammed it into the gap between the wall and the refrigerator.

"I'm going to call them later. I need to see how he is." He raised a hand as if to placate her with a truce gesture.

"Do what you want, Spiros. You always do." She yanked Calliope up off the ground and held her to her chest.

"It's a catch-up with friends. Nobody's mentioned getting the band together again."

"Don't you bullshit me, Spiros. I know you. You can't say no to anyone, least of all your friends when they cry poor."

"Baby, that's not fair and I'm not going to enter into that discussion. You know full-well that I may have to meet my obligations and record another album, so I will call them, and I will see my friend." She had started breathing through her nose. "Pandora, my love, I swear, I will not get 'caught up' in the band again."

"We'll see." Halfway up the stairs, she paused. "You better not let me down."

Johnny Woodrough, affectionately known as Chops, was

probably the least connected of all the band's members. He'd joined late after the band's first drummer, Josh Roberts, decided he'd rather get a university degree and a real job. He'd barely written any music and had always maintained an air of distance from the close-knit relationships the other members shared, so when he'd received a call from The Violent Dead's vocalist, Henry Traine, and been asked if he wanted to catch up for a bit of a jam, the answer was simple. *Fuck yes.*

When he arrived at Symbolic Studio and Jam Room, Traine was smoking a joint in the car park with the band's bass player Scott Maddox. They sat on a handrail running the length of the stairs leading to a raised loading dock. The entire studio used to be an old warehouse and the current tenants had made it a glorified outdoor lounge-room and al fresco area. It was littered with salvaged garden furniture. The concrete wall and steel roller-doors had been graffitied and blanketed in tags and street art. Chops parked the van next to the loading bay and signaled the two friends. "Traine, Scotty, how are you?"

Traine, clearly blazing, raised the devil horns. "Sup, mofo? Glad to see you made it." He took another hit from the joint. "Park her there for now, bro. We'll get your kit out and then you can move her wherever." He tittered. "You wanna hit this?"

He did. Twice. He shook Traine's hand and stepped over to Scotty who was waiting by the rear door of the old van. "Good to see you again, my man."

"Hope you bought your double-kick. The new shit's fast." The bass player pulled equipment out of the van and took it up the stairs.

A couple of hours later, Chops and the other three members of The Violent Dead sat at one of the recycled tables, chopping a fat bowl of weed and sinking a few beers. As far as jam sessions went, it had been solid. Before leaving home this morning, he'd been worried the guys would be a level above him technically and, as a result, would think he wasn't good enough. That hadn't been the case at all. Whenever Scotty or the band's guitarist Ricky Marko had pushed him for a quick time-signature change or wanted to play faster, he'd matched them every step of the way. He pulled a chunky bud from his own baggie and threw it into the bowl. "What's the go with Howie?"

The other guys looked at each other for a moment, clearly communicating with facial expression, before Scott shrugged and Traine answered. "He needs some time. Got family shit to deal with."

"Yeah, well, we know how that goes."

"What's happening with Oaks? He off the stuff?"

Chops opened both palms and assumed a 'who knows' pose. "I dunno, but he's out of the clinic. He was hanging with Nate last night." He brought the photo up on his phone. "Fingers crossed he's clean and stays clean."

The bong bubbled and the smoke swirled inside, initially in cycling wisps before it became a concentrated grey cloud. Just as abruptly, it vanished. Scott took the hit, coughed politely and passed the Macgyvered juice bottle to Traine. "How about Polyphemus? You guys still jamming?"

Chops met the bass player's eyes. "We haven't spoken about it, but it seems kinda done to me." He watched Traine spark the lighter and pull the cone. "We've jammed a few times since, but it hasn't been the same since the last night we played with you dudes."

"You haven't talked about it?" Ricky asked. He was the quietest guy in The Violent Dead, and Chops felt like he barely knew him despite the fact they'd toured together on a couple of occasions. Traine had done the talking when it came to getting him here, but Chops knew that it would be Ricky who had the final say – and the power of veto – when it came to any future opportunities he had to jam with The Violent Dead. The guitarist passed him the billy. "What do you want to do?"

Chops pinched some weed and packed a cone. "Man, it's not easy. The other three guys, they're tight as hell; known each other for years, but as you know, I came across from Bone Totem." Bone Totem had come to a fiery end shortly after their vocalist started fucking the guitarist's wife. Before that, they'd been reasonably successful within their own little niche. Slightly more of a hardcore band than a metal one; they'd gone a lot further and sold a lot more records than Polyphemus. "Seems to me that once a guy goes down after something like that, you need to reconsider. I don't think they'll continue without him, and I don't know if the road is the best place for him." It felt disrespectful to talk about Oaks this way. "All that aside, I want to play the drums. I want to hit the road; nail some groupies. I've got to worry about myself and I can't wait forever for them to work it out." He hit the bong and passed it to Scott.

"It seems to me," Ricky said, "we've got a mutual interest in doing this again. Howie's going to be out of action for a while, and we've been asked to play some shows. We need a good pro to fill in. Why don't you do it while Oaks works out his demons and the others make their minds up?"

Chops nodded. He knew what he wanted to do; but he didn't want to seem too eager. A shot at joining The Violent Dead was impossible to turn down. With three gold records and regular inclusion on the big festival bills, it was a no-brainer.

CHAPTER TWO
DEMANUFACTURE

Oaks hated cockroaches. With their shiny backs, long antennae and spindly legs, they had creeped him out ever since he was a kid. The fact his new room was in a house full of them was only one of many downsides about the place. The protocol for the rehab center he'd spent the last six months in was that every client leaving had to spend three months living in an approved facility with certified personnel. Apparently, this would ensure recovering addicts could live on the outside and reintegrate into society without relapsing into addiction. He knew bullshit when he saw it, though. This place was rife with two things: cockroaches and junkies.

In the week he'd been here, he'd seen several strangers come, hang around long enough for a coffee and leave again after disappearing down the hallway with nurse Amielle. There was always someone on-duty to ensure Oaks wasn't getting on the gear, but if Amielle wasn't selling drugs, he didn't know what she was up to.

She was a squat little mouse of a woman. Her hair was a birds-nest and her eyes constantly darted from left to right. If she was selling drugs, then staying here wasn't going to be easy. He still wanted to get high. He'd done the six months, and he was clean and sober and past the withdrawals, but he remembered the drug fondly. He wasn't sure that was ever going away. He fidgeted with the earphones adorning his shorn head like satellite dishes and dialed the volume to ten. Hopefully, he'd be able to wash thoughts of using away with a cacophony of noise.

Hanging out with Nathan had been a great distraction. More than that, it had been a chance for him to reconnect with the man who had always been a brother to him. Oaks knew the way things had broken down at the end of The Violent Dead tour was solely down to his own addiction and more than anything he wanted to atone for that. Given some clarity on those events by his time in the clinic, he'd been able to reflect on how he'd blown the chance the band had of becoming big. Even if they didn't make it huge, they would have been a widely respected player in the scene. The reality of playing in a band like Polyphemus was that that level of success was pretty much the best you could hope to achieve. Sure, occasionally a metal band blew up like Mastodon or System of a Down, played some mainstream festivals and received a Grammy, but any real fan knew those bands were only the tip of the iceberg and the best stuff was in the shifting sands of renown beneath that apex of success.

If he hadn't fucked it all up, there was every chance the tour with The Violent Dead—who were firmly entrenched in that second tier, selling out shows across the world and posing for the cover of magazines like *Decibel*—would have cemented his band in that echelon. He could picture thousands of fans wearing black Polyphemus t-shirts as they moved around their various cities and attended other bands' gigs; he could picture the Dan Seagrave album cover adorning the record that'd be hailed as their breakthrough; and he could imagine himself, the well-loved vocalist, posing in the forefront on their own magazine cover. All he needed to do was show the other boys that he was clean and that he'd never let them down again. He tore out the page he was writing on, balled it up and flicked it at two cockroaches copulating at the foot of the coffee table. They scuttled away, darting underneath the television cabinet. He needed to get through these next few months if it was ever going to happen.

He was scribbling lyrics in his notebook when the front door opened and nurse Amielle came home. She'd brought a guy with her this time. A skinny little dude with a balding pate, nosferatu ears weighed down with jewelry, a simple black business shirt over black jeans, calf-high leather boots, and half a dozen rings studded across long, slender fingers. The man sauntered in like a proud tomcat, a half-sneer on his face. He levelled his cold blue eyes on Oaks then came across to shake hands. "You're the rockstar. Stephen, isn't it?" His hand was clammy. Uncomfortable. "Anton Pieralski."

"I wouldn't go that far, but yeah, I played in a band."

Anton made no attempt to hide the fact he was eyeballing Oaks's arms. He wouldn't find any track-marks here. "I see you're writing. You getting straight into it?"

Oaks closed the notepad. "Just jotting some shit down."

"Anton," the nurse said. "Stop scaring the houseguests." She nodded at the bedroom down the hallway. Anton smiled in response.

"You'll have to excuse me, Stephen. I do hope we can continue our discussion later. I'd certainly like to hear all about life on the road." He gestured at the notepad. "Perhaps I can see some of what you're writing?"

Sharing his lyrics with this guy was the last thing he wanted to do, but despite knowing full well that Anton's being here meant he was up to no good, he couldn't help but feel pleased that he'd been paid some positive attention. So far, no one except Nathan had treated him with any degree of respect since he'd entered the clinic, let alone left it. Even the counsellors and doctors there thought he was nothing but a filthy heathen scumbag. "There's nothing worth sharing in here. Not yet, anyway."

Anton shrugged with a jovial smile. "When it's ready. No stress here." He gestured to the clearly agitated nurse. "I'd better get to business. I'll be out soon."

Oaks watched the two of them walk down the hallway. His belly tightened when he noticed Anton had a small satchel with him. He rubbed his hands and focused on the notepad on the coffee table. One of the cockroaches had climbed up a table leg. The other was tentatively poking its head out from under the television cabinet. He had to get some fresh air, some exercise, anything. He crunched the roach with his pad. Goo spurted over the book's cover and onto the table. He wiped it up and went out into the suburban night where he could sit on the driveway and pretend everything was okay.

Unlike the city, where he'd spent the greatest part of his adult life, he was struck by the silence of everything in the suburbs. The sound of cars droning up and down the highway could be heard in the distance and bats fluttered overhead, but for the most part it was the rustling of leaves in the balmy breeze, the crackling of a bug-zapper on a porch across the road and the occasional swell of canned laughter from a too-loud television. Last night, he'd kept his fears about relapsing to himself. Nathan had always been quick to check his negativity with an obsessively positive attitude. Nathan wouldn't understand how much the urge to search the house tempted him. Shit, on a number of occasions he'd directly asked the nurse if he could scum a boost. *Just one fix, man*, like the Ministry song. It was all he needed to remind himself that he hated it. That he didn't want to get high again. But how could he tell anyone that?

"Taking a breather?" The hard heels of Anton's leather boots clipped the concrete as he approached. "Mind if I sit?" He held out an open cigarette packet. Oaks took one and the black-clad man sparked it for him. "It's not easy getting on your feet again."

"You've been there?"

Anton hesitated. "Not in the same way you have, no, but many of my friends have been there and we all have our own vices. There are things in my life I would never give up. Things that hold me under their sway and insist I give them everything I have. Your addiction is no different."

Again, Oaks felt he should hate what this man was saying to him. What did he know about addiction? How big were his balls if he would comment on it so freely? The only time he'd ever met anyone with similar confidence in openly discussing the weakness of others was the priest who doubled as a school chaplain at St Quirinus, where he, Nathan and Spiros had gone to school together. This guy, this Anton, spoke with the same self-effusive manner, but for some fucked-up attention-seeking reason it came across as charming. Oaks had no doubt Anton would be a hell of a salesman. "I know what you mean," he said. "I've never submitted to it, though. I was never under its sway; I just like to get high."

Anton wrapped an arm around his shoulders. "I'm not going to argue, semantics, but while I admire your courage in refuting its dominion over you, my point stands. Somewhere down the line you believed sticking a needle in your arm was more important than achieving your dreams." He dragged on his cigarette and casually exhaled the smoke from his nostrils. "If I could be so forward, I know your story. When Lisa told me you were coming to this house and that you were in a 'famous' band, I took the liberty of looking you up."

He was so smug, but Oaks listened anyway. "I wouldn't say we were famous."

"Oh, no, of course not. I doubt your music—if it can be called that—has ever made you a cent. Don't get me wrong, I know there's plenty of talent in what you metal guys do, but there are few who translate that into serious money, and you were small-time. Yes, you had some good records according to the indie presses, but you weren't in danger of breaking into *Rolling Stone* any time soon."

"It's not the point of the genre though is it?"

"That's the usual catch-cry when people say they don't like it. I've worked with enough fans of bands like yours to know that's what they all say when they have to defend its lack of popularity among the wider masses."

Oaks nodded his head. He'd used the argument himself on many occasions before this conversation and he'd no doubt use it again. Shit, he'd told people that half the fun was in 'blowing the minds' of those who didn't get it. "It's not wrong to say that, though."

Anton patted his knee. "You're right, maybe it's not, but I can't help but think that's because of those who don't dream big enough. Some certainly make it to the top of the charts, but it's become a self-fulfilling prophecy. By this point, you play music no one likes for people no one likes." A dog across the street barked.

"That's not a fair assessment. People do like it. Maybe not tons and tons of them, but it's music that has meaning for millions. It's not like you have to travel far to find metal-heads."

Anton checked at his watch and fiddled with one of his rings. "Maybe you're right. I may be giving away my predispositions to something I find so gaudy and juvenile, but it's neither here nor there, and perhaps I haven't been polite. What I wanted to do, rather than insult you, was offer the hand of friendship. I work with many who are in situations like yours and I think you should come and hang out sometime. There's a group of us. We all work to ensure we're getting the best out of life and we make plans to give ourselves the best chance of getting what we want."

It sounded like pseudo-Christian bullshit to Oaks, but considering the satchel and his certainty this man was providing the nurse with her stock of drugs, there couldn't be anything Christian about him. And yeah, it sounded like psycho-babble, or at least the early stages of it, but the idea seemed tempting. Company outside of his remaining circle was exactly what he needed to ease himself into the real world. "Yeah, I think I'd like that," he said.

With the lapping splash and hiss of the tide rolling in beyond the sand dunes, Nathan jerked lightly on his fishing rod and enjoyed the late-night squawking of the seagulls. This particular spot of the river overflow, tucked in behind the beach-front and obscured by mangroves, had long been a favorite. They had first been brought here by Spiros's old man when they were school-boys and he had shown them how to bait a hook, cast a line, and sit around talking shit for hours. Since then, they'd maintained the tradition. To his left, Spiros fumbled around in a tackle-box. "Are you gonna shine a light down here any time soon or would you like to wait until I stab myself with a fishing hook?"

"I didn't know that was an option." Nathan sipped on his beer, flashed the light obnoxiously in Spiros's face, and then flicked it off. "Fuck, dude, battery's dead. You're gonna have to stab yourself."

"I can hurt you. I can hurt you real bad."

"Oh, wait, here it is. All fixed." Nathan shone the light on his upraised middle finger and laughed like a filthy old man. Spiros, never one to resist roughhousing with the boys, leaned across and flipped Nathan's chair. The pony-tailed bass-player landed on the sand. His beer spilled out in hiccupping glugs. Laughing robustly, Spiros snatched up Nathan's phone, shone it in his friend's face and stuck his own finger up.

"This is what we call 'chairing' someone up, Nathan. I hope you are feeling better now." His ridiculous grin did nothing to stop Nathan's laughter. He'd never claim it was the joke, but he'd definitely make out like there was nothing wrong with it at this moment in time. He shone the torch on the tackle-box. "I'm glad we could use this moment to lighten up the mood." He plucked a swivel and a night-lure from the box.

Nathan stood up and brushed the sand off his clothes. "See, this is why Pandora doesn't want you coming out to play, my friend. She knows you're a rogue." He picked up his rod and turned the reel a couple of times to tighten the line.

"Don't joke about it. She thinks the band is done and she likes it that way. I am at home when the band is dead, and to her, the band is dead."

Only yesterday, Nathan realized how long it had been since they'd considered booking in a practice session. He'd never considered that the band might be dead and buried, but this wasn't the first time he'd heard others say it might be. "Is that what you think?"

Spiros paused contemplatively. "I think 'limbo' is the word I would use."

This made sense. In the weeks right after Oaks's overdose they had held off on their regular practice sessions out of respect for their friend. Like everything, though, without paying specific attention to the time that had passed, it had fallen to the wayside and been forgotten like a molding container of take-out in the fridge. Nathan's mum had never let him throw those containers in the trash. Instead, he had to clean out the shit and scrub away the mess until they were as good as new. It was strange how a little lesson like that could bleed into your morals, but it had. From shitty girlfriends he'd dated too long to an inability to give up on riffs he hadn't been able to sell the rest of the band on, Nathan could never forsake something. He was not a quitter. He hardly ever bought new containers and he couldn't imagine playing in any band other than Polyphemus. "Okay, so limbo. Is it time we rescued it?"

Spiros cast his line into the water. "Stop beating around the bush. Tell me what you discussed with Stephen."

Nathan knew Spiros's gift for quick banter came from an astute mind. When it was time for a serious chat, the Greek was always a step ahead. "Pretty simply, he's keen to get it happening again."

"It's not so simple, though. At the moment, everything is on hold, but we have contracts and obligations. We cannot have the same thing happen again. Remember the bad press last time. Websites and magazines that had never so much as reviewed one of our albums happily wrote us off, and our name is somewhere close to mud for many. That shit does damage." He slapped at a mosquito on his leg. "Our name is a brand. Do you think that I could sell people shit veggies or, worse, invite them into one of my stores and give them empty shelves? That's what happened at that concert. People expected to see us play and they saw a man collapse thirty seconds into the set. I would fire a staff-member who did this. On top of that, I have to consider my family." He jerked his line and slotted the base of the rod down into a stainless steel rod-holder he'd pressed into the sand. "This time at home; it's been good for me. I am getting to know my daughter and my wife is happy. I can't say she will stay that way if we go on tour again."

Nathan, in his desire to create one of the most impressive death metal bands in the world, had always eschewed the trappings of relationship, family, and career. Listening to Spiros liken the band to a job felt strange. For him, the desire to press ahead was all important and nothing else mattered. "I don't see how it would affect your relationship."

"Because you can't, Nathan. You've never had one. You don't know what it is to think of others before you think of your own desires. I sometimes wonder if we would have remained friends if I had left when Josh did."

That hit Nathan hard, but he knew what Spiros was doing. "It's not like Josh ever gets in contact. It goes both ways."

"No doubt, but what I am driving at is that you have a one-track mind when it comes to this band. The facts of the matter with Josh are arbitrary. It's not about who's right and wrong, it's about whether you are judging this as you should be. You want to move forward regardless of if it's right for me, right for Chops, right for you, and right for Stephen." He grabbed Nathan's shoulders. "I love you, my friend, but while Pandora thinks I'm obsessed with this, I always have your obsession to reflect on. What has this band already cost you and what more might it cost us if we press ahead?"

Nathan reeled his line in, shone a torch on the unbaited hook and speared another prawn onto it. He cast the line into the water again, loving the whirr of the reel unspooling through the night air and the splash the lead weight and baited hook made as they dropped into the softly churning water. He slotted his rod into the rod-holder, cracked a fresh beer, and pulled a joint from a tin box in his pocket. "I get what you're saying with it all, and I'll be honest and tell you, I'm not sure this is what's right for everyone at the moment, but I need to make music. You have your stores. You've got it made. I'm broke as hell. We came so close last time and then it all went to shit. You didn't see Steve last night." He lit the joint. "He needs something in his life. He was practically begging me. Shit, he brought lyrics, dude. If we say no, then I don't know what sort of message that sends. What that'll do to him." He passed the joint over to Spiros. "I've been writing riffs. Good riffs. We owe the label one more and we have notoriety now. We could call it something cheesy to make a statement. *The Comeback* or some shit like that."

The Greek faltered. "It's a bit out of tone with the other titles. Still…" He caressed his manicured beard and took a hit from the joint. "Were these lyrics any good?"

"I took photos. They're personal, as they should be, but you know how he is; hiding it all in metaphors and allegory. Motherfucker was always a talented writer."

"Send them to me. Let me see them." He passed the spliff. "You know I need to talk to him, yes?"

Nathan's fishing rod bent down and sprung back. The spool spun as a fish took the bait. He snatched the rod up and jerked it, reeling it in with a grin on his face.

CHAPTER THREE
THE NECROTIC MANIFESTO

Oaks had thought long and hard before dialing Anton's number, but despite his reservations, he couldn't think of a reason not to call. If worse came to worst and Anton wasn't a life-coach as he'd advertised, then Stephen would be able to test his willpower and refuse the opportunity to poison himself. After all, wasn't that his biggest concern? Wasn't he scared shitless that this was all a ruse to get him hooked on the smack again? As his cab moved closer to the city, he watched the landscape change from isolated houses on the outskirts of the suburbs to clusters of commercial and industrial buildings, and then to strip-malls, nightclubs and apartments. When it came to a stop at the address Anton had given him, he was dwarfed by high-rises. He thanked the driver, paid him, and got out of the cab.

It was a warm night. The street around him ebbed with the absorbed heat of a hot summer day and sparkled with the lights of gentrified restaurants, trendy bars and opulent marks of wealth. There were wine bars here. Craft breweries. Not a dive-bar in sight. The patrons, half-pissed and seemingly unfettered by the constraints of broken homes, low income, mental instability, and the chemical dependencies he'd always thought of as real-life, moved freely along the streets. They weren't hunched with their hands in their pockets and their eyes down. This was the kind of place you could move around without fear of being jumped or mugged. There were no homeless people and no junkies lounging in the doorways and alcoves of the streets. People seemed happy.

The bar he wanted, the Exchange, was ahead. Its deliberately understated signage certainly didn't stand out in the way he'd been taught advertising should; instead, it was a small sign with the bar's name in simple white font. The sign itself wasn't so small that you could miss it, but it didn't seem to be inviting every passer-by inside either. In the doorway, a hulking security guard wearing a smart button up shirt and chinos surveyed the street as if there might be a threat coming at any moment. Having spent his time in the rougher parts of the city, Oaks knew what sort of nonsense bars in dodgy areas had to deal with when the undesirables came knocking. He found it hard to believe a bar like this had ever dealt with any trouble at all.

The security guard observed his approach, casually raising a hand and requesting identification when Oaks stopped at the door. "You got a booking?" he asked.

Oaks craned his neck. It wasn't easy to see around the guard. "I'm meeting someone here. Anton Pieralski? Do you know him?"

The guard grunted. "ID?" He waggled his finger, encouraging Stephen to pass it to him. He scanned it into the machine and handed it back. He pressed a few icons on the touchscreen then stepped to the side, allowing Oaks to move past him. "Go to the counter. You're on the door-list."

He hadn't been on a door-list for a while, and the mere fact of it gave him pause to bask in a little satisfaction. Perhaps he was someone special after all. Someone certainly thought so.

The girl at the counter took him through a door leading to some stairs. He followed them to a room where Anton and several other people lounged on plush couches, laughing and drinking in small groups.

Around them bottles of wine rested in ornate ice buckets, bizarre statues haunted pedestals and recessed alcoves, paintings hung from walls, off-kilter lights cast down their cold glow at odd angles and strange ornaments rested in bizarre repose across side tables and shelves. It was, he decided, markedly different from what he had expected.

"You made it!" Anton clapped his hands together and beckoned him to come and join the party at his plush leather couch. "These are some of the people I was telling you about. The ones who make sure their lives give them everything they want." He introduced about five people with a quick namedrop in perfunctory fashion. Handshakes were exchanged and, from somewhere, a drink was thrust into Oaks's hand.

When he had left home that night, he had assumed his usual reluctance to get involved in a social setting would see him hitching an early ride home, but the easy affability and genuine openness and humor of Anton and his friends made sure Oaks felt like he belonged with people like this. They were so welcoming it would have been impossible not to want to stay, but it didn't hurt that soon after his first couple of drinks he'd found himself alone with a petite little chick named India.

She squeezed herself in between him and the others after returning from a bathroom break, but as time had drifted and the night went on, she sidled closer and closer to him until she was practically sitting on his lap. Oaks was no stranger to the overtures of women in bars, but while he'd had no shortage of girls—and sometimes guys—throwing themselves at him, this wasn't exactly what she was doing. The vocalist for a band gets to know that kind of behavior pretty quickly, but India wanted something different. At first, she kept both of them engaged in the general conversation at the table, but when it lulled and some of the others went to play some pool, she planted a demure little kiss on his cheek. "Tell me," she said. "What do you think of this place?"

Oaks let her study his face while he considered his

response. "Truth be told, it's not the kind of place I'd have picked to hang out in on my own." He'd usually hang out in dive bars and live music venues, but he couldn't complain. The drinks here were strong, and after drinking at Nathan's and not relapsing, he felt confident with alcohol in his system. Especially when the drinks were free. "I'm glad I came, though. I wasn't sure how it'd turn out, but I've had a blast." He held her gaze as she bit her lip.

She leaned in as if she was going to kiss him. When he followed suit, she pulled away and pressed a finger to his lips, forcing him to pause. "When did you get out?"

"A couple of weeks ago." He leaned in, tried to kiss her again. He couldn't remember telling her about that. "Did Anton tell you?"

"Nuh-uh, we've all been there. I've been out about eighteen months. Couldn't have done it without him." The life-coach nodded and tipped his drink to her. "He's helped me achieve more than I ever thought possible."

There it was again, that idea of making the most out of life, of getting 'what you wanted'. "How so? I've heard him talk about getting everything life can give you, but I can't see what that means."

"You see that painting on that wall over there?" She pointed to a work of art hanging above a fireplace. "That's mine. I gifted it to him after my first gallery show." The painting was a vivid and somewhat ghastly take on sacrifice. It featured dozens of figures leaning over a prone woman on a blood-stained altar. The sky was black, roiling with clouds and winged reptiles. "I'd never been able to make my paintings pop the way they should have, you know? Thanks to the work I've done with Anton, I've been able to paint better than ever before, and I've been getting recognition for them too. I have a gallery coming up at the Modern Art Museum. I'll take you there during the week if you want." She leaned in, brushed her lips lightly against his.

How the fuck could Anton help someone become a better

painter? It seemed ridiculous, but he could see in her eyes she was telling the truth. "What does he do exactly?"

"Shit, I couldn't spill his secrets, but it's all mental. He gives you the belief in yourself and I guess you'd call it the tools to make sure you get what you deserve." Oaks inspected her painting again. It was good. He could easily picture it in a museum. "It's not easy though," she said. "It's worth it, but you've got to have the dedication to make it work. I guess that's why it's so effective with those of us who've been addicted in the past. It's like he gives you a new addiction. A new obsession to dive into and immerse yourself in. If the thing you want is linked to your passion, there's no way it can ever go wrong." She climbed properly onto his lap and pressed her lips firmly against his. "I haven't used since before I went in. Considering I relapsed the first few times I tried rehab, I'm happy Anton's been there since I came out."

Oaks could feel his cock getting hard underneath her and judging by the way she subtly ground her pelvis against it, she'd felt it too. "What does he do in his sessions?" He kissed her neck.

"I'm pretty sure it differs from person to person, but you only have to ask him."

Anton seemed to be watching the two of them intensely. Again, Oaks wasn't bothered when Anton did the sort of thing that would usually make him feel terribly uncomfortable. You get used to making out with people in front of your mates when you're in a touring band but having someone watch so intently was weird. India leaned in to nibble on his earlobe. The coach nodded to Oaks and went towards the restroom. "What did he do with you in your session then?"

India tapped her nose. "I can't tell you." She hopped off him and pulled him to his feet. "It's a trade secret." She grabbed her empty glass from the side table and poured the last minuscule drops onto her extended tongue. In the soft light of the club, and with the way she caught his eye as she did it, it was a titillating and overtly sexual thing to do. "Come on," she said. "We need to get more drinks."

Anton was at the bar when they arrived. He had his arm around the shoulders of a young man with a skull tattooed onto his head. "The two lovebirds have arrived," he said. "Tom, you already know the beautiful India, but this newcomer is Stephen. It's his first night here."

Tom shook Oaks's hand and hugged India. "You two certainly seem to be hitting it off," he said. "I never got a welcome like that when I first came here." He laughed, and India slapped at his arm. "Did India show you her painting? Tell you about her art show?"

"Not up close, but I have seen it. She mentioned a gallery at the Museum of Modern Art. Impressive stuff." Oaks drew her close. "She says a lot of it is down to Anton."

"No," Anton said. "I may have cleared the path for her, but it's all her own work. She made the sacrifices. It would be wrong of me to take any credit."

"You can take some for my work though, can't you?" Tom asked. "One year clean and I've already claimed my first title."

"Again, my friends, I know how to show you which path to take. This is where my influence ends. You make the decisions from there."

"He's too modest," India said. "My gallery is opening this week. Thomas is seriously hurting people in the ring. He has helped us both more than he'll admit. He'll help you too if you give him a chance." She nuzzled his neck.

"If Stephen would like to talk about coaching, I'd be more than happy to accommodate. Tonight, though? Tonight is for fun. Why don't you two run along and find somewhere to get to know each other a little better?"

"Just remember," Thomas said. "If it ain't on, my friends, then *it* ain't on."

Laughing, Oaks led the girl to the couch where they had

first met. He brushed her dark hair, shot through with a red streak, from her face and kissed her again. He didn't know why he felt so open to letting go of himself, but he knew that he wanted more of this girl. He leaned forward and whispered into her ear. Moments later, they were waiting outside The Exchange for a cab.

With Spiros all but on board, Nathan dropped the filleted flathead into the pan with relish. He'd missed playing live shows and recording songs in the studio. If all of this went according to plan, he'd have the band jamming again within the week and that made him happy. Of course, the biggest roadblock was probably going to be Chops. He was a bloody good drummer, but he'd always seemed to be with them only because his other options were limited. Nathan sometimes felt Chops thought he was better than Polyphemus, and he'd move on as soon as he got the chance. When he'd voiced his thoughts to the others, he'd been shut down quickly. Spiros, in particular, told him he needed to give people a chance and that, in all honesty, they were lucky to have the drummer at all. And they had been. It had been his contacts through Bone Totem that scored them higher profile gigs. Nathan flipped the fillet over then spun through the list of contacts in his mobile phone, stopping at Chops's number. He saw the date of the last call. Could it have been two months since they'd last spoken?

He tapped out a quick message to the drummer. By the time he'd taken the fish out of the pan and dumped it on some scrambled eggs he had a response. He sent another, scarfed his food, and flicked on his guitar amp. The perfectly crisp hum of the amp's internal circuitry always gave him a little thrill. It reminded him of a well-oiled machine and the fact it sounded so good at low levels made it perfect for use in his apartment. He fingerpicked his way through some warm-ups and eyed the bass in the corner. Later on today, if luck was on his side, he'd have to give that thing a serious workout. While he always played guitar in his spare time and wrote most of the guitar riffs that weren't exclusively lead-work, the bass was his weapon of choice when the band played live. They'd toyed with the idea of a dedicated bass-player and on occasion, Rusty Walker, another friend of Chops's would do some work in the studio for them, but to most people who knew the band, Nathan was the bass-player. If he could get Polyphemus going again, he would have to change that. Rusty had always threatened to become a full-time member and having two guitarists gave any band a wealth of melodic options in a live setting. On top of that, having Rusty as a member might be the sweetener Chops needed to commit to at least one more album. If anything could provide the double-tap and make sure Polyphemus were well and truly defunct, it would be searching for another drummer.

When his phone went off again, he thought it might be Chops letting him know he'd changed his mind and wasn't going to come for a jam at all. It wasn't. It was a groupie chick he'd banged a few times, Lisa. To say they'd dated would be overstating things by a long stretch of the imagination, but he'd kept her around on the casual for a couple of months. When she'd started acting like she wanted it to be more serious, trying to engage him in actual conversations and asking him what he wanted from life, he'd cut it short. She was a hot little number, but the last thing he wanted was a girl to leech his time away from him. That was the fast train to low productivity, and if there was one thing he had to be, it was productive. In the last few months, he had written a good dozen or so songs structured with the necessary framework and a few embellishing riffs for when he could get everyone together again. As far as he was concerned, having a chick around would mean none of that shit was possible. He'd seen how Pandora had affected Spiros and his dedication. That shit could piss right off. He'd have the band on its feet soon, and no one was going to stop that. He replied, telling her they'd have to catch up some other time: he had plans this afternoon.

Chops arrived a short while later. He'd grown his beard out since Nathan had seen him last, and his hair had matted into thin dreadlocks. "How the fuck are you?" He clasped Nathan's hand in both of his and dropped in an affectionate shoulder-bump as well.

"I'm good, man. How about you? Long time no see." It honestly was good to catch up. Despite his mistrust of the drummer's commitment to the band, he'd always liked him as a person. He had his eccentricities, but he was a good bloke and when he was playing, his neck-snapping precision and drive for excellence made sure the wall of blast-beats that burst from his kit gave the band a bone-crushing heaviness.

"I'm not gonna complain," the drummer said. "I've been keeping myself busy. Making sure I have work coming on the side: teaching kids, doing some labor hire, a little bit of studio work. You know how it is." He handed Nathan the framework for his electric kit and went to the van to grab the rest of it.

By the time they were set up and ready to play, they were two beers deep. Nathan hadn't broached the idea of having Oaks come for a jam to try to repair everything that had happened, but there was an easy brevity to their jam session. They ploughed through some of their favorites and a few covers before Nathan ripped out some of the song skeletons he'd been writing. Chops listened intently, head cocked like a dog hearing something on the horizon as he concentrated on the groove. He started tapping out a basic beat, tricking out the metronome standards Nathan had used when writing them, before adding the double kick and blast beats that hinted at the power the riffs would possess when they became fully fleshed songs. When they got to the end of the first song, Nathan was left with a satisfied grimace. "I've been thinking," he said. "You think Rusty would wanna jam some, consider joining full-time?"

Chops leaned on his stool. "You're up to something, my man." He rolled a hairband off his wrist and pulled his dreads into a ponytail. "What did you and Oaks talk about the other night? He want to sing again?"

There it was. Open. Ripe for debate. Nathan briefly considered how he should answer but figured this wasn't a time for bullshit. "You know he does." He let it linger in the air while Chops mulled it over.

The drummer started to speak. Paused. "I can't say I've ever heard of any dude who had an episode like that go out on the road and have everything be fine in such a short amount of time." He beat the two drumsticks against the palm of his hand. "I mean, I'm open to it, these songs would sound great and he's a great vocalist, but I've got to worry about my career too. You guys are tight. I've joined midway through your journey and I'm not sure where that journey is headed yet."

Nathan swigged from his beer. "How do you mean?"

Chops was clearly squirming through an awkward situation. "I love playing with you guys," he said. "The songs are great, and you're good dudes. Too good." He gripped the sticks with the palm he'd been beating them against. "But I don't know if it's going to end well. You're like high-school sweethearts who got married. Everyone can see it's going to end in tears, but you keep at it anyway. Spiros has a kid. He got married. You, you're sound. You could join any band you wanted."

"*This* is my band."

"Yeah, it is. And I get why you're obsessed with it, but tons of bands need a guitarist—a songwriter—like you, and I feel like you're stopping yourself moving forward because you think you owe it to Oaks not to let him go." Chops winced as he said it.

Nathan peeled the label off his beer. "I can see why you think that. I can. But this isn't about whether he's in it for the long run or not. He's a dude with no one apart from us, and if we keep going and he's not at least given a chance to show us he's all good, then I'm scared about what'll happen to him." He was worried about Oaks, that was true, but he'd go on with the band with or without him. He met Chops's eyes. "I tell you what," he said. "At the end of the day, this is my band, but that doesn't mean it can't continue without Oaks. Help us record. You've heard some of the new stuff. There's no commitment to that. It's only demos for the label. You don't want Oaks in, we find someone else." He could work on the Oaks angle later, but in an ideal world, it'd be him on the mic when they started to record. Nathan had always hated when bands he dug changed vocalists, but he needed Chops to commit first. "That fair?"

Chops started rolling a smoke. "You want Rusty in?"

Nathan nodded.

"Okay, but I'm not going to bullshit you. I'm not sure I'll ever commit to touring with you. I'm inclined to record so long as you understand that it might only—and I mean only—be studio-work." He tugged at his hair. "I don't think you're going to like hearing this, but I'm probably gonna cover for Howie on a three-week run with The Violent Dead."

Nathan blew air from between his cheeks. It was a kick in the balls, but there'd never been any doubt Chops would be asked to play with other bands. In the industry they were in, there were always solid pros who would tour with other bands, record in the studio, and produce. Chops was one of those guys. Shit, it was how they'd got him to join Polyphemus in the first place. "Chops," he said, "that shit doesn't bother me. You helped us out when we needed it. You're a damn good drummer and you've always been ambitious. If it's anything more than a short tour, then I wish you luck." He would be a huge loss if he left for good, but you couldn't stop anyone from touring with a band as big as The Violent Dead.

"You sure?"

"Shit, dude, if I wasn't, would it stop you?"

Chops laughed. "Get Spiros in. Howie's only out for a few weeks – had a tendon issue or some shit like that." He splashed out a quick little fill on the kit. "You want me to get Rusty in? You wanna go guitar full time?"

"Hell yeah I do." He increased his volume. "Tell me what you think of this one." He plunged into a staccato riff marked by wicked bends and sweep picking. Chops nodded his head and picked up the beat.

Spiros

Spiros was in the studio ripping out guitar licks and playing through a few of his favorite tracks to perform live when Pandora arrived home. Feeling great about the fishing trip with Nathan and the potential of jamming with the boys again, he'd been tooling around on the acoustic all day. Pandora had gone to work early, as she usually did, and recently she'd been working late too. Spiros couldn't understand her desire to work in such a rigorous career. They were already more than financially comfortable, but he accepted that her counselling job was important to her. On many occasions, they'd argued about it, but the short answer was that she felt like she'd go insane if she stayed home all the time. It was funny then, he thought, that she didn't understand his desire to play music.

Once Calliope was in bed, he'd gone into the old jam-room. It had been abandoned too long and the weight of his BC Rich on his lap and the quick action of the strings as his blurring fingers wrung intricate webs of sound out of every pitch bend and dive-bomb made him feel like he'd returned home after months in the trenches. Whereas some guitarists thought of their instrument as something that needed to be caressed and loved, he was violent with his. He practically strangled the notes out of it and when he performed live, he swung it like an axe, threw it in the air and dove into the crowd with it hanging from its strap like a machine gun. With the headphones plugged into the pre-amp so he didn't wake the baby, he didn't hear Pandora open the door to the studio. When he eventually noticed, he felt like he'd been caught jacking off. "Shit, babe, I didn't see you." He rested the guitar on its stand and shut down the amplifier. "How long you been there?"

"Long enough." The scowl on her face wasn't good. "How long have you been at this?"

"Since Calliope went to bed."

"Any *reason* you're at it so long?"

He checked the time on his phone. Saw the collection of calls he'd missed from her. "Shit, babe, sorry. I didn't hear the calls. You okay?" He went to her, but she shied away from his touch.

"No, Spiros, I'm not. If you don't answer your phone for me late at night, how do you know I am safe? I could be broken down on the highway. I could be in trouble and I could be calling you for help."

"Honey…"

"Don't you 'honey' me. You know you should be answering my calls. You know what happened to me. If there is one thing I need from you it is the ability to answer your phone. Instead you are here playing with your fucking guitars. You have responsibilities."

He pulled her close.

She struggled against his grip. "You don't touch me."

"Well, are you going to tell me what happened?" Palms open, he raised his hands. "Are you okay? Is something the matter?"

"No, Spiros. Nothing happened." She gestured to the boxes of takeaway food she brought home on the kitchen counter. "I called to see if you wanted dinner, but you're obviously not hungry."

Now that he was up and away from the guitar, he realized how hungry he was. He would usually prepare dinner for them both once Calliope went to bed, but this time he'd played right through the hour or two between the baby's bedtime and her arrival. "I can eat." He opened the boxes. Chinese food. "You're a star." She was. She'd have been well within her right to assume he'd eaten.

"Lucky I felt like takeaway food. You clearly didn't cook tonight." Her piercing stare penetrated right through him. "So why were you so caught up? You've hardly touched your guitars recently." She opened the cutlery drawer with a clatter. "You told those idiots you'd play with them again didn't you?"

How could he explain to her that it wasn't that simple? He *was* going to tell Nathan that he was in, but there was nothing set in concrete yet. Besides, there was no point explaining it when she was in a mood like this. "No, I haven't told anyone anything like that." It wasn't strictly a lie, so at least he wouldn't have to feel guilty. "But, yeah, catching up with Nate did make me think about how much I love playing the guitar and how good some of our songs are." He cracked open one of the Chinese containers.

"So what did you talk about if you remember these things you love but you haven't promised anyone anything?"

"That's not what I said."

She tipped her container full of honey chicken into a bowl and jammed her fork into one of the pieces. "Did they ask you?"

"Did they ask me what?"

"They did. They asked you to join the band again, didn't they?"

He had to wonder how the fishing trip he'd taken last night measured against the one in her imagination. She'd probably pictured them all sitting around pounding beers and talking about the good old days. He speared a piece of broccoli with his own fork. "I'm not going to lie to you, babe," he said. "But first of all, it was just Nathan and I." He held up a hand to pacify her when she tried to interrupt. "He told me that Oaks wants to jam again, and he asked me if I'd be interested." He crunched the broccoli.

"And?"

"And you know the answer. This has been our dream for years, and I'm in a position where I know my family is already provided for. I have the financial freedom to do this. So do you. You choose to work in the career of your choice because you are passionate about it. I am passionate about this."

"It's the band or me, Spiros."

This was the threat he hated most of all. She used it whenever she wasn't getting her way. Up to this point, he'd caved in on nearly every occasion. There'd been small things he'd demanded she deal with and, so far, she'd never followed through with her threats, but he'd never tested the waters with something as big and meaningful as this. "Honey, we are talking about a few jam sessions. That's all." He plunged his fork into a piece of beef. "If Nate can get everyone together, I'm going to have a jam with the guys."

"And that's your choice? Your stupid band and your stupid friends over your wife and baby?" She plucked the chicken and noodles off the bench. "I'm going to eat in the bedroom. You can sleep in the guest bed tonight."

He thought about Calliope. He found it hard to believe he was in any real danger of losing her. The money the grocery stores made were a more than tempting enticement for Pandora, and at this stage there was no danger of the band going on tour. It was a jam. What harm could there be in that?

CHAPTER FOUR
DEATH IS THIS COMMUNION

Nathan hadn't long finished his jam session when Lisa texted him again. He was feeling good about the way things had panned out with Chops and thought things were going to dovetail nicely with the band. Rusty would come in on bass, letting him slide over to rhythm guitar. Chops would help them record some demos, and there was every chance Oaks would be able to resume his position as frontman. Lost in a reverie of how this would pan out in the studio, he'd been annoyed when his phone chimed again. When he opened the text, Lisa was pictured there, spread-eagled on her bed in revealing lingerie. Between her crotchless panties and suspenders, she trailed a lone finger tantalizingly close to her pussy. *Are you sure you don't want to catch up today?* the accompanying text read. *Goddamn* she was fine. She'd always been a good lay too. The first time he'd had her had been at the end of a long boozy day at a local festival. Polyphemus had been somewhere in the middle of the bill, but when they performed, she was right there at the front of the stage. Thanks to the festival crowd, their audience had been bigger than usual, but she'd fought her way to the front barricade. Anyone who'd ever spent more than a few songs fighting off the press of the moshpit behind them and kept their position right in front of the stage knew that it took some serious effort. There was no way you were coming out of it without bruises, but Lisa had done exactly that. Early in the show, she'd fought hard to get Nathan's attention, and once she had it, she did everything she could to make sure she kept it, including flashing her pert little tits at him. They were shaped to perfection. For his part, Nathan had kept her hydrated with swigs of his beer. Once the set was finished, he'd climbed down off the stage and helped her climb the barrier so he could take her backstage. Aside from the obvious caveat of having to cancel a tour because of your mate's overdose, it was the most rock 'n roll thing he'd ever done. They'd spent the day drinking from the rider, but instead of watching the festival headliners close out the show, he'd got in a cab with her and taken her straight home. She hadn't left for three days.

He read the text message again and remembered all the times he'd buried himself in her. Her prowess in the sack had been the only reason he'd kept her around as long as he had. Thinking about those times after receiving an SMS like this one was a hard temptation to avoid. Thinking about them after a half-dozen beers wouldn't have ended well if he'd wanted it to. His fingers tapped out his response without thinking about it. *No, I'm not sure. What other great memories have you got to convince me I'm wrong?* He sent the message.

Another one arrived a couple of minutes later, sounding its arrival with a familiar *ting*. In this one, she was fondling her breasts. A lacy pink blindfold adorned her face. At any other time, he'd have considered how such an impractical accoutrement could be so hot, but instead he wondered how she could possibly be so cold. He replied, this time telling her to come over.

A short while later, when there was a knock on his door, he answered it in his usual fashion: with a beer in each hand. When he swung the door open, he was confronted by something unexpected. Before he'd clicked it into the catch on the interior wall and allowed her to step through, he paused, leaning on the door as if for support. It was her all right. Her hair was styled in her classic loose fashion and her face was as heavily made up as it always was. Her short sleeves left her tattoos visible to the world and he vividly remembered the bouquet of flowers adorning her left underarm and the montage of Disney Princesses on her right arm. On top of that, the comically oversized matching earrings and necklace were so ridiculously chunky they could have come out of a vending machine. All of that was perfectly normal. The part that blew him away; that shocked him so much he could barely function, was her belly. She was heavily pregnant. "Surprise," she said. "You're going to be a father."

"Bullshit! This is a joke, right?" He leaned on the door, letting it swing with his weight. "There's no way that thing's mine." He shook his head, willing her to disappear; to fade into memory. The last thing he needed was bullshit on this level.

"Are you going to let me in so we can talk or are you going to send me away like I knew you would?" She rubbed her shoulders absently.

He stepped out of the doorway and took her bags off her. He felt like he'd had more guests in the last few days than he'd seen all year. "I don't see how…"

"We fucked, Nate. We fucked a lot, you remember?"

They had. He'd had her in every room of this house and in plenty of other places too. She was a glutton for it. "But the photos you sent…"

She came in through the hallway and dumped her handbag on his couch. "Old ones." She grimaced at her surroundings. "Good to see you've cleaned up," she said. "Your toilet clean? I'm busting for a piss."

He told her to go ahead, necked the remains of his first beer, and cracked the other one instead of giving it to her. He sat on the couch and stared at the white froth, deaf to the sound of the carbonated bubbles hissing as they swam for the surface of the amber liquid and escaped in a steady stream.

Anton grinned at the girl as she gazed up at him from between his legs. She was a useful one and her work with the new kid would bring him into the fold. She was, in general, always willing to do whatever he needed her to, and who could blame her? He'd gifted her with everything she wanted, and she was—to an outsider—living a charmed life. He elicited a groan of pleasure as she jerked her wrist faster and faster, then he pushed her head down and closed his eyes, enjoying this human pleasure as a base bit of hedonism. She was, despite her willingness to obey, inconsequential, if not for her use as a tool in helping him 'feed the beast' as he liked to call it. Yes, even her artworks, as disturbing as they were with their graven images and depictions of sinning heathens, did their bit in luring people into the fold. There were acolytes everywhere, and the art world had always been a magnet for those who were searching to fill a void in their lives.

This line of thought brought him to Oaks. Tonight's meeting would be the first real test for the singer, and he couldn't afford for the pathetic little man to be scared away or to turn down the offers they would present to him. He had seen glimpses of what the future could hold for his new obsession, and in order to make the best ones come true, he needed Oaks on board quickly. Once that happened, he should be able to manipulate the piss-weak little junkie idiot into doing exactly what he wanted and maneuver him towards the most desirable outcome. Thinking about this, he held the girl's head down and came with a thrust of his hips. He pulled a knot of hair he'd balled up into his fist, grunted his appreciation as she gasped for air and grinned when she wiped her lips. Yes, this one would swallow anything. He stood up without a word, patted her on the head and zipped up his fly. "You're certain he won't baulk?"

She licked her lips and wiped her hands on her skirt. "We can never be certain, but he's crying out for love and acceptance. I think he'll jump at the chance."

Yes, it was obvious to the most casual observer that Oaks was a needy man, if indeed 'man' was the right word for him. To an astute eye like Anton's, the cause of that neediness may well have been tattooed on the little piss-ant's forehead. The singer missed his mummy. Anton had seen it in seconds. Yes, it helped that he was able to read people so well, but he knew without a shadow of a doubt that if he got Oaks talking about his childhood, the results would be textbook. As for the girl's confidence, he'd need to knock that out of her soon enough. She was becoming cocky. Brazen. That wouldn't do, not when there was so much at stake. "We've seen failures before. Remember there are risks when it goes wrong, and not everyone can be bought off. I'd hate to think rash decision-making might be the cause of another mistake." He levelled his gaze on her briefly, trying to see the inner workings of her mind. He grunted again and gestured at the corner of his mouth with a bony finger. "Go and clean yourself up. You've got shit on your face."

She touched her own finger to it. Bowed her head. She went in the direction of the bathroom, slinking like a chastised child.

As he considered the huge night ahead, he watched her self-consciously make her way to the bathroom. "I'll see you there tonight," he said. "Make sure nothing is amiss when you go to him." As she left, he added, "I shouldn't need to say it, but he doesn't need to know you've been here."

She nodded and closed the bathroom door behind her.

The eight-foot-high glass window panels of his penthouse provided unfettered views of the city, the coast, and the hinterland from all angles. As he traversed the open plan lounge-room, running a hand along the top of one of his plush leather sofas, he watched the waves crashing onto the beach. Lately, the tides had eaten away the sand dunes everyone loved so much. With practically nothing of them left, he would no doubt see dredging equipment doing everything it could to turn sand onto the shoreline over the next few days. Goddamn he loved this place. He was an observer, and when he needed to, it let him see everything.

"Blinds," he said. "Down."

The voice-activated motors at the top of each window panel hummed, and the blinds rolled down from within their sleek plastic compartments. Satisfied, he barked another order at the technology.

"Stereo, play Ligeti." The speakers in his room came alive with a single discordant note. Eerie chanting bled into the soundscape, and Anton stripped. "Volume up to full," he said, walking into his bathroom. Turning the hot water to temperatures he could never have borne without years of conditioning, he stepped into the frameless shower and shaved every inch of his body clean of hair beneath the vast eternities and voluminous power of the music that beat down from the ceiling's built-in speakers.

When he was dressed, he exited the bedroom to find his apartment empty. The girl had left, hopefully to collect Stephen and prepare him for the night's festivities. He racked and snorted a large line of coke, draped a garment bag over his arm and made his way to the elevator. Before he swiped his key over the magnetic lock, he looked across the room to the ancient desk that served as his altar. He wanted certainty he'd done everything he could to ensure the night went as planned and hated the fact he had to rely on others. He knew the girl was currently loyal, but there was a part of him that worried she was jumping the gun in an attempt to prove herself indispensable to him. She was ambitious and she wanted a seat at the table of whatever she thought was happening. It was an admirable trait really. He'd never mentioned the idea there was a plan in motion to her, but she'd decided something was happening anyway. While those ambitions would suit him for the present and made her a compliant servant, they could be a threat later.

The jam session with Nathan had been a great warm-up for practice with The Violent Dead, and Chops was in fine form as he showed off the fact he'd brushed up on some of the band's stalwart live songs. With Ricky buzz-sawing distorted riffs across the practice space and Maddox's thick bass-lines rattling underneath in a peristaltic groove, he felt like he was running a marathon as his burning calves pumped the double-kick and he rolled across the cymbals, toms and snare with the relentless pace of a semi-trailer hurtling down a long straight. After Traine waited the requisite eight measures and joined the maelstrom with the kind of grunt Geroge Fisher would be proud of, Chops dropped the beat to half-pace and the thick groovy riff of their regular closer "Providence in the Fall of an Angel" took shape.

"Right on, dude," Henry said in the brief moment before he had to shriek out the opening lyrics. This track had been their closer since their major-label debut had broken big. It was, Chops had said on many occasions, a fucking ball-snorter of a tune. As much as he was happy to tell Nathan he'd go into the studio with them—and he wasn't lying, he genuinely loved recording—he couldn't wait to see the wall of death "Providence's" breakdown would spark from his position on the drum riser. He'd seen it from the ground and from side of stage plenty of times but providing the fill on the cowbell would be awesome. It closed off what sounded like uncontrolled chaos before the band came together in a devastating crescendo. The riff they dropped a beat later was one of the biggest since Pantera's "Domination" breakdown at Moscow's 1991 *Monsters of Rock* festival. At his command, the crowd would careen into each other like atoms in a heated test-tube. How could that not feel good?

Once they'd reached the end of the song and it faded out with Ricky finger-picking his way through a simple minor scale chord progression that transposed the main riff into a lilting coda, the three core members of the group took turns high-fiving the drummer and praising his performance. "Thanks guys," Chops said. "I don't want to go all fan-boy, but there's not a metalhead alive who doesn't think that's going to sit alongside the classics in twenty years." He wiped sweat from his face with a microfiber towel. "You have no idea how much I enjoyed that."

"Fuck you, brother," Traine said. "You have no idea how much *we* enjoyed that."

"Shit was tighter than a nun's nasty," Ricky said. He upended a bottle of water and drained it. "How'd you go with "Dissolved Soul?" You learn that bad boy too?" "Dissolved Soul" was the title track to their most recent album. "That's the one we'll be opening with when we hit the road."

The drummer laughed. They'd better believe he had. He'd locked down that one and a few more. His visit to Nathan's place had marked the only time he'd been away from his practice kit for so much as a brief period in the last few days. In truth, he'd never felt so productive and in-tune with his instrument. He felt like he could go toe to toe with some of the greats. Shit, he'd spent time jamming with Rusty before Hank had invited him to come and do The Violent Dead thing. He was on top of his game. "Dissolved Soul, you say?" He pointed the stick in his right hand at Ricky. "Turn that guitar up loud and get ready to distil the essence of self, motherfucker."

"You want my job too?" Traine asked.

Chops had referenced the opening line to the song in his comment to Ricky, and Traine, who was as high as a kite thanks to his constant intake of edibles and steady stream of joints, had clearly enjoyed it.

"Let's do this shit," Traine said to the others.

Chops counted them in, and the song, another slab of brutality riddled with groovy riffs and blast beats filled the practice room with its wall of noise.

When they were done and their allotted time in the practice room was up, Traine led the way to the same table they had sat and smoked at last time. As always, he was the first to pull a bag of weed out of his pocket. He dropped a fat bud into a little rotating grinder-tin that shredded it into crumb-sized portions, twisted it until it was ready to go, and tipped it into a little plastic container. "First hit for the guest of honor today," he said.

Chops checked his watch, shrugged his shoulders and obliged the man. He let Henry pack him a cone, pulled it and blew smoke in a long plume. "So we're doing this?" he asked.

"If you want in, we'd be stoked to have you on board," Ricky said, fiddling with his nose piercing. "It's only a short run around the state, and we're expecting Howie back in the fold afterwards, but yeah, he's cool with it and we don't want to miss out on the shows." He flexed his knuckles and pulled a piece of gum from a packet in his wallet. "Did you get the chance to catch up with Oaks?"

"No, not yet. I caught up with Nathan though. I went and saw him earlier today." To be truthful, he felt bummed that Howie would return so soon. He was hoping he'd be able to stick around for a little longer and cement himself in the band, but as he'd feared, that shit might be too good to be true.

She hated the drive out to Oaks's place. Memories of the time she had spent in the shitty little share-home were fresh. Life for a former junkie fresh out of rehab was tough at the best of times, but for a woman who'd done some more than unsavory shit in the name of getting a fix, it was worse. When it came to casual sex, she was pretty liberated, but some of what she'd done for cash stung, and in her weaker moments, shame's incessant little voice crept into her mind. Taking the turnpike, the taste of Anton lingering in her mouth, she tried to push the thoughts out of her sub-conscious.

The halfway house hadn't changed. The patchy lawn was long and unkempt, probably more thistle than actual grass. Old junk-mail had fallen out of the letterbox, never to be picked up, and free local newspapers melted into the ground where the paperboy had thrown them. No doubt, it was the same shithole inside that she remembered. Cockroaches owned the place. The window-tracks would be full of dead flies and the skeletons of house geckoes.

She swiped her phone, ready to text Oaks and the front door opened. Amielle stood in the doorway, arms folded, staring at her. The nurse called out to Oaks, who came outside only moments later. She grabbed the needy prick by the arm and whispered something into his ear. Oaks shook his head.

India stepped out of the car and walked over to greet him. Throwing her arms around his neck, she kissed him passionately on the lips. When he nuzzled her neck in response, she cast a glance at Amielle then strutted to the car.

She reversed out of the driveway. "Still cockroach city in there?"

"It's crawling with them. You know the place?"

She slipped the car into fifth and headed in the direction of the highway. "Yep. Amielle still selling?"

"For Anton, right?"

She nodded her head. "I always thought that too. You

gonna question him about it?"

"Fuck no." He wound his window down a crack and lit a smoke. "Doesn't bother me. At first, I thought it would be bad news, and I'm tempted by it, but I haven't felt compelled at all. It's not like she's offered me a hit, either."

India sighed deeply. "*Yet.*" She merged onto the highway. The roads were clear and they'd be at the Exchange in no time. "She will. She always does, unless she's told not to." She'd always found it weird how Anton seemed to have his fingers in both pies. For some people, like her, he did everything he could to get them off the drugs and take them under his wing, but others weren't so lucky. If he didn't think he could use you, he hooked you straight on the smack. It kept money rolling in and the halfway house gave him a steady stream of clients.

"So what's the big initiation like?" Oaks asked. He was staring wistfully out the window, trying to hide it, but she knew he was nervous as hell. "Why do I feel like it's going to be like something out of *Illuminatus*?" He could see she didn't have a clue what he was talking about, so he said, "Cult book. Awesomely paranoid and full of satirical conspiracies. Great stuff."

"Can't say I've heard of it." City towers appeared on the skyline. "It's hard to say what it's like. Shit's different for everyone."

"Sure, but what's the big deal? It's only coaching. You guys make it seem like some sort of weird cult or something."

"It's just Anton's way, man." Her own initiation had been terrifying, but she was here to make sure that Oaks was on board. She wasn't allowed to talk about her experiences, probably because if everyone did, they'd find the weak spots in Anton's methods. "Don't worry. It'll be worth it. He'll show you how to make your dreams come true."

"So you keep telling me."

Solemn was the only word he could think of to describe the Exchange when he stepped into it this time. The pumping music was gone and there was no one milling around enjoying a social drink and laughing with friends. It was somber. Serious.

"Is it always like this?" he asked India.

"It's a formal occasion," she said. "Don't worry. Nothing bad is going to happen."

Anton appeared, bald and freshly shaved, garbed in a black robe. What was that for? This *was* some pseudo-Christian bullshit. What the hell had he gotten himself into? "No one told me it was fancy dress. You going to sacrifice me?"

Anton laughed. "Oh, yes, my friend. It's all been an elaborate ruse." He swept aside the door to the private area, revealing a dozen or so others all similarly garbed in black robes. "Come. We love a bit of ceremony. Your own robe is inside."

"Did you know about this?" Oaks asked India.

"Surprise," she said, pecking him on the cheek. "Anyway, hang with Anton for a bit. I need to get myself ready." She disappeared down a corridor.

As stupid as the whole robe thing seemed, he'd go along with it. He'd done way dumber things on tour, and those ridiculous nights in more and more ridiculous costumes were some of the best times he'd had. Before the smack had hooked its claws into him, last night on tour had usually been an excuse to get wasted and dress up. Tarzan leotards, ballerina outfits, construction crew get-up, it didn't matter. It was good fun and it gave everyone a laugh. This shit didn't seem quite the same, but he could make it work.

Anton led him to the bar where Thomas was pouring

drinks. "They got you into a robe too, huh?"

Thomas asked him what he wanted and handed him a bundled robe. "Think of it as a satanic toga party, my friend. A heavy metal guy like you should totally be able to get into it."

It didn't matter what the reality was. The legacy of Satanic panic was that heavy metal always was and always would be the devil's tool. It was easier to mock the whole thing than to try and fight it. "Oh yeah, we're real heathens. I can't wait to visit Norway and burn down a church."

Thomas passed him a tall glass of whiskey, but as he reached for it, Anton closed a palm around it. "First, we add a little something." He withdrew a small vial from a pocket on his robe and unplugged the cap, swirled it and held it under his nose. It had a strong eucalyptus smell.

"I can't, Anton. Whiskey is fine."

"Relax. This won't hurt you." He poured several drops into his own drink and sipped on it. It will only clear your mind and prepare you." He tipped some into Stephen's glass and passed it to him. "Cheers," he said. "To good health and personal riches."

Was this how it started? Would Anton be so blatant as to try and rehook him on narcotics in such a clumsy fashion. "I shouldn't…"

"This is not a narcotic. Think of it as an essential oil. An herbal medicine. It's mostly wormwood and eucalypt." He raised his glass again and grinned.

What the hell? Although he couldn't profess to have been expecting any of what was going on, he'd be fine. "Cheers," he said, tipping the shot down his throat. "Now where can I get changed?"

CHAPTER FIVE
RITUAL

Spiros hadn't had this much fun in ages. Nathan's new riffs were killer and with Chops and his mate Rusty already smashing out the kind of rhythms that'd make Morbid Angel proud, his first time playing with a full band since Oaks had fallen off the stage couldn't be going any better. Nathan was slaying it on the axe as well. He cracked a fresh brewski from the ice-bucket on one side of the room and tuned his weapon up a notch. "Rusty's better at bass than you ever were. You might have to stay on guitars. Just hit the open strings in time with the double-kick and we might finally have a good band." He swigged a healthy guzzle of the beer. "We might make you the vocalist. You got some trauma you want to clear out? Maybe the pain of waiting to hit puberty in your early thirties?"

"Oh, hey, Spiros, I brought you something," Nathan replied. He reached into his pocket and rummaged around, finally withdrawing his hand to reveal a middle finger. "That's for you, man. That one's all yours."

"Fuck me?" Spiros said. "You're going to need to buy me flowers too, dude. And a nice meal. I don't come cheap."

"Bastard fucks on first dates, though," Chops added. "Your mum told me all about it."

Nathan swung the finger in the drummer's direction. "There's plenty of this to go around, bro. Plenty of it."

Chops put his hands up like he'd been threatened with a gun. "Okay, man. Okay. I don't want nothing I can't handle.

I'm a lover, not a fighter."

Spiros started noodling on the guitar. An old riff from the first album. Chops slipped into the groove and started pounding out the bouncing intro beat. Spiros pulled a face at Nathan, counted out the bars and when there was a brief pause in the wall of sound that would usually be dominated by a chest-beater grunt, courtesy of Oaks, he stepped up to the plate. A beat later, Nathan and Rusty were on the groove too. "The Sacrifice Poles" was one of their big crowd-pleasers. Full of fast verse-riffs for the pit and a breakdown that bordered on slam, it was for the scene-kids who weren't messing around and went to gigs to blow off steam. When it dropped, the casual bystanders cleared the deck pretty quickly. That wasn't the only reason he loved this particular track, though. His solo had made number three in Guitar Mag's list of the year's best solos. An achievement he was yet to top. The profile page he'd featured on, alongside some of the biggest names in the business, was framed in his practice-room at home. He worked his way through it, and together with Marsh, moved into the palm-muted outro.

"Fuck that's a sweet song," Rusty said when they finished. "I wanted to run something by you guys, too. I was talking to Chops on the way here. I know there's some debate on what's going to happen with Oaks, but if you guys want to give someone solid a trial on vocals, I know a dude who's after a new gig."

Spiros stomped the mute button on his pedal. "He has experience?" He could practically feel Nathan's eyes burning into him. "I think it's worth considering."

"Spiros, man, if we're going to try out new vocalists, don't you think we should let Oaks come for a jam session first?"

Spiros could only meet Nathan's gaze with sadness. The risk was too much. "I don't see what harm a trial could hold. If Rusty's friend is good, we have a safe bet. If he's not, then perhaps we let Oaks trial."

"I don't think it's fair. He's been here since the start," Nathan said. He fiddled with his tuning pegs. "Chops?"

The drummer rested his sticks on the snare and stretched his arms out in front of him, cracking his knuckles in the process. "We've spoken about this, and I think you're thinking with your heart and not your head. We all love Oaks, but I can tell you, man, as soon as we hit the road again, he's going to be faced with his demons on a massive scale and the support mechanisms he's guaranteed in town won't be there for him."

He'd said when 'we' hit the road. That was interesting. From the conversation he'd had with Nathan—the same one as he'd heard—Chops had said he wouldn't be touring. Hopefully he'd had a change of heart. "Why don't we go for a smoke? We can talk about it and maybe Rusty can call his friend. Is he far from here, Rusty?"

"Spiros?" Nathan made a face that said *come on, dude, don't do this.*

"A casual chat. Maybe a casual jam. We all want this to work. These songs are good. The label is waiting for us." Lord knew they needed to record something. They were already in massive debt to the label. Failing to meet their contractual obligations would be expensive. There was only one guess who'd have to bear the brunt of that – and it wouldn't be Stephen Oaks, the man who was ultimately responsible for leaving them up shit creek without a paddle. "Rusty, is he solid?"

"Yeah, man. Corey's sound. Played in Rabid God for years. The other dudes settled down and got married. He's left with no band to play in. Good vocalist, too. You know the band?"

"I may have heard one or two songs."

"I do," Nathan said. "They're good. Vocals were sick. Highs, lows, cleans, not that we need those." He rested his guitar on its stand. "Come on, I need a smoke."

Outside, Spiros searched for Rabid God online and found

an album stream. "This is him. Corey, Rusty's friend." He placed the phone in the middle of the table and let the album play while they passed a joint around. The band itself was a little punkier than Polyphemus, blending more hardcore into their sound, but Nathan and Rusty were right. Corey was a good vocalist. Bringing a straight to the point style with his lyrics, his vocals ran the full spectrum in their range. "This dude is excellent. He brings a lot to the table, and with Rusty coming on bass, assuming he wants to, and you taking up guitars, it's the perfect time to bring someone else in. I tell you, man, this excites me."

"Want me to call him?" Rusty asked. He drew on the joint, coughed, and passed the spliff to the side. "I don't want to cause trouble, but I told him I'd find out what was going on. He loves Polyphemus. I bet you he knows all the lyrics."

"Call him," Nathan said, resigned to the notion that Oaks was firmly on the outer. "Put him on loudspeaker."

Something was hovering in Oaks's periphery. He'd tried to see whatever it was that loitered there like an indistinct shadow, but so far he'd had no luck in catching it. Coupled with the collection of black-robed guests milling around the exclusive area of Anton's nightclub, not to mention the way the perspective of the room had subtly shifted, he knew he was under the effect of something more than alcohol. Whatever Anton had put in his drink, there was no way it was herbal oil. If anything, it had some sort of meth feel about it, but he didn't have the clarity of mind he was told it would give him; the thing creeping in the fringes of his perception, the billowing motion of the walls and the apparent wrongness of the room's dimensions saw to that, but he felt charged. He'd booted up enough times to know the sensation. If he didn't feel so good, he'd have been pissed. And besides, what harm could there be in a little whizz or acid or whatever it was on a night of celebration? It wasn't like he was addicted to anything except the smack, and this was as opposite to that as you could get.

"Stephen, how are you feeling?" Beneath his hood, shadows obscured Anton's features so that his gaunt and hairless visage may as well have been the reaper's own. To add to the effect, the dilated pupils of his sunken eyes blazed. "We'll begin the ceremony soon." He handed the vial to Oaks. "Drink this."

Oaks took it. Held it up to the light to try and see how much was left in there. "You've drugged me." It was half-full.

"I've prepared you for the ceremony. It's all part of it." He rested a hand on Oaks's shoulder. "Besides, you seem to be enjoying yourself."

"I'm tripping balls." The shadow in his peripherals felt close. "I don't need any more." He held the vial out for Anton.

"Please, I insist. It's an important part of the ritual." He gestured around the room. "All these people have done it. It's perfectly safe."

"What is it?"

India approached and sat on his lap. She took the vial, popped the cap and smelled the contents. "I remember this. It's good."

"As I said, it's an important part of the ritual. Joining us isn't as simple as filling out a few forms. Of course," he eyed the exit and raised his hands apologetically. "If it's not for you, there are no hard feelings."

There was no way he wanted to leave his new friends. They were good people and they'd embraced him with open arms. It had been a long time since anyone had been so welcoming and stoked with who he was. India was amazing. So pretty and so smart. He knew that giving up on this would be giving up on her. Anton could help him get back in Polyphemus. Get him back in front of crowds, rebuilding the relationship with his old band mates. He could help him. Show him how to make Polyphemus way bigger than any of the modern bands they were associated with. Shit, they could be as big as Slayer with a little help. He needed to be here. Needed Anton for that.

India motioned towards one of her nearby paintings. "I wouldn't have achieved all that I have so far without it. And I know there's a lot more to come. I'd love you to be part of that journey."

Oaks took the vial. Weighed it in his hands then drank the contents. The thing in his peripheral vision seemed to swell, pregnant with anticipation. How strange. Why would he think that? The loiterer, whomever it happened to be, was excited. He knew it inherently. Felt it in a strange way, and in turn, that excited him. He felt the head of his cock beat, curious as to what was going on. The presence could have been male or female. It could have been both. It didn't matter. It wanted him and this drug was good. He wanted to fuck it too. To be inside it. To be one with it.

"You need to know that once the ceremony begins, it cannot stop. You will see things and you will be spoken to and propositioned. Do not resist, my friend, not if you want to achieve your wildest dreams and show the world there is far more to Stephen Oaks than the nothing junkie who ruined everything for his friends." Anton took one of Oaks's hands and let India take the other. Together, they led him to the center of the private area where the rest of the black-robed guests had formed a circle.

As Oaks approached, the circle parted, allowing him ingress. He surveyed his surroundings. He could make out little of the people wearing their hoods like cauls. The whole scene was spooky as hell. If he didn't know better, he'd have sworn the thing hiding in the liminal space of his peripherals was leering at him, tumescent as a lecher and as wet as a willing whore.

Anton momentarily disappeared and the deep bass of a ritual drum began to pound. There was movement outside the circle and then it parted again. Anton, his hood down and his face daubed in smears of blood-red paint, reappeared and stepped forward. On a rope, he led the biggest fucking goat Oaks had ever seen. It must have weighed two-hundred pounds. It was the size of a great Dane; built like a brick shithouse. Screaming and skittish, it jerked at the rope like a dog that wouldn't heel. Its fur was stygian black and its four horns reached out from its head like the star in Baphomet's sigil. The spike of its beard tapered into a terrifying fifth point. As if it were a fly disturbed from feasting on putrescent roadkill, its dilated pupils capered from side to side, but always alighted on that one focal point. For the goat, that point was Oaks. But as much as it jerked its head, trying to escape Anton's hold on the tether, it kept focusing on Oaks. No, not at him. Beyond him. As if there was something huge and predatory there. Oaks tried to catch a glimpse of whatever the goat was seeing, but he couldn't find it. There was only that hungry, horny, desperate shape loitering there like a monkey.

Anton dragged the screaming beast into the circle, and the ritual drum pounded as slowly as a dying man's heartbeat. The hollow booming hung heavily in the air. The lurking shape swelled with each resonant thud. The goat bleated, apoplectic with fear. It reared and kicked its forepaws, but Anton kept pulling it forward, unperturbed. Then, when the next drumbeat struck, the entire black-robed audience chanted in unison. With each successive strike, they chanted again and again. A single ominous 'Om'. The hairs on Oaks's arms and neck stood on end and the shape began to coalesce. Wispy tendrils of black smoke crept in front of his eyes.

Anton gestured for him to stay put and remain calm as he approached with the scrambling, bucking goat. He produced

a long and ornate knife from inside his robe and shortened the goat's leash by winding the rope with looping twists of his wrist. The wailing animal was dragged inexorably closer and closer to the blade and there was nothing its braying could do to stop it. A stream of piss sprayed out from beneath its shaggy belly. An acrid stench steamed up from the growing puddle, then its bowels released and the smell grew worse.

Transfixed, Oaks wondered briefly if India's initiation had been anything like this. Was she watching him; a black-robed voyeur of this bizarre and electrifying ceremony? He had goosebumps. He could have sworn the entity that had followed him all night was caressing him. The hair on his neck stood on end and his balls tightened. Anton's knife flashed and arced through the air. The goat gave a pained scream then fell silent. It had shat and pissed everywhere, but that made nowhere near as much mess as the blood spraying arterial geysers of red.

The goat tried to thrash. To escape. Anton was too strong for it. He held it firm, stoic determination on his blood-drenched face. He pushed his hand into the wound and reached down, feeling around for something. When he pulled his hand free, he pulled the beast's heart with it. He threw the sinuous thing to the floor and let the goat fall to its shaking knees. Its hind legs scrambled in the mess. It slipped, collapsing onto its side. Using the heart, Anton painted a bloody pentagram onto the ground around Oaks. When it was complete, he plunged his hands into the mutilated animal. When he withdrew them, his arms were blood-red.

Oaks watched, wide-eyed. Barely able to process what was happening, he stepped forward as Anton reached for him and grabbed his face. As the bald man drew a spiral of blood on his forehead, he felt the shifting shape from his peripherals manifest and become corporeal. Something seized him and as the booming drum and the strange chanting continued, he felt himself pass out of existence.

Nathan let the phone ring for the fourth time then checked his Messenger, wondering if Oaks had seen the messages yet. If he had, he was dodging calls. The alternative, though, didn't bear thinking about. He scrolled through his contacts and when he couldn't find what he wanted, he tapped open Google.

"What are you doing? It's late."

Lisa was leaning on the doorframe of his bedroom.

"I told you. The bed's all yours." He polished off the beer he had sitting beside him and wiped the condensation off the bench with the sleeve of his shirt before turning his attention to his phone.

"You need time to get used to this, I know, but trust me, I'm not bullshitting you. This baby's yours."

"Can't you see I'm busy?" He'd found the number for the rehab center. He selected it and shrugged his shoulders at Lisa. "I'll take the couch. Tomorrow, you can go to your mother's house. Or Jarrod's."

Her eyes narrowed. "You don't know shit about that, so don't bring it up." She stepped forward, her finger wagging. "What, are you stalking my shit?"

"Stalking you? It's all over your Facebook. You think I'm dumb enough to believe you haven't been shacked up with someone else for the last few months? I know you, Lisa."

"You don't know shit."

"I know you're trying to pass someone else's kid off as mine." He stepped off the stool and walked to the fridge. "Girl like you ought to have better prospects. I'm a no-hoper. I'm not a dad. You're better off lying to someone else." He cracked another beer.

"You think I *want* to be here? Like this? You think that if I didn't know it was your kid in my belly I'd come crawling back to you?"

"You're here, aren't you?" He drank deeply. "What's the matter with Jarrod anyway? He beat your ass or something?"

"Fuck you," she said. "Fuck you."

"You've been fucking some piece of shit. You're so worried about the goddamned trophy you got for it, go and see a doctor. They'll lance it like a boil."

"You're a cunt, you know that?"

"Yeah, baby, I know that. Guess it makes two of us. Now go to sleep. You're gonna need all the energy you got to get the fuck outta here when you wake up in the morning." He swiped on his phone. When she slammed the bedroom door closed, he hit the call button.

The voice on the other end was sleepy and slow. "Hello, Maverson Clinic. Our guests are currently sleeping, so unless it's an emergency, the best I can do is take a message."

"I'm chasing the phone number for one your out-patient's hostels; Stephen Oaks?"

"Unfortunately, sir, we aren't at liberty to pass out phone numbers for anyone outside of the facility. I can take a message and have him contact you."

Nathan squeezed the bridge of his nose. "I get it, but I'm worried about him. His name's Stephen Oaks and something's up. He's not answering his phone."

"I see. Why does that make you think something's up?"

"What?" He wanted to throw the phone.

"It's late, sir, why don't you try again in the morning?"

"You don't get it. He doesn't skip calls from me. Shit, he wants this call badly and he knows how to answer the telephone. Can't you pull your head out of your ass and understand that this is important?"

"I'm sorry, sir, I understand your distress."

"You don't understand at all. He's my friend and we put

him in your facility. If he's using again; perhaps overdosing in a gutter somewhere, you'll regret brushing this shit off so simply."

"With all due respect, if a client uses again within their first few weeks outside of the facility, they're not ready to be reintroduced to society."

The rage coiled in his gut. He could probably crush his phone with one hand if he wanted to. "Fuck you then. Let's hope for all our sakes that he's fine." Imbeciles. Morons. He ended the call, skulled his beer and went to the couch. He hit play on the stereo remote and closed his eyes. The sound of atonal distortion washed out of the speakers and over him. He'd have to hope Oaks was okay. There was nothing else he could do.

CHAPTER SIX
UNDERNEATH A MELTING SKY

He was naked. Around him, the audience had melted into a watercolor smear of black and grey. The lights of the club were stars in a distant sky that glowed blood-red and baleful while the ominous drum pounded on. Soaring above that, the voices of those surrounding him chanted as one, but individuals were manifesting around him. He could hear the tones, pitches and accents of people he knew—India, Anton, Tom—as well as a hundred more, but beneath that, other voices chanted at a lower, stranger level. It wasn't like he was hearing them with his ears. They were in his head. In his mind. The goat lay amidst a circle of blood and the shifting presence that had been shadowing him all night, shimmering in his peripherals had come into full view. It kneeled beside him like a lover. It had no face or any definable features that remained if he tried to focus on them. It was, to Oaks, something that *seemed*. At any given moment it could have been any of the millions of faces he'd seen in his life, but the next it was a blur. A shade of grey pencil an artist would smudge into a smoke-swirl. A scribble. A presence he couldn't define. It had wings and a tail and then it didn't. It had eyes and horns and then it didn't. It was male, then female, then something else entirely. It *seemed,* he thought.

It *seemed.*

The only thing he could say with any clarity was that it wanted him. It exuded a lust he couldn't resist. Cold and squamous hands caressed his face, his neck. It trailed a finger along his larynx, his jugular, his clavicle. The sensation was magnetic, tempting, enticing. He groaned and his cheeks flushed, and then, as if given consent, the sharp claw at the end of that eternally cold finger pressed on his breastbone and shuddered as it cut towards his navel.

In his mind, he knew this was wrong, perverse, disgusting, but it felt so good. The thing buried its face in the cut it had clawed into him and nibbled at his flesh as if it were a labium. When it reached his belly button, it pressed harder. Oaks tried to push the thing away. He shouldn't be enjoying this. He should run and run and run, but as his belly swallowed the icy hand and it slowly slipped, scale by profane scale, through his insides, he felt his cock throb and stand to attention. The creature mounted it, taking it inside a carnal orifice as empty and void of warmth as anything Oaks had ever encountered. As it did so, he realized the creature had removed its hand from inside his navel and replaced it with another writhing appendage. Its hands, coated in the slime and ichor of his own guts held him by his face and the pulsating tentacle stretching inside him quivered, lurid and peristaltic.

The pounding of the drum reverberated across the floor, through the coagulating goat's blood and into him. The creature—it wasn't a shifting presence anymore, it was something corporeal and demonic and *seeming*—thrust in time with the beat. The chorus of chants set the pace for Oaks's heart. He didn't know if the blood he wallowed and rutted in was his own or the goat's, but he knew the thing riding him was changing. The weird, insubstantial flesh of its chest had torn. Teeth and a tongue had appeared in the wound, and it had split into a mouth. It gaped, huge. Too huge. Somehow it was bigger than everything in the room.

Bigger than it could possibly have been. It was the size of a world. As Oaks stared into it, it reached for him, stretching wider and growing exponentially. Teeth lined its gums and a forked tongue twisted suggestively as it came closer and closer. It yawed like the maw of eternity and closed over him.

He was on a stage in front of an audience of thousands. There were so many watching, they spanned his entire field of view. Like a black ocean, they swelled around the sound tent; a current of people flowing towards the stage, all trying to reach the moshpit and be as close to the action as possible. Anton had promised him a way to make his dreams become reality, and this was exactly what he wanted: to lead Polyphemus on festival stages like this. The energy in the air was palpable. Dusk was falling on the tail-end of a sunny day; the beer would be flowing in the bars and a good show here would mean selling records and t-shirts. Then there was the word-of-mouth marketing that followed a summer on the festival circuit.

The familiar boom-boom of a double-kick sounded, and he felt his heart swell. This was it. He would return to Polyphemus, and they'd make it happen. He gave Chops the horns. Seated behind the drums, the drummer was slick with sweat. A large pedestal fan whirred behind him. A massive backdrop hung beyond that. It bore The Violent Dead's logo. Their name, blocked in all caps adorned an image of a monstrous spider perched atop a mountain of severed heads. Chops clicked his sticks four times, and the wall of amplifiers exploded with a riff he'd recognize anywhere: "Providence in the Fall of an Angel".

Oaks snapped his head to glare across the stage. That

loser Hank Traine stalked the lip and the rail with the cocky assurance of a rock-star. Ricky had one foot on the fold-backs while he windmilled his hair. The others were doing the same choreographed bullshit and Chops, *his* drummer, was there with them, playing to a crowd of thousands. The moshpit at the front of the stage was a churning cauldron of bodies and Chops was driving the whole thing. Shit, he seemed happy. That prick *never* seemed happy.

Oaks stepped onto the riser and reached for the drummer, but the scene changed before he could grab him, pull him through the kit and ask him what he thought he was doing. He was back on the floor and the creature was riding him. Its hands were buried deep in the sides of his face and it slid that cold and slimy void up and down his cock; explored him with that terrible appendage. "What are you?"

It didn't respond, but the chorus of strange voices he'd heard without truly hearing rose in babbling titters.

The mouth swelled towards him again.

Pandora Coumantouros shut down her computer and checked her phone. She fired off another message and threw it into her handbag. If that moron was on his guitar again, she would stick it so far up his ass he'd be able to use its strings as dental floss.

"Another late one, babe?" Sebastian Connors leaned confidently into her office, his hands gripping the top of the doorframe. "Anyone might think you were staying late so you could see a little more of me."

He was getting too forward lately, but when he grinned as cheekily as that, it was hard to hold a grudge. "I have seen quite enough of you, thank you very much." She slung her handbag over her shoulder. "Now, get out of the way."

"You know I can't let you go without a kiss." He pointed to his cheek. His wedding band flashed under the office's halogen lighting. "It's tradition. And I don't know about you, but I don't want to make the gods angry." He stepped towards her. The top two buttons of his shirt were undone already. He'd come in expecting the usual, but tonight she was too pissed off.

"I have to go."

He stepped in front of her and swung his arm around her waist, drawing her close, leaning in.

She pulled her head away and pressed a finger to his lip, pushing him off her. "I told you I don't have time." She jerked out of his arms with a shimmy. "It is already late and I need to go home. Now get out of my way."

"C'mon, we don't need long. A few minutes is all. He thinks you're working and it's still earlier than it has been on most nights lately."

"And tonight I need to leave." She pushed past him, ignoring his forlorn gaze as she waited for the elevator. "Tomorrow," she said, stepping beyond the sliding metal doors and blowing him a kiss.

She needed to do something about Sebastian. What had started as an innocent fling was growing out of control. He was becoming needy and infatuated. At least his marriage meant he wouldn't be inclined to blurt it out and he had the decency to keep it hidden when anyone else was in the office, so she would deal. She had bigger problems at home. Spiros was becoming obsessed with his guitars once more. Fuck Stephen, the stupid junkie. If he'd hurry up and get himself into trouble again, that'd do nicely. She might be messing around with a colleague, but that was harmless. She had no doubt Spiros had bedded dozens of women on tours with Polyphemus. This was a transgression, but little Calliope and Spiros—and his money—would be around long after Sebastian was forgotten.

Pulling into the driveway, the first thing she noticed was

that the curtains were closed and there was no glow of light from behind them. That meant the bastard was in the spare room. Probably with his headphones on and his guitars as loud as possible. The house was dead, and tonight, she hadn't brought dinner home. He was supposed to handle that. She opened the garage and beeped the horn. Nothing. Fighting the urge to scream, she stormed into the house. Everything was shut down and locked down. On the kitchen bench, he'd left her a note.

Pasta in the fridge.
Calliope with Vasilis and Selene.
Love you lots, but don't wait up.

She screwed the note into a ball and swiped to Selene's phone number with clacking strikes of her acrylic nails. Before she pressed the 'send' button, headlights washed over the driveway behind her. He was home.

Anton watched the junkie writhe on the floor, delirious and as high as a kite. Despite the attentions of the posers standing around the bloody circle, only he knew what was happening. This needy little puke, though, should prove interesting. At times, the visions you were granted mid coitus with the entity could be vague and nebulous, but sometimes they were crystal clear. When he had walked into Nurse Amielle's roach-infested little hovel, he had recognized the vocalist straight away. What happened from here was anyone's guess.

"He's been down for too long." India stepped forward, as if to go to him.

Anton grabbed her arm, jerked her towards him. "Don't break the circle, you stupid bitch. He pressed his fingers deep into the meat of her arm, enjoying the grimace on her face.

"He'll be down for as long as he needs to be. Whatever is happening in there is happening for a reason."

"Look at him." Foam bubbled from the corners of Oaks's mouth. The chords and muscles visible in his throat and face were taut and strained. "He's not okay. We have to get him out."

He squeezed her arm harder, eliciting a meek whimper of pain as she tried to jerk away from him. "You don't have a clue what is going on here. If you break that circle, there's no telling what will happen, so close your mouth and watch, or, if you don't have the stomach for it, get out of here." He gave her arm one last good squeeze and released her.

She cowered away from him and turned towards the moaning rock star.

Stupid bitch.

With a wail of guitar feedback closing it off, Oaks recognized the riff instantly. "A Gift for the Darkness" was one of Polyphemus's recurring openers. At only four minutes, it wasn't their longest, but it was written to crush the pit. When they kicked things off with this bad boy, the audience only needed to get to the fist-pumping chorus to know what they were in for when they came to see Polyphemus.

As Spiros bent his feedback into a melody that tortured the high-end of his eight-string and Nathan picked his way through a polyrhythmic bassline, Oaks realized the sound was fatter somehow. More powerful. That's when he saw Nathan wasn't playing the bass at all. He had a second eight-string, was hitting the bass-line's root-notes, beefing the rhythm out with palm-muted triplets and muffled strings. Rusty was on the bass, and he was killing it. Chops was here too. He was smashing the double-kick, so in this trip, he was still Polyphemus's drummer. One thing was new, though. Some dude Oaks didn't recognize was on vocals. When the chorus kicked in with the weight of a brick wall, he shared the job with the audience, holding the mike out to them for alternating lines. He delivered the "Kill the pig!" line and they responded with "Cut his throat!" When he gave them the "Kill the beast!" verse, they gave him a reply, "Drink his blood!"

When had he ever interacted with the audience like that? This guy was giving them everything they wanted and the energy coming off them—and the rest of the band—was intense. Shit, he could see it. It was a steam of sweat, a mist, a presence encompassing band and crowd alike. If this was Polyphemus, they might have been at their peak. He couldn't have that. Not if he wasn't involved. The thought pinched like a headache in the frontal lobe, travelled down his spine like an icy finger and settled in his guts where it festered and grew. "Nate!" he called. "Nathan!" but his old friend was lost under a huge weight of decibels; caught up in a moment that saw him windmilling his way through the next riff.

Sensing the vision fading, Oaks tried to see if he knew the dude on vocals. For some reason, remembering him seemed important. As the stage seemed to melt, he felt the presence shifting through his peripherals. For the first time, there wasn't a sickening sensation accompanying it. This time, he gave himself willingly to its control and instead of coming to on the blood-soaked floor of the darkened club, he stayed where he was. The stage had shifted somehow. It wasn't that Polyphemus were playing underneath a night-sky and had clearly moved up the bill. It wasn't that the sky was a mud and ochre chancre that roiled and writhed, it was that the presence that had shadowed him loomed over all of them. No longer a place where people performed for entertainment, the stage had become an altar where his band offered up souls to the entity – or other things like it.

With the presence directing his gaze, it seemed vital that Chops pounded the skins for Polyphemus in the near future. The drummer had always been a machine, but he was hitting the kit with precision, clean and clear. Ahead of him, Nathan, Spiros, and Rusty ploughed their way through riffs. Finally, standing atop a foldback speaker with his arms stretched like a crucified martyr, he saw himself. This audience was *his* audience, and they would do whatever he told them. A shifting spotlight bathed him in the palettes of hell and cryo jets pumped smoke so it swirled around him. The figure he struck was menacing and powerful and the crowd ate it up. With their horns raised, they pumped their fists in time to the music. The song was reaching its crescendo. He thumped his chest as the breakdown hit three pounding notes. He brought the microphone to his chin and the drapery fell. He came to in a mess of blood on the floor of The Exchange. The circle of robed onlookers was a swirling smear. The chorus of demonic voices chittered in whispers that surrounded him. The entity rode him.

"*Stephen,*" it said. The words floated in his head without ever passing his eardrums. "*You have seen the variables. You know your desires. So do we.*" It trailed a clawed finger along his jawbone. "*There will come tasks. You owe completion. Your desires will become reality.*" The image of a remote cabin appeared in his head. "*In this place, you will deliver your first part of the bargain. They will all submit, and you shall have your desires.*"

He was dressed. He should have been naked. Last time he'd seen them all, he'd been naked. He shifted inside his cold, slimy underwear and realized he was soaked in sweat. And worse. Whatever he'd been feeling in his mind all night was gone. He felt as clear as day.

"Welcome back." Anton stood over him, smiling a shark-like rictus.

CHAPTER SEVEN

THE INHERITED REPRESSION

To put it simply, breakfast bongs were the favorite part of Chops's day. What could be better than waking up to some trash television, drinking a warm coffee and dropping a couple of buds into the grinder? After last night's jam session and the discussion about bringing in Rusty and Corey, he was feeling good about his options. The tour with The Violent Dead was going to be a shitload of fun. Even if it didn't pan out to anything else, it'd put some more kudos behind his name, and then the ball would be in his court. If he liked what was happening with Violent, he'd be able to decide whether or not he should, like the Clash, stay or go. Shit, the way things were, he could probably exert a bit of influence over Nathan and the others if he decided to stick it out and go on a couple of tours. If there was one thing those guys needed, it was someone objective to have a voice. He liked Nathan and knew the dude's heart was in the right place, but his allegiance to Oaks was a problem that needed sorting before it festered. If they could get that shit right, they could break some festivals and make some magazine covers.

Decked out in a Tool hoodie and a pair of old slippers, he kicked up the recliner's footrest, found an old re-run of Jerry Springer, packed himself a fat cone, thumb-screwed it, and sparked it up. He sucked down on the bong and exhaled the aromatic smoke as Jerry introduced his first guest: some weirdo who wanted to have his limbs amputated by trains. This one was a good one. Dude was a proper redneck, and later on when Jerry invited out a real amputee, the two fought. He cranked the volume and grabbed his phone. He'd read that the guests used to get free alcohol to limber them up. A quick Google search could confirm that shit. It'd make for a good bit of trivia next time he saw the boys. Before he could search for that, though, he had a message from Rusty. "Yo, dude. Got in touch with Corey. Wants to jam ASAP. U down?"

He hit the call button. That texting shit was a pain in the ass. He couldn't spell at the best of times and he was so stoned his fingers couldn't have tapped a sentence if his life depended on it. He put the phone on speaker mode, sat it next to his bowl and packed himself another billy. He was smoking it when Rusty picked up.

"Yo, this is Rusty."

"Sup, dude?" He coughed like a coal miner. He pounded himself on the chest to help get it out of the system. "Whoo! Shit, that was a good one."

"You okay there, brother? Sound like you're choking on a dick or something."

He laughed. "Nah, man, ain't had no dick here since your mum left an hour ago. Gotta cough to get off; open up those capillaries. Get the THC in where it makes your balls clench."

"You're a freak. D'you get my message?"

"Yeah, man, I got your message. Shit's tight." He drifted off for a moment. The second amputee, on the show to talk the first out of his fetish had arrived on stage. "Put Jerry Springer on, dude. About to be a cripple fight."

"I'm out, man. Getting some new Ernies for the axe. You keen on a jam sesh or what?"

"Fuck yeah, I'm keen." He muted the television. "Tell you the truth, I been feeling kinda down on the whole band lately, but your shit with Corey's got me excited about Polyphemus again, dude."

"That's good to hear. I think we can knock this shit out of

the park. You think we can do something tonight?"

Chops grinned as the amputee ran across Jerry's stage swinging his one good arm back and forth trying to punch the phantom limb fantasist. "Yeah, man, I don't see why not. Ain't got anything else on. You want me to hit up the boys?"

"Yeah, do that. Feels a bit weird for me to arrange shit."

Chops was all too happy to get the ball rolling. "Leave it with me. I'll make it happen." He increased the volume, watched Steve-O separate the two losers and laughed as the audience chanted the host's name.

Nathan waited for a waitress to scoot past him, then placed the two pints on the table and smiled at Calliope as she pointed at him with one hand and bounced her sippy cup on the table with the other. He really was a selfish bastard. Apart from visiting Spiros and Pandora right after their daughter's birth, he'd paid bugger-all attention to the family. He'd kept in touch with Spiros, but aside from asking about the girls out of common courtesy, he'd treated them like an inconvenience. With that in mind, he was kind of lucky Spiros was about. The Greek was a good dude, everyone knew that, but here with his daughter, he was exhibiting a whole other side of his life.

Spiros grabbed one of the beers and held it out for Nathan to clink with his own. "We should have done this more often." He took a deep swig.

Nathan drank his greedily. "You have no idea how much I need this beer. Nah, don't look at me like that. I don't mean I need a beer or I'm gonna get the shakes or anything." He swirled the glass, watched the foam run down the sides. "I mean it's been a stressful couple of days."

"Relax. It's no secret you like your drink. I can't

remember the last time I saw you without a beer in your hand, but I'm not judging." He dropped a rusk stick in front of his daughter. "You're worried about Oaks?"

"Did you see the email from Cormac?"

"No. Should I have?"

"Yeah." He drank a deep swig of his beer. "They're bringing the album demo submission deadline forward to the end of next month." He gave Spiros a 'can you believe this shit' lift of the eyebrows.

Spiros zipped up his hoodie. "Fuck. They know what's been going on. That's ridiculous."

"No shit. And we're back to where we were: two months to get into the studio and record the fucking thing without a vocalist before they start fining us and we end up in court. That shit's broken bands bigger than us. We can't do it."

"Well, if all goes well today, then at least we can offer Corey a recording gig. It might not be so bad."

Nathan pinched his bottom lip, rapped his knuckles on the table. "That's it, though. This Corey shit—it's gonna have to be me who breaks it to Oaks—and that's going to kill him."

"You're a stress-head, we all know this, but let me tell you that if you're worried about Oaks, you don't need to feel bad. You have to put the emotion aside and remember that this is a business decision. I think the Corey thing is good news. Shit might be falling into place at the right time, but you don't have to talk to Oaks alone. I'll help."

"Yeah, well, we need to find him first. I've been trying to get hold of him since last night. Dude is AWOL. You don't think he's…"

"Nate. What he's doing is his decision. Despite all his flaws, he's a grown man. You can't wrap him in cotton wool, and neither can I. Personally, I noticed he's been offline since the other night. Maybe he's moved on already. Wouldn't he have been pestering us if he *really* wanted this?"

Nathan cracked his knuckles. "It's not his style. You

remember our first jobs as telemarketers. He got the flick because he couldn't bear trying to convince people."

"Of course. He said it wasn't up to him to force people and that if they wanted it, they would buy it without being convinced." He shrugged his shoulders. "You might be right, but there is nothing we can do except perhaps wait for him to contact us." He wiped some drool from Calliope's chin. "When he does, then we'll talk to him together. We're betraying him. Married couples fight and disagree all the time." This time, he drank. "Trust me. I know. This band, man, this band...Pandora is not a fan. Last night we had it out over us jamming again, but what it comes down to is that if someone's worth having around, they'll respect your choices even if they don't like them."

Nathan knew he should dig deeper here. It'd be exactly the kind of thing a good friend would do, but at the same time, fuck that. The last thing he needed was to add worry about Spiros's position in the band to his list of issues. "Okay, so there's Oaks and you'll help with that—not that I don't feel like a piece of shit about it. Do you remember Lisa?"

"The groupie chick you were banging?"

"Yeah."

He drank, finishing his beer. "Well, she turned up the other night. Lures me in with these dirty pictures and then, when she turns up at the door, she's up the duff; claims it's mine."

"You're kidding."

Nathan watched Calliope. There was no doubt she was a cute kid, but she was also a little shitting, pissing, eating machine. When she wasn't being cute, she was hard work. All kids were. "Nah, man, I'm not kidding. Crazy bitch hasn't gone home."

Spiros slapped both hands on the table. "Dude, you cannot allow this. Please tell me you have not been sleeping with her."

"Do I look like an idiot to you?"

"Well, no, but I know you are one." He laughed his goofy hee-hawing laugh and pushed Nathan's shoulder. Calliope laughed too. "My friend, the real danger with this is that if she is in your house and the baby is yours, she could make your life very difficult."

Nathan called the waitress. "You want another beer?"

Spiros glanced at his watch. "Just a schooner. We have to drop Calliope off before we go to jam." He threw a twenty on the table. "On the way, you can call Chops and talk to him about Corey and the new timeline."

After the party, he'd gone to Anton's place in a limo to keep drinking and racking lines with some of the others. It had been a blast, but for some reason he couldn't remember, India had bailed on him. He'd have to catch up with her later and find out exactly what had happened. As it was, though, he had a bottle of whiskey beside him and he was gonna sit in Anton's kick-ass rooftop spa drinking and enjoying the view. Pouring three fingers for himself, he wondered if he could see the halfway house from his position. What a joke. He'd been partying all night and he didn't feel at all like shooting up. Matter of fact, he'd never felt this clear-headed and confident. Clarity, man, that's what he had sitting there in the steaming, bubbling water. Well, clarity and all the world he could see beneath him. He'd catch up with the boys later and let them know that everything would work out. He hadn't seen Spiros or that loser Chops, but today seemed like a good day to feed the drummer's ego and grovel a little. He quaffed the whiskey. That shit with the other singer in last night's dream was troubling him, but that prick Chops was central to everything.

Once he was done there, he'd have to get in touch with India and find out what her problem was last night; why she bailed on him. The whole thing had been pretty important, so if she couldn't stomach it—although she'd supposedly been through it—he'd have to ask her a few pertinent questions.

Reaching for the whiskey, he noticed he wasn't alone. For a split-second, he'd thought it was Anton, but as soon as he realized the faceless presence was already staring at him, his pulse quickened and his breath caught. It was the same feeling of awe he'd got from his earliest crushes: a nervous fear melting into a longing for touch and the sense that only this smoky shade could fill the void in his heart.

"*Do not forget,*" it said. "*You owe. You are obligated.*"

A coldness spread through his chest. What did he owe? How was he obligated? He needed to ask, but with all his blood rushing to his cock and the overwhelming desire coursing through his veins, he leaned forward instead. The presence moved toward him, but instead of kissing him, its hideously clawed hand snapped tight around his throat. "*Do not sit idle. Failure to meet your end of the bargain will not go well for you, Stephen Oaks; this is not some genie's wish. You must act to affect the outcome yourself.*"

"How you doing in there, Stephen?"

Anton. The grip on Oaks's throat loosened. The presence disappeared and the life coach leaned on the side of the Jacuzzi. "I've got some business to run. I'm heading into Amielle's. Thought I'd give you a lift if you were done."

"Better drop me off in town. She doesn't need to see me drinking yet." Yeah, town would work a treat. Nathan had been trying to get hold of him for a few days. He'd better go see him and let him know that he hadn't fallen off the wagon.

CHAPTER EIGHT
SLAUGHTER OF THE SOUL

Whatever last night had been, it wasn't what she'd expected. She'd seen more than a few initiations and none of them had gone like Stephen's. Anton had drugged him or something. The way he'd writhed on the floor, the raging boner, the way he'd startled awake at the end; the bastard had done something and Stephen had paid the price. She ought to call the pigs on the prick; an anonymous tip that let them know a few unsavory things about the billionaire life coach.

She poked the bruise on her arm for what must have been the five-hundredth time and touched a paintbrush to the palette. She'd been asked to contribute a piece to a themed gallery display, but shit wasn't working for her today. She would usually have finished a decent amount of line-work by this time of the morning, but all she could visualize was the intensity of Anton's eyes as he'd grabbed her by the arm and told her *there was no telling what would happen if she broke that circle.*

It was far too soon for all of that, though. All she was doing was whining, and if her mother taught her anything it was that you only whine and carry on when you're using that shit as a tool. Anything other than that and you were giving people what they expected of a skinny little bitch. Far better to repress the emotion, let it harden into a dagger you could use later. That's what Mum had done when she'd beaten Dad's head in with an ashtray. The blood-spatter had painted the brick mantelpiece in the lounge-room with a galaxy of skull fragments, brains and crimson stars.

India wasn't beaten, but Anton regarded her the same way her dead father regarded her mother before that final explosion of violence. She planted an angry smudge of black onto the canvas and swept it across the raw image coming together in her mind.

Despite the fact he had been alone when Anton dropped him off, Oaks had company soon after he hailed a cab and told it to head to Nathan's place. As the vehicle cruised through traffic on the way out to the suburbs, he was watching the highway scenery melt into a blur when the seat next to him shifted with the feeling of a weight pressing on it. A finger caressed the line of his jaw, up the nape of his neck and down his spine. The grey presence leaned into him; licked the inside of his ear and scratched a claw along his clavicle.

The cab-driver was oblivious, but India was there beside Oaks. The vocalist didn't know how or when she'd gotten into the cab, but he wasn't complaining. He needed her touch. Pushing his face to hers, desperate for the kiss, he was disappointed when she pulled away. "*You have work to do first.*" The claw that had been circling his nipple, pressed into his chest, drawing blood in a trickle. "*You're slow, but today you will see what you need to motivate you.*" India's face started to swirl and ripple. The shadows in its recesses grew, and the ink-stain presence that had hounded him since last night coalesced into view. "*When you arrive, make the driver wait. You won't be there long.*"

Oaks came to reality, unsure how the driver hadn't noticed anything. A sensation of dirtiness had settled deep within him. It was as if cockroaches and worms crawled in and out of his skin, nesting there, burrowing, rooting for purchase. Outside, the highway had given way to suburbia. The normality of it all sickened him. He was destined for bigger and better. The fact that even a few months ago, he'd accepted all of this and had thought he'd made it because he had released a couple of records and done a few interviews for street-press magazines was the biggest mistake of his life. If he'd made it, would he be broke as fuck? Living in a halfway home while he recovered from the kind of addiction only the lowliest scum got sucked into? Not a chance. Thankfully, though, that shit was done. From here, it was serious business.

"Take the street on the left. Park her out front and wait up. I'll need another ride if no one's home."

The driver took the left.

Nathan's house was a shambles. Wedged back in the corner of the little street, the hedgerows lining its boundaries needed trimming. The grass was worse. There was a car there he didn't recognize, but that didn't matter. He knocked on the door, and a pregnant chick came to the window, peeling the curtains aside, not bothering to open the door. "He's not here. You missed him."

He thought he recognized her but given that he'd been high for most of his recent life, she could be anyone. Especially without the dark lighting and haze of most clubs. "Shit. You know when he'll be back?"

She rolled her eyes. "Am I his Mum? They're, like, testing a new singer or something. He'll probably be late. You want me to take a message?"

That presence was once again loitering in the peripherals of his vision, shifting, laughing. He ignored it. "Stephen," he said. "Stephen Oaks."

"Wait, you're Oaks? What happened to your hair?" She smiled weakly. "Sorry, man. Sucks to be you, huh? Nathan should have his phone if you want to call him. If not, I'll take a message."

"Nah, but tell him I came round." Oaks returned to the

taxi. "Drop C Studios," he said to the driver. "Take me there."

When they arrived, he could already hear Chops's signature drum-rolls squeezing their way out of the room's small ventilation window. They always jammed in the back room bordering the forested parkland behind the studio, so he knew exactly where to go. At first, he could hear only instrumental music. That was promising, but when the vocals cut in, his stomach sank. How could they? This band was his everything. He'd been there since the start at St Quirinus when the band had been nothing but a logo scrawled in his math book. And Nathan, fucking Nathan should have had the balls to tell him, to front up and own it rather than act like a scared little child and avoid the issue.

"Do you see the dilemma facing you?"

That voice. He couldn't see the presence, but he could feel it caressing its way across his thoughts. What was he supposed to do? Clearly the Anton thing had been for nothing. That was it, he would never be at the front of Polyphemus again. He'd go home, find someone to score off and wipe himself into oblivion. It was the only thing he could do.

"You'll do no such thing. You will stay. Have your faith broken. The bargain will be honored and you must act to facilitate it. One way or another, you must bring them into the fold and that means you will watch the things that transpire here."

The band was tight. Shit, they might have been sounding better than they had in a long time. Corey was killing it, and Chops, well Chops was always a true professional, but he was damn sharp lately. It was no wonder The Violent Dead were trying to poach him. He'd always known the guy was a machine, seemingly growing extra arms and putting out unimaginable amounts of energy—all while staying calm as fuck—but seeing him up close and personal with a full band—including Rusty and a vocalist with the intensity that Corey brought to the table—was something else. And, yeah, while Chops was hitting every skin-rattling stop on the classic covers the boys were putting out, Nathan had to give Corey some credit too. The guy had absolutely crushed the Slugdge, At The Gates, and Fear Factory songs they had burned through, and as much as Nathan might not want to admit it, he was a good fit.

While Corey caught his breath after doing his best Burton C Bell impression for a cover of "Self Bias Resistor", Nathan fired a text to Spiros and Chops, then stomped his overdrive off and drank from the beer on his amp. "You ready to try some of our shit?" he asked once he'd plopped it down.

Spiros rattled out the intro riff to "The Sacrifice Poles" and raised the horns. "You know this one?" His fingers swirled effortlessly across the fretboard as he fired the jumpy little rhythm out a couple more times.

"Count it in," Corey said to Chops. "Let's do this."

Chops obliged and Spiros started the song off properly. A couple of bars later, Rusty brought in the low end and Nathan smashed his distortion pedal on and doubled over the line with a palm muted riff before the whole thing built up to an early crescendo and Corey gave the opening line everything he had. *"Ritual skulls! Impaled on the sacrifice poles!"*

Spiros was making impressed faces at the others and trying not to grin by halfway through the song, and with the chorus fast approaching, Corey had a big test coming up. When it landed, the whole thing would need to alternate between shrieking demon vocals and a throaty bellow. *"A lonely stretch of coastline. An island, home to torment and a twisted mind. A vicious game. Of life and death at the whim of the vespiary. You cannot escape! What you are! Your lifetime! Your life a lie! You'll fall victim to the call of the wasp factory!"*

In his mind, there may as well already be a pit in front of him. He could picture it churning and pulsing, writhing like a great peristaltic blob ingesting the multitude of black-garbed bodies as they pressed together, heads thrashing and fists pumping. The song finished, and Nathan peered out the window. There was someone there; he could feel them watching. He moved closer to it, peering out, trying to see who it was. No one. Maybe in the tree line? "Did you see anyone outside?"

Spiros shrugged. "You're tripping balls, man. There's no one out there."

Nathan wasn't so sure. Fuck it; whatever. He emptied his beer. "You think you've got "On the Shore of the Black Ocean" down, Corey?"

"Try me."

This one ought to pose a bit of a challenge. It was a breakneck speed moshpit song with barely a second to pause for the vocalist. Chops counted it in and everyone jumped on its opening groove.

Nathan felt eyes on him again. Someone watching. He shook off the sensation and slammed into the next riff, breaking a string as he tried the sweep-picked opening lick. "Fuck!" He unslung the guitar from his shoulder and thrust it onto its stand. "Some fucker's out there, man," he said as the others came to a crumbling stop.

"Don't worry about it, dude. I think you're nuts, but let them listen if they are. What harm could it do?"

Nathan grunted and whipped up another guitar, this one an Ibanez. Chops counted them in. Nathan went through the motions of the song, but he kept turning to the window. Could he see a man-shape out there?

"Sorry," he said when they were done, "but I've gotta get some fresh air. Why don't you guys have a smoke break?"

"Good idea," Chops said. "We can talk to these two

clowns then as well."

"Fuck you," Rusty said. "If we're clowns, you're the bearded lady. Small-dick bearded lady at that. What you think, Corey?"

"Man, I don't know about the dude's dick, but I think bearded lady's a damn good call."

Nathan snatched another beer out of the cooler and made his way out onto the balcony. There, right on the edge of the tree line, he could make out the shape of a man. *Oaks?* Goddamn, had he come here and found them jamming with another singer? Was he listening to the whole thing?

The wind gently gusted and the shape melted into the shifting shadows of the night. If it was Oaks, he needed to talk to him. The balcony was on the second story, but it was an easy climb. If he lowered himself down, he'd only have a short drop. He threw a leg over the rail, spinning so he was holding on with both hands.

"What the fuck are you doing?" Spiros asked when he made his own way onto the balcony.

"Chill, man, I gotta check something."

"Use the stairs like a normal person. And I'm taking your damn beers, dude. You've been drinking too much."

Nathan let that slide. "Back in a second." He lowered himself and dropped down to the bitumen below. He found the tree Oaks—if it was Oaks—had been loitering behind. No one. Wait, yes there was. Someone—*something*—huge. Hulking. Not Oaks anymore—if it ever was—but something bigger, more powerful. Its barrel-sized shoulders were silhouetted against the light bark of the moonlit tree. The branches above its head forked out like horns. Another breeze blew. The susurration of the leaves surfed across the foliage. The shape disappeared again.

Approaching the spot, a chill ran up his spine. He checked his shoulder. He could hear the general chat on the balcony as a murmur. Nothing in crisp clarity, but a general hubbub punctuated by barking laughter. The boys telling jokes.

Something rustled beside him. Big. Heavy.

"Yo, Oaks, is that you?"

The rasping growl of a possum croaked through the otherwise still night.

"Oaks, if you're out here, we can talk."

No response. There, though, that shape again. He moved towards it; chest tight.

"Hey! Nathan, get your ass back, we need to talk, remember!"

They were right. What was he doing out here? Did he think Oaks was listening or did he have a guilty conscience? Worse, was he scared that Oaks had gotten up to mischief again already? "All right, I'll be there in a second!" He focused on a spot where he could have sworn the hulking shape had reappeared. Again, there was nothing but a swirling grey mist. Localized fog in a cool spot. *Something like that*. He made his way to the studio.

That was *too* close. Despite all logic, Nathan hadn't seen him. At times, he was certain his friend, well, the man he had thought was his friend was staring straight at him. The thing in his peripherals had enveloped him somehow; had masked him. With Nathan—the traitor—returning to the studio, he found himself walking around the perimeter of the property, the presence shifting and shimmering in and out of his peripherals; its claws digging into his shoulders.

"You must see this. Listen to this."

Before long, he came to a low hedgerow that hugged the building and led to a concealed shed within hearing range of the balcony.

"In there. You will listen. Then, later, you will act."

Inside the shed, the studio's bins were locked away. Oaks

squatted down, leaning on one and ignored the smell of
rotten garbage as he listened.

Corey laughed with the rest of the guys as Nathan made his
way through the corridor and out onto the balcony. Spiros
wrapped an arm around the guitarist's shoulders. "I mean
what I said, man, are you drunk?"

Nathan laughed him off. "Nah, well, I'm tipsy, but I
needed some fresh air. Thought I saw someone out there.
Must have been punk kids."

"Fuck 'em. Maybe they're making a bootleg."

Corey hadn't heard of anyone making a bootleg for years.
In a way, it'd be kinda cool. He packed a cone for the
guitarist and held the bong out. "We saved you a couple,
chief."

Nathan thanked him and punched the billy.

Chops took it from him and packed another. "I was telling
Corey that we haven't had someone hit the vocals with the
intensity he does in a while."

The singer thought he saw Nathan shake his head a little,
but he supposed it was more at Chops's enthusiasm than
anything else. He knew Nathan had been keen on getting
Oaks back, but the idea had been vetoed by everyone else.
With that in mind, he was surprised when Nathan concurred
with the drummer.

"Chops is right," he said. "You're nailing it, man.
Everyone knows this has been a huge period for us, but it's
good to have you on board. If I'm honest with myself, Oaks
hadn't been on the ball for a while before he crashed." He
raised his beer towards Rusty. "You too, dude. Anyway,
Spiros, myself and Chops had to have a pretty serious
discussion earlier. We got an email from the label this

morning and they're only giving us two months to get the new album recorded. While it's awesome that we're gonna have some of these new tracks out there in the public consciousness sooner, it means we've got to make some decisions on personnel in a pretty timely manner..."

"What he means to ask," Spiros said, "Is do you motherfuckers want to be in our heavy metal band?"

Corey did. He definitely did.

CHAPTER NINE
EXISTENCE IS FUTILE

Apart from Nathan's weird little venture into the trees, the night couldn't have gone better. The band was sounding good, they had set a recording date, and although Rusty had been a casual member for a while, they had formalized everything and secured Corey as a vocalist. Polyphemus was a real band again. Shit, it was more than that, it was one that was going to drop a new album in the next few months, and that was a feeling he'd never grow tired of. He had to explain it to Pandora, but with the flowers sitting on the passenger seat, that should be a piece of cake.

Once he got inside, he saw Pandora sitting at the kitchen bar, a bottle of wine almost empty on the bench beside her. As she swung her eyes across to him, he realized they were heavy with contempt. His heart caught in his chest. "You all right, babe?"

She guzzled the remains of the glass in front of her and poured another. "We're done, Spiros. I told you that it was me and your daughter or your stupid band. You still want to be a teenager playing at getting famous. We deserve better."

He dropped the keys on the lounge-room coffee table. "You have everything you could want. How can it be so difficult to let me have this?"

"I let you have this," she said. "It failed. Your idiot friends let you down and you could never be better than another run-of-the-mill band. This is something that will always cost us money."

"Money is not an issue. You know that." He held the flowers out to her. They seemed to have wilted, their brightness dulled by the situation. "Think about everything we've been through. I don't get it. We have a kid."

"You should have thought of that."

"You're drunk."

"No, I'm not, and my mind is made up. You can't change it."

He thrust the flowers towards her again. "But, babe, I bought you flowers."

"They only mean that things are about to get worse. If you had gone and hung out with your friends and returned in a bad mood, I would be happy." She poured the remnants of the bottle into her glass. "It would at least mean your jam session had turned to shit. As it is, though, it's obvious what has happened."

"The label is going to sue us. Who do you think wears the brunt of that?"

"You said it yourself; money is not an issue, and honestly, I would rather be sued—especially on something we could probably defend—than see you return to your band and your junkie friends."

"That band existed before you came along, but more importantly, we have a kid."

"You *had* a kid."

"You can't do this."

"I can, and I am. I thought about telling you that if you wanted to fix this, you needed to say goodbye to this stupid obsession of yours, but it wouldn't matter. Nothing will stop you re-forming, writing another album and touring the country while you leave me at home with Calliope. When will I matter, Spiros? When will my goals not play second-fiddle to yours?"

"Give me this one last chance. We have to do the album, and the deadline is so close, we wouldn't be moved out and separated before it had to be finalized."

She glared at him. "And then what? You tour? Take us all the way to square one? How long does a tour take?"

"Give me until the album's done, and then we can figure out the rest. You're afforded a good life. You don't have to work. You can come with me on the road. We can hire a nanny; make arrangements."

She glared at him.

"This album, babe. That's all I'm asking for."

She walked into the yawing darkness of the stairwell and disappeared. When she was gone, Spiros slumped onto a stool at the breakfast counter. Why could nothing ever be simple?

It was all wrong. He had done everything that Anton had said. Why was *his* band doing this? He had met his side of the bargain and allowed that *seeming* thing into him; shit should be happening. He had paid for it. He had *earned* it. He waited for his phone-call to ring out and kneaded his forehead with hard knuckles. When Anton didn't pick up, he threw the phone at the couch and bit his lip.

Unable to ask what he was supposed to do, he made his way to his cockroach-infested bedroom. He couldn't pussy out of this. He'd been told time and time again that if he sat idle, things wouldn't end well. One of the big lessons they'd taught at St Quirinus—and at the rehab center—was that the Lord would help those who helped themselves. The entity that had shadowed him since last night must feel the same. Whatever he was going to do, he had to do alone.

If only he could settle his mind. If only he could calm down and think straight. Make a rational decision. He slammed his door. Opened it. Slammed it. Opened it again. Amielle could help him when she came home. Would help him. Would give him something to help him settle.

But he couldn't wait.

He crossed to the master bedroom, opened the door, and slipped inside.

There was nothing in any of the drawers. In the cupboard. Under the bed. Goddammit. He knew she had some gear here somewhere. She had to. He went into the ensuite. The cupboard below the vanity was padlocked. Fucking bitch.

He thought about searching for a key. He'd seen collections of keys around the place, but what was the point? If he got on, she'd know anyway. No point trying to hide things.

He kicked the low cupboard as hard as he could, aiming for the padlock, desperate to smash it free. *Stop it,* his conscience chided. *You've come so far.* But what did it matter? This was who he was. *Nobody. Nothing. A hack.* He kicked again, and the handle broke from the cupboard door, letting the padlocked chain tumble free. Inside, a tan leather bag was tucked away. He opened it up. Bingo.

Fuck the band.

Fuck Anton.

Fuck it all.

The whole kit and caboodle was there. He took it all and ran to his own room, barricading the door with his bedhead. Certain he couldn't be disturbed, he slipped into his familiar ritual.

"No."

The edges of his vision melted into fog. A smoky smudge of *seeming* loomed over him.

"No."

Yes. He needed this to think; to set him right before he made his plan. He pressed the needle into his skin.

The entity flared, angry.

Oaks pressed the plunger on the syringe and fell onto the pillow, waiting for euphoria to wash through his bloodstream. In a few hours, his mind would be clearer. He'd know what he was going to do. He'd start fresh again tomorrow.

A cold hand closed around his throat. Another grabbed his upper arm. *"You will not shirk this."* Tremendous pain flowered around the tiny hole he'd pierced in his inner elbow. His muscles contracted. Pulsed. Mud-colored liquid oozed from his pores, running down his arm in sickly trickles. The fog that was already settling over him cleared.

As soon as the hand released him, he shot up, wiped one of the runnels, and licked it clean. "I need to think! What are you doing?" He slurped at his inner elbow, tried to gather the last of the ooze trailing his forearm.

Something like a punch impacted his sternum. He fell, wheezing. Once more, that cold hand wrapped around his throat, and then, that penetrating feeling in his chest returned. The entity had him pinned, was pushing its clawed hand inside, wrapping it around his heart.

"When your work is done, and your side of the bargain fulfilled, you will control your own destruction. Until then, you are mine to toy with."

"What can I do?" Oaks writhed, his skin crawling with the wrongness of his lot. "You saw what happened. Corey is the band's vocalist. You failed me. I cannot give what was promised if you don't help."

The hand around his heart squeezed.

"Okay, okay. I just...I don't know how to get rid of him. I need to think."

The entity chuckled. *"Kill him."*

He couldn't kill anyone. Shit, he'd never punched anyone. Wouldn't hurt a fly. "I'll go to jail. Never be able to give you what you want."

"Find a way."

Oaks rifled through the kitbag he'd found in Amielle's bathroom. *An overdose?* "How? I don't know where to find him?"

"Find a way."

Oaks's phone rang. He snatched it up. Nathan. By the time he shifted his attention to the entity, it was gone. Despite everything, he felt a swell of hope that his old friend had changed his tune since earlier and was calling to invite him back into the fold. He took the call.

With Corey all but confirmed, Nathan had to break the news to Oaks. He had decided with Spiros that they'd take him fishing and talk to him there. He'd put it off for as long as he could, responding to emails from Cormac about potential studios to record in, arguing with Lisa, and practicing some of the new material. Sooner or later, though, he had to make the call, even if he didn't expect his old friend to answer.

"Hey, shit, Oaks, how you doing? Been trying to get hold of you for days."

"I'm good, man. Good. Busy, you know."

The vocalist sounded flaky. Short of breath. Was he high? Was that why he'd disappeared?

"Yeah, man, I know how it is. Anyway, the reason I'm calling is to hit you up for a fishing trip tomorrow. Spiros is keen to head out to the overflow and catch up. He's bummed he hasn't seen you yet."

"Is that where you plan on telling me you've got another vocalist?"

Motherfucker. He was *lurking in the shadows earlier.* "Steve...I..."

"You don't have to mollycoddle me. I get it, man. It's not your fault that I'm out of *our* band. The one *we* started in high school."

Nathan's skin crawled. The sensation of otherness he'd experienced in the bush behind the studio earlier settled on him again. That vague notion of something huge loitering in liminal spaces. "Hold on a minute. It doesn't have to be something permanent. We're under a ton of pressure. The label wants the record, man. They're hounding us for it. Threatening litigation."

"Well that explains everything."

This wasn't going the way it was supposed to. Seriously, why couldn't shit be easy for once? "C'mon, man, this isn't all on us. On *me*. I've fought for you. Stood by you. Done everything I could to make sure you were catered for, while you self-destructed and nearly took us with you. I mean, you've already dropped off the face of the earth again."

"You're wrong there. I came by your house earlier. How do you think I knew about your little jam session?"

Lisa. Why hadn't she told him that? "Okay, whatever, but this is the first I'm hearing of it. Why haven't you been in touch? How am I supposed to know you're not dead in some gutter with a needle in your arm?"

"Fuck you."

"No, fuck *you*. We need someone now, and you're so selfish, you don't give a shit. Not that you could, but while you're wasting away in your own private hell, you don't care about the rest of the band and the fact we have bills and goals and aspirations. That's on you." He noticed Lisa walk into the room and glared at her. She smiled and sat on the couch.

There was an awkward pause on the other end of the line before Oaks answered. "I see how it is. You're probably right. I could have been in touch. I could have shown you that I'm not the big flake you all think I am and that this shit's important to me too. I just...it's tough, man, seeing everything you love get palmed off to someone else. I've got so much to offer. So much to apologize for, and I feel like I could make that up to you if I had another shot, but I get it. I get it."

"Dude, I'm sorry too, but you have to understand. I tried. It's people's livelihoods here. They didn't want to take the risk of having you collapse on us again, and I can't force that."

"Promise me one thing, man. If you guys need me, you'll ask. I've been working on some shit that'll help us, man. It really will."

"Why don't you come out for that fishing trip, and we'll talk about it there? It'll be good for Spiros to talk to you."

Oaks agreed, and Nathan hung up.

Lisa, who was sitting on the couch absently rubbing her pregnant belly smiled at him. "Who was that?"

"That was Oaks. Why didn't you tell me he came over?"

She shrugged her shoulders. "Dunno. Didn't seem important."

"I want you gone. Get the DNA test done, and then you can move on. I don't know what you're trying to do here, but if you want to rip someone off, there are better options than me."

She threw a cushion at him. It whizzed past him and bounced off the wall. "Do you think I don't know that? Do you think you're the pick for number one Dad? You're a loser. A hack. A no-good, alcoholic piece of shit who couldn't last long enough to pull out. You're the bottom of the barrel. The bottom."

He wanted to slap her. Could feel his hand twitching with anger, but he couldn't do it. He'd never struck anyone, let alone a lady, but she'd cut him to the bone. He walked to the fridge, pulled out a beer and popped the cap. "Get the test. If it's mine, we'll work out some payments. If it's not, you owe me rent. Now fuck off."

"Classy, Nate. Real classy."

The guitarist flipped open his phone and sat on the couch facing away from her. He had a new notification from the band's manager, Cormac. He'd booked them into Tomb Studios, out in the sticks, as far away from Drop C Studios, their regular jam-room, as possible. Better still, it was a step up from Symbolic, where The Violent Dead jammed and recorded too. The label must still have some faith in them.

With a studio like that, they'd be able to get away from all the bullshit and focus on what mattered out there: Polyphemus. Everything else could go to shit, but if they recorded the best album that place had ever seen, he knew things would work out fine. They had to.

He forwarded the email onto the others and drank his beer.

Corey couldn't believe his luck. The jam session yesterday had been a treat, and the band was dead serious about having him record on the album. Nathan had already sent him a calendar appointment via email, and the label had booked them in to Tomb Studios to start recording. It was a dream come true, despite the residual guilt over taking Stephen Oaks's place in the band. There was clearly some underlying tension going on around that, but then everyone knew that Polyphemus's ex-vocalist had fucked up on their tour with The Violent Dead.

The way Corey saw it; he'd been as disappointed as anyone. He'd loved Polyphemus's last album, cranking it daily, and Oaks's vocals were a huge part of that. He respected the guy; thought he was one of the best in the business. He'd tried to bring a lot of what Oaks did into Rabid God's more death-influenced breakdowns, but he'd never thought he'd be taking his spot in Polyphemus.

Flipping through Nathan's friends list on social media, he thought about sending the dude a message. It'd be good to talk. To ask him his vision for the band. It felt right. After all, the split was more about health and circumstance than any acrimonious nonsense.

Someone pounded on the door.

He checked his watch. Almost midnight. What the hell?

He jogged downstairs and stuck his eye against the peephole. Oaks was standing there, leaning against the wall, waiting for him to open the door.

"Yo, Corey," he said. "It's me, Stephen Oaks, I wanted to wish you well."

There was a word for when you saw a person shortly after you'd been thinking about them: synchronicity or some shit. Whatever it was, it was weird. Still, he couldn't leave the guy standing there. He opened the wooden door. "I didn't know if you knew, I was thinking of messaging you. How'd you find me, though, man?"

Oaks waved his hand dismissively. "It's not that hard these days. You can find anyone if you want to."

"Well, yeah, I hope there's no hard feelings. I mean, I was about to try to get in contact with you online, see if we could talk."

Oaks rested a hand on the screen door handle. "Is it an okay time? I just…you know, with everything, I thought I should talk to you, so it seems like…y'know."

Was there something in the dude's eyes? Was he high? "I'm not far from bed, man."

Oaks appeared crestfallen. "Ah, well, maybe some other time."

Corey's heart sank. "It's all right, dude, I don't have much on tomorrow. RDO. Come in, I can sleep after." He pointed to a small plastic table next to the tiny kitchen. "I'm afraid the digs aren't crash-hot but make yourself comfortable."

Oaks fiddled with something in his jacket's breast pocket. "You said you wanted to ask me some things; what were they?"

Corey poured a glass of juice, swirled it, and sat down. "I hoped I might be able to pick your brain. But you came all the way here. You start."

"I wrote a shit-ton of lyrics while I was at the center." He drew a Moleskine from a small satchel. "I know I'm not gonna get to use them myself, but it'd mean a lot if you'd use a few on the record."

Corey let his eyes drift over Oaks's inner elbow as he reached out to grab the pad. He might have been thinking the same thing himself, but it was a big ask when it wasn't invited. "I can read 'em, but I'm not sure it's up to me." Realizing that Oaks was watching him closely, he made a show of opening the notebook and inspecting the lyrics.

Oaks reached into his inner pocket and fiddled with something. "Can I use the bathroom?" he asked, standing up.

As he walked past, Corey saw Oaks whip something from his breast pocket. Whatever it was, it glinted in the bright glare coming from the down lights as Oaks lifted it high in the air and plunged it down. He could have sworn it dripped venom like the fang of some great snake.

He didn't have time to confirm.

It bit into his shoulder. He jerked away, but it was too late. By the time he realized Oaks was holding an empty syringe, the liquid was sweeping through his bloodstream. Within seconds, he couldn't be angry with the bald vocalist looming over him. A pleasant sensation had settled over him. His skin prickled with warmth, and his arms and legs felt heavy. "You drugged me," he said, grinning.

"No, *you* drugged you."

Where Oaks had been standing a moment ago, something else stood, engulfing Corey in its voluminous shadow. It was huge, towering above him, and if he didn't know better, he'd swear it had fangs like tusks. Horns erupted from its head in grasping claws, black fur coated it, eyes that gazed down like bullet-holes held him in disdain. "You're not Oaks."

Creeping tendrils of swirling smoke weaved their way in and out of his peripheral vision. He shook his heavy head, realizing that it *was* Oaks in front of him and not a monster. "Funny," he said. "You seemed to be something else there for a second."

Oaks grasped Corey's arm and exposed the inner elbow. He shook a vial of liquid and slipped the syringe inside it.

"I don't think that's how you do it."

Oaks pressed the needle into Corey's exposed arm, injected the milky solution, and gently lifted Corey's face by the chin. "Beggars can't be choosers, Corey. Sometimes we have to play the cards we're given."

Corey's body bloomed with warmth. This was amazing. Then he realized something was all wrong. Oaks pressed the needle into his other elbow. "You're killing me, aren't you?"

The monster was back. It held his numb face between giant hands. In Oaks's voice, it soothed him as it seemed to melt into the shape of Oaks. It was as if the creature existed and wasn't only a manifestation of the former Rabid God man's addled brain.

"Hold this." Oaks, behind a swirling grey cloud of nothingness passed him the needle. "I'll make sure I write a song for you. We'll call it "The Usurper Falls". Or something like that.

As soon as Oaks released his grip, Corey's head nodded down to his chest. He was so sleepy. His limbs were so tired. He wanted to sleep. He started to drift off, only to feel himself coaxed to his feet, and led to his bed. He was guided into position, lying prone. His mouth gaped open, and Oaks poured what was left of the drug into his mouth. He tried to swallow it. Tried to spit it out, but his body was useless. His gorge pushed against it, but there was no strength in his muscles. None at all.

Aware but uncaring, Corey realized he was choking to death. Asphyxiating. The last things he ever heard were Oaks's footsteps as the vocalist left the room, and the gentle closing of his front door.

CHAPTER TEN
EARTHBORN EVOLUTION

India rolled towards Stephen and draped an arm across his midriff. God only knew what he'd been up to last night, but he'd been stone-cold sober when he called for a ride.

Right now, he was sleeping like the dead. A line of drool ran from his mouth. Not even the sounds of garbage trucks rattling bottles and trash, traffic rumbling past, or several phone-calls to his cell could wake him, so when the phone rang a fourth time, India picked it up, recognizing the name of Stephen's current—and her former—case manager. "Hey, Tina, it's me, India. He's with me. We met up last night. No, no, he's sober. He's sleeping, though."

She put down the phone and rolled out of bed, leaving Oaks where he was. The conditions of his release into rehab meant that Tina was going to have to report him, and he could find himself back in the center. That was the last thing he needed. Anyone could see how close to breaking he was.

She rubbed the bruise on her arm, and snatched up her own phone, punching in Anton's name. "Anton," she said. "You need to talk to Tina. Stephen came here last night. He wasn't on the gear, but he was out and about late at night. He called me to come get him and I brought him home. Amielle's pissing herself over the rules, and she's about to call the clinic."

"I'll sort it," he said. "In the meantime, talk to that idiot and tell him I want to see him later."

She ended the call and washed her hands. She didn't

know exactly what Anton's plans were, but she couldn't have all this nonsense affecting her own life. It was well past time she cut ties with Anton and his bullshit rituals. She had made a name for herself as an artist. It was never easy remembering he was a life-coach and that she didn't owe him just because he knew a few things about the occult. That was the problem, though, wasn't it? He knew how to make you *feel* like you owed him.

When she had been through her own initiation, she could have sworn she'd felt the presence of the entities he claimed were there. She'd felt invigorated. Sexually charged. Completely possessed by the presence of something otherworldly and all-knowing, but she was no longer sure it hadn't been psychosomatic.

After her mum had caved her father's head in, there'd been a long period where she had been dragged to church weekend after weekend. While she had hated it, she had to admit that when everyone put their hands in the air and the music hit the right notes, you could feel the presence of something in the room. She had never thought that was proof God existed, so why had the opposite been true when it came to Anton and his claims? It had to be about more than the drugs he plied you with. Unquestionably, if you dosed up on hallucinogens before visiting your local congregation of happy clappers, you'd come out convinced the swaying mass was celebrating something real, something all-powerful, while they were asking you to empty your wallet, and spread the word. Anton never asked for money. He only asked you to keep your mouth shut, and that was something the born-agains could learn from.

Now that she had seen what had happened during Stephen's initiation, she wasn't so sure her own had been the same. He was distant. She had been imbued with confidence. Belief. It was no secret that within days of smearing herself in goat's blood she had sold paintings to galleries, had started spreading the word about her art online. All of that, though? Correlation. And it was possible that was all it was. Any decently connected life-coach could have delivered that.

She brushed a finger across a half-painted canvas. Swirls of thick black paint spiraled madly around flaming galaxies, scarecrows cavorted on the bank of a blood-red river, and a bonfire burned brilliantly in the center of the image. She'd never thought about Eliot's *Hollow Men* until recently. It had occurred to her that the only thing stopping her from leaving her own purgatory was Anton. His insistence that she kept providing him with service, luring Stephen into the fold with her body and providing Anton himself with favors had become an obstacle to her goals. And in the name of what? The promise of some better life? Just as the hollow men of the poem had forgotten their prayers, she'd forgotten that all the talent she possessed was innate in her. She'd paid her obols. She could cross the Styx on her own.

"Hey." Stephen was awake. "Thanks for last night," he said. "I was lost there, and I don't know how I'd have gotten through the night."

Did she have to cross on her own? If Anton had used and abused her, she couldn't imagine what he wanted with Stephen. Whatever it was, it was going to break him into pieces. Could she leave him; condemn him to that?

"You okay?" he asked.

"Yeah, I'm fine," she said. "Just thinking. You need to call Tina. She's worried sick about you. I should have taken you home last night."

"It doesn't matter. I'm clean. I'm not going to rehab again. No one can force me."

He was wrong. If it wasn't for Anton, who would undoubtedly cinch the net tighter over this, plenty of people could force him. It was literally how the process worked. "You've gotta jump through the hoops. It's the way it is."

"You have coffee in this place?"

"There's a café down the road. We'll go there. Anton's

wanting to see you too."

He became pensive. "You know why?"

"I think he's pulling strings for you with Tina. Undoubtedly, you're going to end up owing him."

"I already owe him. He's been amazing for me."

She sighed. "Yeah, I get the feeling. You know, though, that you shouldn't see him as more than a coach. You're your own person. Owing him too much…it's not a good place to be."

His eyes narrowed and he cocked his head to one side, scrutinizing her.

Could she trust him?

"Don't worry about it," she said. "Let's go get coffee."

Chops hung up the phone and took a deep puff on his joint. "I hate leaving messages, man. No one checks 'em. You sure he knows we're coming?"

Rusty took the turnpike and maneuvered through the roundabout and into the estate Corey called home. "Dude, we're bringing him the baggie he asked for. Of course he knows we're coming. Give me a hit of that."

"He's not answering his phone, man." If it was him waiting to score, he'd be hanging on the phone like a limpet.

"He's dogshit at answering his phone, bro. He'll be there." Rusty slowed as he navigated his way past a chicane in the road and hit pause on the Inferi album he had playing. "Serious question, dude. This shit with The Violent Dead goes well this week, you gonna see your commitments through with Polyphemus?"

Chops tapped the joint's cherry on the window's edge. "I gotta be realistic, dude." He knew what the correct answer was, but he also knew the answer Rusty wanted to hear. He'd be gone in a second, but the reality was he couldn't dare to hope. "They've asked me to fill in while Howie's out of action. That's it. If—and it's a minimal chance, dude, like negative infinity chance—they want me to extend the tour or play with them for longer, then I've got some real questions to ask myself. But, if that was the case, they'd be down with me recording with Polyphemus anyway. I'm a session muso, man, it's what I do."

Rusty nodded his head. "I got a good feeling about this shit now that Corey's on-board." He flicked the indicator on and came to a stop outside Corey's place.

Chops took the last hit from the joint, blew the smoke out the door and hopped out. "Yeah, man, I do. I'd be lying if I said anything else."

Approaching the house, he called Corey's phone again, letting it ring out. "Yo, Corey! Answer your phone, dude!" The house remained quiet. "That's his car ain't it?"

Rusty nodded. "Yeah, man, must have his earphones on or something." He rapped on the window and rang the doorbell.

Nothing.

Chops slapped at the door handle. "Should I try it?" The screen door opened effortlessly.

Rusty nodded.

It turned.

Chops pushed it tentatively open. "We're coming in, Corey! You better not be pulling your dick, man!"

It was dark inside. The blinds were drawn, and no lights were on. Exactly as it would be if you were shutting the house off for the night.

"Listen." Rusty gestured down the corridor. A fan whirred noisily.

"Corey, man! We got your weed, dude. You wanna get high or not?"

Only the fan answered.

Rusty pushed open the door to the room the sound was

coming from. Corey's body lie still, grey, and lifeless on his bed.

"Fuck." Chops jumped forward, and shoved Corey's prone figure. His whole body rocked unnaturally. He was stiff as a board; skin cold and clammy. "Call a fucking ambulance."

"His hand, Chops."

A syringe lay loosely in the dead man's fingers.

"Call a fucking ambulance!"

"He's dead. Ambulance ain't going to do shit."

"It doesn't matter. Who else do we call? The cops? Just call someone. Ambulance, cops, fire brigade; it doesn't matter. We've got to call someone." What was up with this band? Was every vocalist cursed? "Why didn't you tell us he was a smackhead?"

"He's not."

"He clearly was."

"No, he wasn't. It doesn't make sense. We have to take it away. Throw it out."

"Call emergency services." He pulled Rusty close. "Don't touch anything, man. The cops will be all over this, and you don't want to get caught fucking with evidence."

Chops ran outside to get some fresh air. This couldn't be happening. Not when everything seemed to be coming together. He knew it was selfish, but he couldn't help but think what this meant. They were screwed. They were literally screwed. The label was going to press charges; the media was going to have a field-day with another drug-related drama in the band's narrative. He had to get away. Yeah, he liked to blaze up and do the occasional line of coke, but this was bad. His own career was going to take a huge hit. The Violent Dead might not want anything to do with him. They were known to party, but they were pros, man. Pros.

An ambulance appeared on the street, sirens ominously silent. He flagged it down. Two paramedics came out, their faces grave. "Are you Rusty?"

"No, Rusty's inside. With Corey."

"Take us in."

They stopped at the door to Corey's bedroom and slumped their shoulders.

"It doesn't make sense," Rusty said to them. "He wasn't a junkie. He didn't shoot up."

The first paramedic's face didn't lack compassion. "You'd be amazed how often no one has a clue. People hide it well. Sometimes for years."

"No," Rusty said. "It's not right. This is all fucked up. What about his family? What are we going to tell his Mum?"

The paramedic wrote something in his notepad. "In cases like this, there's often compassion for the parents and some things are kept quiet. Had he spoken of being unhappy at all?"

"What? No. He agreed to join our band last night. We're recording an album."

Chops led Rusty out to the lounge-room. "Get some fresh air, man. Don't tell 'em what they don't need to know. Polyphemus is associated with drugs enough."

The paramedics came out. "In cases like this, we need to call the cops, and they'll call the morgue. Until then, no one can touch the body or the paraphernalia. We know this is hard, but I'm guessing the cops will want to ask you a few questions. I have to take your names for the report."

Chops gave him the necessary details. The cops arrived within moments. While the paramedics spoke to the two officers, he sat down at Corey's dining table. "If you haven't stashed the buds, I'd go and do that, dude. They're going to search every crevice of this place – and us."

"It's not right."

"No, it's not, but do you want to be charged with dealing. Because if you've got the weed on you, they're gonna make your life hell. Go and put it in his drawer, man."

Chops watched Rusty make his way to the bedroom and

fired off a quick text message to Nathan and Spiros.

Dudes, shit going down. We have a jam session booked tonight if anyone asks. Don't call. Cops involved.

That done, he waited at the door as the cops came up the driveway. He invited them in and led them down the hallway. When he got there, Rusty was crouched over the body, caressing Corey's hair, and crying into his shoulder. "How did this happen?" he asked. "How the fuck did this happen?"

Sliding the barbed hook up underneath the prawn's tail, curving it around and pushing it out below its head, Nathan admired the calm water. With no breeze in the air, and a blue sky above, the surface was like glass. It was, to be fair, the antithesis of how he felt. He cast the line into the water and wedged the butt into the sand. "What do you think's happening?"

Spiros gauged the tension on his own line with a finger and sighed. "I don't know, man. I'm guessing they got pulled over with buds in the car."

Nathan pulled on his beer, an already lukewarm can of Extra Dry. He pursed his lips, swirled the warm remains and downed them. "Nah, man, that's a ticket. We've all been there and done that. They'll confiscate them, but you ain't going anywhere."

"If you carry a little bit. Chops carries ounces."

"Yeah, well, hopefully they call soon." He reached into the cooler and cracked another tin. "I got a bad feeling, man. So bad. As soon as we start to make some headway, some bullshit reams us."

"You can only worry about what you can control. You can do nothing about this except wait."

"We should call 'em."

"No, we shouldn't. Chops will call when he can."

Nathan swallowed a few mouthfuls of his beer. "All right, man, let's change the subject. Between Oaks, that stupid bitch at my house, and whatever's got Chops needing excuses, we need some good news. Tell me about the kid, man." It was only the other day that he was thinking about how often he forgot to ask after Spiros's family. "How are Pandora and Calliope?"

Spiros drank from his own beer. "Well, considering you want good news, perhaps you should ask a different question."

"You're kidding me?"

"You notice how I am slow to turn to the right? The couch might be plush leather, but it's a bitch to sleep on. My neck will be sore for weeks."

Nathan couldn't help but laugh. "In the doghouse again! What this time?" He spun the reel, moving his bait a little.

"The same thing as always. She thinks the band takes away from our relationship; that I earn money in the family business, and therefore I shouldn't treat this like a lifestyle. The other night she gave me an ultimatum."

"And..."

Spiros grinned. "Tonight, I'll need to find a more comfortable solution if I want to sleep. I might need to grab an air mattress on the way home." The guitarist laughed.

"I don't know how you can be so blasé about it. I'd be doing my nut. Shit, I am doing my nut with everything that's going on. I keep telling that psycho to leave, but she sits around causing problems."

"As for me, I figure that Dora will get over it. She always does. It'll take a few days, but we've been through a lot more, and she'll be there, waiting on the other side of all this. Fact is, there's a contract to honor, and she can't honestly expect me to renege." He reeled his line in. The bait was gone. "She'll be over it before the kinks on my neck disappear. Let me ask you a question, though; play devil's advocate for a moment."

"It's not my kid, dude."

"Sure, but what if it is. What if she waits around till it's born, takes the test, and proves to you that it's yours? Will you be confident in your actions then? Will you honestly be able to look yourself in the eye?"

A couple of seagulls squabbled over something nearby. A boat cruised up the waterway. "Seeing as it's hypothetical, I'm going to say yeah. Bitch ain't going to be able to prove shit, and there's no way I'm settling down with her. This cheap skank's suddenly supposed to become trustworthy because she fires out a kid. Fuck that."

Spiros shuffled uncomfortably. Flicked his fishing rod. "I'm not saying you should totally change your frame of mind on this, but I think you need to consider the possibility."

Nathan swigged from his beer. Grunted.

"Think about it. What does this girl have to gain from coming to you? It's not like you're loaded."

What an asshole. Nathan sighed. That was exactly the same shit Lisa had pulled on him. "I don't know, Spiros. We don't all get our father's businesses handed to us, but any port in a storm, you know." He skulled his beer and reeled his line in. The prawn was attached, soggy and limp. He firmed it on the hook and cast it again.

"I'm not trying to be a dick, Nathan. I told you, you need to get her out of your house so she cannot claim anything later on. I'm not sure how many months the law says you have to be together under the same roof, but you don't want that, and you certainly don't want to fuck her or lead her on in any way. Matter of fact, I'd put your shit in writing, but you should keep a channel open in case this kid turns out to be yours."

Spiros, man. How did he get so smart? There were only a couple of beers left in the cooler. He passed one to the Greek.

"I kinda wish Steve was here, man. Remember how much fun we used to have doing this? No dramas. Just the boys. Just beer, fish, and a few buds."

Spiros nodded. "I do…"

Nathan's phone went off. "It's Chops, man!" He put the phone on speaker. "Yo, what the hell, dude?"

"Dudes, are you in a private place?"

"Yeah, man, only me and Spiros can hear."

"What you been up to, you cocksucker? You got caught with weed didn't you?" Spiros asked.

There was a pause on the other end of the line. Shuffling. "It's way worse, man. Corey's dead."

Nathan leaned forward, stared at Spiros. Grabbed his knee. "Say that again."

Chops sniffed. "Corey, man, we went to see him this morning, and he was in his bed. He OD'd man. He's fucking gone."

He hadn't been to the club since the night he'd been introduced to the seeming. Walking through the front door, he wondered if the presence that had attached itself to him ever since felt as nostalgic about this place as he did. He remembered vividly the way the walls had shifted as he'd moved around the milling crowds of people. The way he'd given in to it. Gone down in the circle after the bleating goat had bled its life all over the floor.

He could feel the shapeless thing in his periphery, watching and waiting, but apart from that he'd heard nothing from it since last night. Even then, he couldn't say he had no control over the things he'd done. He had a crystal-clear memory of everything that had happened: the heroin oozing out of his arm, Corey letting him into his place, plunging the syringe into the bastard and pumping him full of death; but he'd have never done those things without a little urging.

India unwound her fingers from his as they approached Anton's regular spot on the raised couch. The big man hadn't arrived yet, but Oaks remembered what India had said about him earlier. He'd have to unpack some of that shit, but it was pretty clear that his loyalty had to be with Anton. If India wanted to run, wanted to escape all of this, then so be it. Once he'd retaken his spot in the band, and was on the road, there'd be girls in every town. She was replaceable.

The huge security guard offered them a drink from the bar.

"Whiskey," Oaks said.

India took water.

The guard handed them over. "He'll be with you in a moment."

When he arrived, he was clad in a black turtleneck and chinos. His eyes were wide; fully dilated. "I hear you had a big night, my musical friend."

Oaks sniggered. If only he knew how big. In the circles he was used to running with, people joked that they'd kill for a chance to headline one of the big festivals or to make a gold record. Provided everything panned out, he had. No small talk. No bluff. Just blood on his hands and a bold move towards his dream. It was only a step away, and he had to be present as things unfurled. "Yeah, I had a few beers," he said. "Needed to go and check out the old jam room. Try and get in the right frame of mind."

"And?"

Oaks remembered why he hadn't trusted the life-coach when he'd first met him. The prick wore the same patronizing expression he'd had on his face when they'd chatted in the gutter outside of Amielle's place. "And what?"

"Did it work? Tina was worried about you and I had to pull a few strings, so I hope it was worth it."

"It'll be worth it."

"I certainly hope so." He leaned forward. "India. It's lovely to see you as always. I must say you two seem to be getting along well."

She picked her teeth. "Well, you asked me to be there for him. It's not easy coming out of rehab and having no one to rely on. I'm glad we met."

"I have you to thank for that," Oaks said. "I'd have had a long walk home in the cold without you introducing us."

Anton clicked his fingers and the security guard brought over a drink. "Now, there is a more serious thing we have to discuss. Two things. The first is pretty straightforward. You need to realize that despite whatever is happening in here," he said, pointing to his own temple, "you need to follow the rules of your court order. Everything turns to shit if you fuck that up."

"And?"

Anton narrowed his eyes. "The second is that I want you to tell me how you're feeling. From what I understand, the ceremony was huge for you. In the days after that, we can sometimes think that things are more harmless than they are. Whatever *suggestions* have been implanted in your mind, it's important not to give them too much power. Those dreams can seem vivid. The after-effects can seem real. Does it seem like you have someone—or something—with you, talking to you?"

The seeming shifted to the forefront of his mind. He shook his head. "No." What was Anton's game? Oaks knew the thing that had attached itself to him was in service to something bigger, but whatever that thing was, they had enlisted Anton for some reason. He clearly knew more than he was letting on, but what was his goal? "I feel like I have a great sense of purpose, but that's all."

"India, I wonder if you'd give us some privacy for a moment."

She stood up. "I need a bathroom break anyway."

Both men watched her leave, Oaks taking in the dark

surroundings, noting the paintings, the statues, the furniture. "Don't bullshit, me." Something slithered behind his pupils. "We're in this together, and I would like to know if the process worked. You should have one of the most powerful entities we've brought forward yet keeping watch over you."

Oaks felt it come forward again. "I told you. I feel like I have a great sense of purpose. That's all."

Anton nodded. "OK, but you need to know that I am privy to some things. You have been given a task. It must be completed. You need to make sure that you bring the others into the fold, and that you go forth and bring others in with you. We are on a mission here, and its success is imperative."

Oaks thought about the visions he'd seen during his initiation. "And what exactly is it we're doing here? What is our mission?" The seeming moved forward again. He could feel it in the peripherals of his vision. Lurking. "I know that me being back in the band is a big part of it, but what do we do then? I don't get how it works."

Anton waved a hand dismissively. "The ins and outs of it don't matter, but when we're afforded the boons we receive, there's a promise. What we do is give ourselves to the servitude of a higher power in return for earthly rewards."

If word ever got out about this, he'd be a laughing stock. "There's nothing more cliché than musicians selling their souls. I don't know if that's what I need to be doing."

Anton laughed. "If you want to be vulgar in the way you describe it, then sure, but it's a little more complex than that. There's no soul. That's nothing but spiritual mumbo-jumbo. I can't explain it all to you, but I know that it has the power to offer us rewards in exchange for bringing others to it."

"And I'm supposed to get the rest of Polyphemus to take the same initiation I did?"

"Or something like it. The method isn't important, but what I do is bring individuals to it. When I met you, I knew you could help me take this mainstream."

"And what's in it for you?"

"Does it matter? You'll get what you want. Fame. Fortune. The *Rolling Stone* cover. The headline shows. All that nonsense."

He pictured the vision again. The crowd of churning bodies garbed in black shirts banging their heads to a song he was leading. It would all be his.

He was recalled to reality by his phone. It vibrated angrily in his pocket. Nathan. His heart skipped. His hand shook. Anton watched eagerly. India paused as she returned from the bathroom.

"Nathan?" he said into the loudspeaker.

"Yeah, man, it's me. I can't go into everything," his old friend said, "but I'm here with Spiros. I'm gonna go straight to it. We need you, bro. We record in two weeks, and you're our man."

He wanted to scream. To shout. To kiss Anton's feet. He felt the presence inside him purr with excitement. His skin broke out in goose pimples. "You can't be serious. After everything?"

"It's a long story, but we love you, man. And we need you. We need you." Nathan paused.

Spiros came in over the top. "Will you do it? Say yes."

Anton's face was a predatory leer. India's was hidden in shadow, but she'd raised a hand to her mouth. Her eyes, huge and doe-like, watched him.

"Yes," he said. "Without a doubt. You know I will."

CHAPTER ELEVEN
ARISE

Chops was pounding the kit like an octopus when Nathan entered the jam room. He nodded at the drummer, but there was no response. The dude was lost in it, hammering his way through "Goat of Departure", an absolute slayer from The Black Dahlia Murder. Rusty was laying the bass out beside him, but he returned Nathan's greeting, sticking his tongue out and smiling a forlorn welcome. Nathan plugged his Ibanez into the PA and jumped in, chugging away when they hit the chorus.

Chops's face was dark, man. They played to the end of the track and Nathan went over to him. Rested a hand on his shoulder. "Shit's pretty fucked, huh?"

Chops bit his lips. "I don't get it, man. This band's cursed or something. Every step forward is met with two in the opposite direction."

Nathan squatted to his haunches. "It's shit," he said. "But we'll get through it."

"Yeah, but it's not about us. That's your problem, you know." He gestured towards Rusty. "Rusty's known Corey for years. He had a family. And you, do you care or are you worried about what it means for the band? You haven't asked if we heard from the cops or anything."

"Come on, man, you know I didn't mean it like that."

Rusty placed his bass on its stand and lowered the volume. "Chill, guys. We're all messed up. We've got shit to work out. Arguing amongst ourselves isn't going to help."

Chops rested his sticks on the snare. Put his hands on his hips. "I need a smoke, dude. Spiros is on his way?"

"Yeah, he's coming." They'd decided not to cancel the session. Logic said they should, but there was nothing to be done about it. Corey was gone, but the label wasn't going to change its tune. The only way they could cope was to deal with it, and with the news Nathan was going to drop on them, some good angry shit could help them vent first.

The whole conversation was going to be a tricky one, and the last thing he needed was to have Chops quit. With his Violent Dead shit simmering in the background, he had an easy out if he was adamant about it. Polyphemus could always get another drummer, but with everything going on, him bailing could be the final nail in the band's coffin. And besides, there weren't many around who could hit the skins the way Chops could. It just sucked that he'd been the most vocal about keeping Oaks away from the band.

The drummer pulled up a chair at the patio table and pulled a tin of ready-ground weed out of his pocket. He sat facing away from the forest Nathan had ventured into a couple of nights ago. The car park bordering it was empty, but traffic roared on the nearby main road. He lit the spliff and toked deeply. "We were there for hours," he said, breathing smoke out of his nose. "I thought the cops were going to ask for piss-tests and everything. Like, what the fuck? Rusty's adamant the dude wasn't even a user, but that's the second smack-death we've had, man. Who comes back from that? Did Alice in Chains have that many?"

Rusty exhaled smoke. "He wasn't. I swear it." He passed the joint along.

He certainly hadn't seemed like one. Remembering how dusty he'd thought Oaks had been when he was in the thick of it, Nathan couldn't correlate that image with the one he'd gathered of Corey in their few small meetings. "They're keeping it from his parents, though, right? I thought you said that."

"Yeah, but come on, man. Have you been online? They don't have to confirm anything for the entire world to make assumptions. It's what we're known for."

"Yeah, but it's not true. We had Steve with his issues, and this, but are you a user? Is Spiros? Rusty? I know I'm not, so let the rumor-mill spin, man."

"You don't get it. You're too close to this." He took the spliff and ashed it over the balcony railing. "We've got a reputation. Yeah, we can set it right over time, but there's a stigma. How are we going to go forward when everyone thinks of us as smackheads?"

"We play good music. We go on tour, we stay clean, and we kill it on stage. Run interviews and shit. Solid PR, that's what."

Spiros's car pulled up down below them. "You fuckers smoking again?"

"Catch!" Chops flicked the butt of the joint at him. "Get your shit out of the van and hurry the fuck up."

"Did you tell them?" Spiros asked.

Nathan sighed. Played with his ponytail. Spiros's timing couldn't have been worse. He tried to ignore the fact Chops was staring at him.

"Tell us what?"

Nathan hesitated.

"You invited him to rejoin didn't you?" He rattled his fingers on the table. "Did you think about it at all?"

"You know, we've got a pretty huge consequence hanging over us if we don't get this album done." Seriously, though, Chops was probably going to leave anyway. He was only here for the studio; he'd said it himself. "So, yeah, we thought about it. We thought about it long and hard."

"Whatever, man, I'm out."

"Don't be a dick. Please, will you listen?"

Spiros stuck his head out of the sliding door. "He's taking it better than we thought."

"Sit down, Spiros. Sit down and shut up." Nathan pulled

a chair towards the guitarist and faced Chops. "Dude, we know where you're at. We get it, but here's the cold hard fact. We need to record in two weeks. The dude's done his time and he knows the band. You're currently not promising us any more than studio-work. We can't let you dictate everything, and we're in a real bind."

Spiros interjected. "So this is the thing. We need you *and* we need him. We know we're running the risk of you bailing on this, but for us, the financial costs of failure are massive. We know that you're not in on that part, but if you stay, we'll give you full equal credit for everything on the record, no questions asked. We'll let you run as much promo as you want, and we won't keep you when it's done. We're lucky to have you, and we hope we're lucky to have you for the tour, but the way things have gone, we are screwed without a singer. Fucking Corey, that's a tragedy, man. It's a nightmare come to life, but we spoke to Cormac yesterday, and the label is going to fuck us bareback with no lube if we don't deliver."

Rusty, who'd been staring into space, piped up. "Come on. You've been saying you've got a good feeling about it all. I'm gonna stay. All this bad shit can't happen if there's not some positive at the end of it. We can create something that makes it all worthwhile."

"It's the connotations, man. I've been asked to tour with The Violent Dead. I start in three days. I haven't heard from them, but you can bet they're wondering if I'm the man for them. They smoke a ton of weed, but they're professionals. No hard drugs, and they perform sober. Every time. Having Oaks return from his stint in rehab right after Corey…" he shook his head. "I don't know what that's going to do to our reputation, man."

"I know the reputation's huge for you, and I promise that we get it, but bailing is only going to cement that shit. We can come out of this stronger. When we do the press, when we release the album; tour it, the truth will come out. Look at Lamb of God with Randy's alcoholism, man. That shit didn't break them."

"They were already huge. It's not the same."

"Don't bail on us yet. You know the songs are good."

The drummer pushed away from the table. Stared into the forest behind him. "When's he coming?"

"He's supposed to be coming this afternoon. We need as much time as we can get with him in practice."

"If I think anything's awry, I'm going to pull stumps. You know that, right?"

"Deal, man. We've already spoken to him, and he knows it's only recording."

Chops stared out across the forest. "Fuck you guys. The shit I've been through with this band; I could write a goddamn book."

The cockroach scuttled up the wall. It crossed to the light-switch, buzzing and fluttering its wings, scraping its mandibles across the plastic surface, feeding off whatever greasy shit had been left there by the foul fingers of some filthy junkie, and then ducked into an alcove and down the wall, behind a couch. No wonder the pathetic little piss-ants who came here to recover hated the place so much. He pulled a money-clip from the interior pocket of his leather jacket and pressed it down on the table in front of the nurse.

"As promised," he said. "And thank you for your discretion. Stephen is a good kid, and he'll go far."

Nurse Amielle eyed him suspiciously.

"I spoke to him earlier. It wasn't drugs that kept him out last night. He's struck up a bit of a relationship with India. You probably remember her."

"I remember her," the nurse said. "She's a strong one.

She'll help him find himself again." She slipped the money quickly into a pocket.

"How are things here?"

"Truth told, I'm not sure. I know what you're telling me, but someone got into the bag last night. Broke the lock off the cupboard door."

He raised an eyebrow.

"And Stephen is…"

"My only ward at the moment."

"No sign of forced entry?"

"He smashed the cupboard."

"No, the front door?"

She shook her head.

He pulled a few more fifty dollar notes out of his wallet. "That should pay for the damage."

"Have you hooked him again? This one's not like the others. He's not a wastrel, he's just weak." Her eyes were bloodshot and strained.

There was something about the kid; that much was true. Whereas some of the others who came through Amielle's halfway house were little more than career criminals, Oaks was not of the ilk he wanted to ply with drugs. In those cases, he saw nothing wrong with keeping them addicted. They'd be into the prison system once the rehab cycle had ended, and they would be buying their smack from someone. They may as well be lining his pockets. The nurse was right that Stephen wasn't like that, and she clearly had a soft spot for him. "Why'd you wait to tell me this?"

"I know he's been seeing you. He needs something to cling onto, and you've helped others. India. Tom. I hope you can do the same with him."

He nodded his head slowly, taking it in. "I'm doing what I can." The boy clearly hadn't been coming down when he saw him. What had he done with those drugs? "Tell me. Was anything missing?"

"A syringe. A baggie. Enough for a few serious hits."

"I'll have a word with him." He stood up. "Until next time."

"Thank you. You're a kind man."

He stopped as he approached the door. "Do me a favor. Don't mention this to him. Let's keep it between us until I can find out what he did with it."

He exited and made his way to the car. This put a whole new light on things. Stephen had taken the smack, but if he hadn't used it himself, he had to have either stashed it or sold it. He'd have to get India onto this. He reversed out of the driveway and told his hands-free device to call her.

When India dropped him off, he got out of the car to hear Chops pounding the skins off his drum-kit. He threw the horns at the girl and grinned. The drummer might have tried to make Oaks's life more difficult than it already was over the last few months, but there was no denying that the dude knew how to play. Seconds later, when a thick and dirty bassline slithered over the beat, he nodded his head and growled in his familiar guttural voice, showing off the cookie monster for a little pre-jam warm-up. The shadows in his peripheral vision momentarily writhed as the vocalist considered how things would go with the drummer. He'd shat three times before getting in the car, ready for his first jam since he had fallen off the stage all those months ago.

Nathan was waiting for him on the balcony. Oaks walked closer, raising his hand. His old friend lifted a beer and cracked it with his lighter. He tipped the beer up, drinking three or four deep guzzles before resting it on the railing and grabbing another bottle out. "You made it! Get up here and have a beer."

An overwhelming feeling of familiarity settled over him.

Not of before, but of the first time he'd seen Nathan after rehab. He loved the guy, it was simple. The feeling was mutual too, not that he needed anyone to tell him that. It was how things were.

He passed his equipment up to Nathan and scaled the balcony. Last time he'd been here, he'd listened as they invited Corey to take up the vocals. Momentarily, he felt a chill, and spun around to observe the forest bordering the grounds of the studios. From here, they appeared dark and impenetrable.

Taking the last step over the balcony, he latched onto Nathan and pulled him into a bear-hug. "You've got no idea how good it feels to be here, man. I'm pumped."

Nathan grabbed the top of his shaved head. "Wait till you hear the new shit. It's killer."

"That's Chops and Rusty?" he asked, nodding in the direction of the bass and drums booming out of the studio.

"Fucking tight, right?" Nathan passed him a beer. The condensation on the bottle glistened in the cool afternoon sun. Last time Nathan had offered him a beer, he'd hesitated, worried about the terms of his release. This time, he clinked it against Nathan's own, and drank deeply. It was cheap piss, A Nathan March specialty, but it went down like gold.

The music coming from inside shifted in dynamic as a guitar kicked in. A rapid-fire lead from Spiros. The tone was warm. Sonorous. "This is new stuff." It sounded amazing. Chops's blast-beats had stopped. The beat had slowed to half-time. Spiros was wringing anguished bends out of the strings, driving towards an ever-building climax.

"You got those books of lyrics?"

Oaks nodded.

"All right. Let's go inside."

This was it. His big chance to show them he wasn't a liability anymore. And, truth told, that had to happen. His own career wasn't the only thing riding on it. "Nate, I just, I wanna thank you. I know you had to fight for it, man. I won't let you down."

As they entered the studio, the song came to a close with a palm-muted riff that'd make any thrash-band from the 80s proud. Spiros saw him hovering behind Nathan and charged with the enthusiasm of a puppy, wrestling him to the ground and kissing his bald head. "I love this haircut, you slaphead motherfucker! Do I get good luck for kissing it?" He held Oaks down, tickling him as he laughed. "Everyone must kiss the head!" He slapped it. Rubbed it like a genie's lamp.

Oaks rolled him over, laughing. "Get the fuck off me, you big dumb bastard." He whacked his knuckles down on Spiros' head and noogied the prick in return. "I missed this shit. You know that? The whole time I was in there, I was waiting for the day you were gonna try to wrestle me again." He flicked the Greek's ear and climbed off him. "Goddamn, I missed you guys."

Nathan shook his head, chuckling at the reunion. "Boys," he said. "You remember Oaks."

Rusty came over, shook his hand and went in for the bro-hug, pounding his shoulder on Oaks's and welcoming him. He gestured to a bottle of bourbon on his amp. "Shot! You gotta take a shot, man. It's like, the law."

Oaks grabbed the bottle and took a nip. "It's good stuff," he said, pounding his chest. His eyes met Chops's. There was a pause, and then he approached, holding his arms wide. "Come on, man. I got a lot of love for you too."

Chops climbed off the drum stool. For a moment, Oaks wasn't sure how it was gonna play out. The prick wasn't exactly well-known for his commitment to decorum and charity. "What the fuck," he said. "We've known each other too long to carry on with grudges, and we're all here for the same reason. To make a new record, right?" He clasped Oaks's hand.

Spiros whooped like a frat boy. "Let's get some dee-rinks into us, play some metal and raise hell, boys!" He spun off to the Bluetooth speaker set-up on a side-table and scrolled through his phone. "Did I hear you assholes say "Dead Embryonic Cells"?" In seconds the pulsing sound effects of the Sepultura classic's introduction were ringing through the cabin.

"I'm not here for miracles, Chops. I know I screwed up bad, but I'm all good. I'm gonna make it up to you with the best vocals we've ever put on tape."

There was a pause as the two tried to decipher each other's faces. "Mate, I was only ever worried about you. This is a career for someone like me and in all the years I toured with Bone Totem, I never knew anyone who was able to recover from what you did and not relapse without a lengthy break before they hit the road again."

"Well, I'm not hitting the road, I'm contracted for vocals only. I hope that changes, but let's put Polyphemus on the map."

"Amen, dude, but I wanna know that you're fine and healthy. That's the most important thing."

Spiros came over and wrapped an arm around each of them right as the huge neck-snapping breakdown kicked in. "Are we all kissed and made up, because we need to be banging our heads!"

Pandora looked up from where Calliope was playing with her blocks. Was she doing the right thing? Should she let him have his stupid band? No, she couldn't think like that. She'd given him the ultimatum and told him exactly what she needed from him. She couldn't have him out there on tour again, not knowing where he was spending the night, what he was putting in his body. He had a family, and if he didn't want to spend time with it, that shit was going to disappear. "Not long now, my darling. Only a couple more bags."

Her own stuff was packed, and she'd divided the bank accounts straight down the middle. From tonight, she'd be spending the next few nights in a hotel on the coast. Later, she'd find her own place to rent, but in this moment, she needed to get away.

On the walls were dozens of photos of her life with Spiros. In most of them, he wore the usual black band shirts. A thousand dead things, tentacles, monsters, and strange altars took away from the childish innocence that always shone through his stupid grin. His long ponytail was a constant fixture.

Her phone beeped. Another reminder of how annoying Spiros was with this music thing. He couldn't even keep a ringtone like a normal human. He had to have some ridiculous song blast out, embarrassing her whenever it went off in public. It was a message from Sebastian. He, too, was starting to piss her off.

You're at home with your wife, she punched into the response. *Don't be a fool.*

She picked up the two bags she'd packed for Calliope. They contained a few toys and some comfort items. Her clothes were all in the suitcase she'd already packed. She took them to the car, picked up her daughter, and kissed her forehead.

She wiped the tears running down her own cheeks, and took Calliope, buckling her into the safety-seat. She went into the house, wrote Spiros a note, got in the car, and drove for the coast.

CHAPTER TWELVE
THE LUCID COLLECTIVE

The big guitarist swerved onto his street, buzzing. The jam had been immense. As soon as Oaks had stepped up to the mic, he'd reminded everyone of his prowess. Cookie monsters, shrieks, screams, and the occasional chanted clean, he could do them all, and he could do them *well*. Somehow, his lyrics had seemed tailor-made for the songs Nathan had been putting down, and with two guitars, Chops's drum-work, and Rusty snaking under the mix with his distorted bass lines, the songs had been brutal.

He was yet to clear the air with Pandora, but in the mood he was in, that should be easy. A bit of sweet-talking, a few promises, and things would, no doubt, be good. Pulling into the driveway, he checked the time. She should be here, but her car was absent, and the curtains were drawn. No light glowed beyond them.

He hit the buzzer, opening the garage. Pandora's car was missing. She must have gone to her folks. She did that when they'd been fighting. Whatever, it gave him the chance to have some alone time and catch up on some old horror films. Hopping out of the car, he pulled his phone off the dashboard and fired off a text message, telling her to let him know when she was coming home. Before then, he was going to hit up the spa, smoke a reefer, and pour himself a few fingers of scotch.

He made his way into the kitchen, half-expecting there to be some sort of note left on the kitchen table. Something about dinner, perhaps. When he found it, the message was way simpler than that:

I'm gone, Spiros. I've taken Calliope. My phone is off. I'll be in touch to grab the rest of my things. No one else knows where I am, so don't bother hassling them. You chose this. I hope you're happy
Dora.

A weight bloomed in his chest. He dropped two hands to the counter. Breathed deeply. In. Out. In. Out. Half a chuckle escaped his mouth, mutating into a cry as the sound formed beneath his lips.
Fuck, man. Fuck.
He dragged his phone out of his pocket. Dropped it on the bench, flipped open the leather case, and tried to call.
Nothing.
He had to think. Had to get his head together.
Selene.
Dora told her everything. She had to know what was going on. But what if she didn't? If he called and got other people worried, the whole thing would be a shit-ton more embarrassing than it needed to be when the truth came out. No, this was his dirty laundry. There was no way he was sharing it with anyone, least of all friends who respected him.
Pandora was gone. At least until she'd processed it all. She'd understand. She had to. This was his dream. And besides, they couldn't afford to pay out the contract. For the sake of a couple of months, all she needed to do was sit tight. He'd record the album. Make it his best ever guitar-work, meet the requirements of the contract, and then he'd retire from it. Easy.
He typed that into his phone. Sent it to her as a text. She'd understand. And there was no way she could take Calliope from him. Shit, the most deadbeat dads got to see their kids.

She couldn't deny him that.

He pulled the scotch out of the bar. Grabbed a beaker. He poured in two fingers, paused, and poured two more. Heading upstairs, he left the note to flutter to the floor.

Upstairs, he found the door to Calliope's room open. He stepped inside. Her teddy, Stilly, was gone. Her drawers had been emptied. Her little going out bag, a rainbow-colored rucksack with Elsa from *Frozen* on it, was nowhere to be seen.

Spiros pinched the bridge of his nose. Tried to focus. He sat on her little bed and checked his phone to see if Pandora had replied. Shit, he'd be happy if she'd read it and not bothered to reply. At least that would be a start and he'd know she was engaged enough to do that. When he saw the text message symbol up in the top bar, his heart leapt.

He swiped it open. It was Nathan. Whatever, he could read that later. He needed to check one more thing before he settled into the evening and dealt with this bullshit.

In the master bedroom, he made his way into Dora's walk-in wardrobe. As he feared, her wedding ring rested forlornly on the bench. Fuck. He pinched it between his fingers. Kissed it. Fell to his knees with it in his hand. He stayed there for a minute, taking it all in. *It's temporary*, he told himself. *It has to be.*

He rested it on the bench, made his way into the ensuite and ran a bath. The hot water would clear his mind.

Nathan's house felt gross. Ever since Lisa had refused to leave, it had grown more awkward. Several beers deep, and fresh from a killer jam session, he felt immersed in the insidious mist of tension oozing through the house, choking off the corners and sucking the oxygen out of the room.

Usually, he'd chill on the couch, smoke a couple of bucket bongs and read a book until he was ready to fall asleep after a good practice. Now, though, he couldn't get through the first paragraph. The palpable sense of unease in the house wasn't going to disappear unless he did something about Lisa. The first of those things was simple. She could shut that ridiculous television up. She'd made herself at home in his bed, stocking the room with a million different bottles of perfume and candles, but the least she could do was keep it quiet so he didn't have to feel like he was sitting in a *Jerry Springer* story.

"Hey, why don't you turn the TV down?" he called.

When there was no change to the volume, he strolled down the hallway, banging on the wall as he approached. *Why could this chick not understand he did not need her here? Didn't want her, had nothing to offer her, and couldn't possibly be responsible for knocking her up?* He swung open the door. She lay on the bed, sleeping. He killed the television and jostled her awake.

As her eyes adjusted to her surroundings, she spoke. "What do you want? I thought you weren't going to come in here with me?"

He shook his head. Pissed at the insinuation. "I'm not coming in here with you. I came in to shut your television off. You've been making out like you own this place; like me coming round to your game is only a matter of time. Acting like a stuck-up bitch who calls the shots when you're not getting what you want." He moved to the door. "Consider this official," he said, "I'm *done* with your nastiness and your bullshit. I let you stay here because you said you had nowhere else, but I've had enough. The whole place feels toxic. In the morning, you're gone. Find an apartment, or another friend, or anywhere that doesn't mean you're bringing a kid into this shitshow."

She sat up in the bed, her legs dangling over the side. Her heavily pregnant belly poised like a medicine ball. "Where do you want me to go? I'm at thirty-five weeks. This is gonna drop any day."

"That's a problem for you and whoever put it there. You can't be here when it comes." He paused in the middle of closing the door. "Think about it, will you. This is not in anyone's best interest." He pulled the door shut, went to the lounge-room, fished his buds out of the drawer and chopped up.

He lit the first cone and listened to the cherry sizzle and pop as he lifted the halved coke-bottle out of the bucket. Thick grey smoke swirled inside it as the building pressure did its work. And then Lisa started screaming. "Nate! Nate! Come here!"

He lifted the cone-piece and sucked down the smoke.

"Now! Now! There's someone peeping through the window."

His stomach lurched. What the hell was she on about?

"Who?" He made his way to her bedroom. *His* bedroom.

"I don't know. Someone weird. They were under the trees on the verge."

Goddammit. "This is what curtains are for," he said.

"He was there when I opened them, staring in at me. His eyes, Nate, they were red."

The front door rattled.

Nathan met her fearful gaze.

It rattled again.

"Wait here." He made his way down the corridor, grabbing a guitar from its stand as he sneaked towards the door, hefting it up by the neck like a weapon.

The door rattled a third time.

"Nate," came a voice from the other side. "It's me, Oaks. Let me in, man."

"Oaks?" He glanced towards the room. Lisa had stepped into the corridor. "What are you doing here, bro?"

"Can I come in?"

He opened the door. Oaks was leaning on the security

screen. "Shouldn't you be at the house?" Nathan said.

"You gonna let me in?"

He sidestepped and gestured Oaks into the lounge room. "You know your way around, man. Now what are you doing here?"

The vocalist flopped down on the couch. Surveyed the posters on the walls. "I wanted to talk. We haven't done that in a while."

Nathan put the guitar on the stand and sat opposite his old friend. "If it's about the band, there's not much to say. We record soon. Be ready."

Oaks nodded. "Sure, the band's a little bit of it, but I wanted to see you on a human level. I shouldn't be stressing you guys out when there's going to be a baby coming into the house."

"It's not like that."

The singer cocked his head. Raised an eyebrow.

"Lisa's staying temporarily. She'll be out of here tomorrow."

Nathan heard her in the hallway. He twisted to see her standing at the mouth of the corridor, half-dressed in shadow, clutching her arms around her chest.

"You're such an asshole," she said.

Nathan looked away.

Oaks raised his hands up in apology. "Shit, sorry, guys, I didn't mean to start anything. I wanted to congratulate you."

"Yeah, well don't bother," she said. "Your stupid band is more important. Seriously, you're all adults, What the hell is your obsession with this ridiculous music?" She disappeared down the corridor.

"It's yours?" Oaks asked in a hushed tone.

"She's saying it is."

"Shit, man, that's gotta be a royal pain in the ass."

Nathan pulled the cone-piece from the bucket-bong and offered it. "I've told her she has till tomorrow to find somewhere else to stay. She tricked me into letting her stay here and she hasn't left since."

Oaks sprinkled some of the pot into the piece and shook his head. "That's harsh, man. I'm surprised you can focus on the band with all this going on."

Nathan snorted. "Hell no, man. That's all that matters. That's why I haven't focused on getting rid of her." He waited while Oaks smoked his cone and placed it in the drawer. "Anyway, you didn't come here to talk about my bullshit. What's up?"

"Nothing major. I wanted to thank you. I know you've put a lot on this. Fought for my right to be here. I want you to know that's appreciated."

"It's no sweat, man. It became easier after Corey, well, you know. We'd have been screwed without you stepping in. I know Spiros is stoked. Rusty seems to be, and Chops, well, Chops is Chops. I think we would have lost him anyway. The Violent Dead are sniffing around big time."

Oaks twitched, checking his shoulder. "We've gotta keep him, man. He has to stay."

This was interesting. "I don't think we'll have much control, dude. If he wants to go, he'll go." He leaned forward. "Why are you so adamant?"

Oaks's lip twitched. "It'll sound weird," he said.

"Try me."

"I've been having dreams, man. When Chops is there, we're huge."

Lisa staggered down the hallway and into the loungeroom. "You need to take me to the hospital," she said. "Something's wrong."

Nathan followed the angle of her arm, stopping where he saw her cupped hand. "I've been drinking," he said.

"Then call a cab." She raised her hand, revealing bloodied fingers. "I need to go now!"

He hadn't long watched the cab disappear around the corner when a black Chrysler purred onto the street and pulled up beside him. His mind swimming with thoughts about the last few days, he sat on the curb for a while before getting into the passenger seat. Why had he come here to Nathan's? It hadn't only been about jamming again. There had been an ulterior motive. He'd felt egged-on. Driven. Determined to find out if Nathan was dedicated to Polyphemus or if his head had been turned.

There was no doubt. Head and heart, the guy was there until the bitter end. Trapped by it. Obsessed. He'd do anything to make this band work. Despite the girl's cries for attention, Nathan had no interest in the family life. Even if he was the kid's father, which he probably was.

Considering Oaks had already killed to make this thing his own again, that was good. It meant he wasn't the only one with a truly emotional investment. If the others had sacrificed for this, had lost something, they'd fight to make it worth it. And that meant they'd agree with whatever it was he presented to them.

"Feeling pensive are we?"

He eyeballed the driver. "Anton?"

The bald man behind the steering wheel grinned. "Who else?" Effortlessly, he merged onto the highway and accelerated to a ridiculous speed. The streetlamps became white streaks, and the other traffic on the road became sweeps of orange and red light as Anton zoomed past them.

"Why are you picking me up?"

The life-coach sniffed and scratched his nose. "I'm here to keep an eye on you. I'll make sure you get home tonight. Trust me, it's in your best interests."

"You're taking me to Amielle's?"

"The nurse holds a lot of goodwill for you, but it won't last forever. You've already had one night out this week. Let's not make it another one."

He thought of India then. How could the girl think this man was trying to take advantage of him? Hadn't she benefitted from everything Anton offered? And then he remembered how she spoke to him. Out of everyone, she was the only one who didn't judge; who understood.

Nathan, Spiros, the others; they all saw him as a liability. At best, a charity case. To Anton he was someone to patronize and lead by the nose. As for Amielle, there was no telling how the nurse thought of him. She'd never shown enough emotion to make anything beyond a cursory connection. No, to her, he was another body to pass through the halfway house. He stared Anton straight in the face. "Take me to India's."

"Not a chance." Anton's smile faltered. Momentarily wavered. Twitched.

"I'm serious, Anton. Take me to her."

"Don't let your drug-addled brain trick you. You are nothing to her."

He shook his head. "You don't know what you're talking about."

A smudge of ash appeared on the driver's forehead. "You think a girl like that is going to fall for someone like you? She was put up to it. I put her up to it. There's nothing to get you feeling comfortable like the attentions of a whore."

No. It had to be bullshit. She loved him. She might not have said as much, but it was patently obvious. "Don't talk about her like that."

Anton raised an eyebrow. Instead of coming down like it should have, it kept going, sliding up into his hairline. Beneath it, the skin smoldered, blurring into a smear. *"Forget the girl, you fool. You need to focus on that which you want above all. Like your friend, Nathan. There is a man who knows how to prioritize."*

"I went there, didn't I?"

"Wasted energy. The threat does not come from your long-term friends."

Chops. "The Violent Dead. They're going to take him aren't they?"

"There are many paths before us. Only you can narrow them down."

"You want me to kill again?"

The entity pointed out of the passenger window. Dimly, he was aware that Anton was in the car with him, but it didn't matter. He didn't think the man could hear or see what was happening, but if he could, it was inconsequential compared to everything else.

Oaks followed the long finger. Outside of the window, there was no road or traffic. Instead, he saw the pathways of a park he recognized. Moths and other winged bugs flittered in the harsh light of a lamppost looming over a concrete footpath. The sound of approaching footsteps came from ahead of him. Hank Traine came running past, bright orange sneakers glowing in the light. He paid no attention to Oaks, puffed his cheeks in and out as he pumped his arms.

"The park is always empty when he comes. It is dark."

"And if I say no?"

"Your choices are yours. So is the cost of failure. I am here to help you eliminate the pathways that could threaten your goal."

The image melted away. When he returned to the present, Anton was grinning at him. "I'm telling you exactly what she is. She went with you on that first night because I told her to. You need to stop being a child and you need to remember that you have a job to do. How you do it affects both of us."

"Is that right?"

"That's exactly right. Not everyone gets the treatment you have. I was told to bring you in and to make sure you were blessed. You were important, and if you fuck up, you won't be the only one whose head is on the chopping block."

CHAPTER THIRTEEN
DESTROY ERASE IMPROVE

Chops rested the bong on the table and fanned away the last few wisps of smoke curling out. "You guys sure about that?" he asked.

Ricky nodded. "Yeah, man, dude spoke to Hank last night. He's hanging up the sticks. Ligament damage means he can't play blast beats anymore. Shit sucks ass, but it leaves us without a drummer."

"Unless you want in," Hank said. "We've been impressed with your skills, dude. We wanna take you overseas with us."

Chops observed the stars and blew out a sigh. "Fuuuuuck." He pressed his thumbs into his eyebrows. "How soon? That's right after the local gigs here, right?"

Hank packed another billy and grabbed the lighter off Ricky. "Sure is. You in?"

"I got shit to sort out, man. Corey's funeral, recording with Polyphemus; I promised them, man. Any other circumstances, I'd be there in a split-second, but they're in big-time trouble if they don't get their shit recorded."

"How much of that's your problem?" Ricky asked.

"It's not the point. I've gotta do the right thing. They're good people."

"We've got thirty-six dates in Europe: London, Paris, Madrid, Berlin, Milan, Moscow, Prague, Bucharest, and every other little joint in-between. We're headlining Wacken and a festival in the ruins of a castle in Romania, man. Home of vampires and shit."

"You know I want in, but I'm supposed to help them record right after the local tour here."

Ricky pulled another cone and passed the bowl across the table. "I'm gonna play devil's advocate, Chops, how long are you planning on staying with those guys? Our last album went platinum. Their singer collapsed because he had to celebrate getting on the bill with us by shooting smack. This is a no-brainer."

Oaks's overdose got him thinking about Corey again. That shit didn't add up. "I need to sleep on it. I'm in, but I need to think about how I break it to them."

"Take a couple of days if you want," Hank said. "Worst case scenario, we can get a session drummer in for a week or two. The label's got shit in the pipeline for us in case of an emergency."

"Dudes, that's way too kind."

"Man, we're not blind to everything that's been going on and we want you in the band," Ricky said. "Give us a definite answer by the weekend so we can make arrangements if we have to. I'll get the label to draw up a contract in the meantime."

Chops took the bong off Ricky and filled the cone-piece. Maybe he could get the drum-tracks down before it was time to leave. Maybe not. Either way, this was the reason he'd spent most his life leaning over a kit. From here, he'd be the guy gracing *Modern Drummer*, making guest appearances on awesome albums, and playing huge festivals in front of thousands of people. This was the dream. He ripped the billy and slowly blew the smoke into the sky above him. "Leave it with me," he said. "I'll see what I can work out."

The road had been dead for miles. On either side, open fields stretched into rolling foothills, and ahead, in the distance, several volcanic plugs protruded upwards. The setting sun, dropping behind them, cast the monolithic landforms as silhouettes. Spiros drove toward them, a joint hanging out of his mouth and the rushing wind blowing his hair back.

Nathan fiddled with his phone, cueing up the next album. "This place is right out there." He hit play on the app and High on Fire came blasting out of the speakers.

"So she's there?"

"Who?"

"Lisa."

"Yeah, man, in the hospital. I thought she'd miscarried, but the kid's fine. They want to monitor her, find out why she was bleeding and shit." He took a swig of his beer.

"And after hospital, she's still at your place?"

"I thought I could, but I can't kick her out now. I'm a prick, but I'm not evil. She knows my priorities, but once the kid's born, we'll get it tested. If it's mine, we'll come up with a plan. If it's not, well, then she leaves."

The GPS told them they were turning soon. Spiros wound his window up. "Sounds like a risky game. Isn't that kid coming any day?"

Nathan took a hit from the joint. "Yeah, but fuck that. Let's focus on the band, man. Fucking Polyphemus, dude! We're back." He pointed to a road forking off the main drag and leading into the forest. "Turn down there. Seriously, though, I know we're gonna blow up with this one."

Spiros held out his fist for a wordless bump and cranked the volume. "It's about time, man. Now play something fast!"

The turnoff led to a road that sprawled below overhanging trees. On more than one occasion, the interwoven branches of the canopy blocked out the sun, casting shadows that covered the vehicle in darkness. In response, the GPS map switched to dark mode automatically, and Nathan, already several beers deep, bit his fingers in mock fear. "Spooky shit," he said.

He made jokes about that stuff, but when he was younger, he used to love mystical tales. He would eat up stories that tree tunnels were pathways to alternate dimensions and the fairy kingdom could be found through mushroom rings. He still semi-believed it. He'd never admit he thought different realms were a possibility, but if there was something in it, then he hoped it would be the right kind of magic they needed to make this album a killer.

"GPS is offline, man. We're out of service."

"We're almost there, dude. Cormac said there'd be a sign a couple of kilometers after the turnoff."

Spiros accelerated and gestured once more for the joint. The trees outside blurred and Nathan passed it over. By the time Spiros had sucked the last toke out of it and blown the thick grey plumes out of the window, they had whizzed past the sign and skidded off the main drag onto the side road leading to the studio cabin.

A cemetery stretched over the field to their right. Dense forest loomed on their left. "Cormac wasn't wrong," Nathan said. "The place is creepy as hell."

"Hope you brought your corpse-paint. Help us get in the true kvlt mood and channel some demons."

"Find a church to burn."

"I forgot snacks. Good to know we get to eat someone's brain."

Nathan pressed his finger to his nose. "Shotgun not, man."

"No one wants to eat your brain anyway. It's tiny. Like a meatball. We want something big and juicy we can marinate. I nominate Chops. That motherfucker's got a head like an elephant's testicle. Bound to be plenty of meat in there."

"He's a drummer; there's nothing but meat in there."

They laughed, and the cabin appeared as they crested a small rise in the road. Set amongst a stand of Eucalyptus trees, their bark hanging in strips like nooses from gallows. It could have been something out of *Evil Dead*. Constructed from logs and black corrugated iron, surrounded by wild lantana, and serenaded by cawing crows, it would be their home for the time it took them to record. Yeah, there was some shit they had to work out—Oaks getting a pass from the halfway home being the main issue—but this was where they had to make the comeback album work. If they didn't want to fade into obscurity, this record had to be *killer*.

They got out of the car, and Nathan whistled, impressed. "Check the door, dude."

Spiros snorted a syllable of laughter when he saw the goat skull adorning the entrance to the studio. "That was a big-ass goat."

"That was no ordinary goat, man. That was Black Phillip."

Spiros snapped a photo of the bleached-bone idol and uploaded it to his socials. "Let's check it out."

Nathan opened the door and flicked the lights on. Despite the outward appearance of the cabin, the interior was pristine. Decorated like an old hunting lodge, the polished timber floors reflected the glare of the overhead lights, busts of animals leered down from the walls, and framed records filled the spaces in between. The furniture was immaculate: plush leather couches, a large timber dining table, and a gas fireplace.

On the other side of the interior, a sliding glass panel led to a large jam-room. Branching off that were two separate production and recording zones.

Spiros ogled them and ruffled Nathan's hair. "Go and get the guitars. We've gotta test this shit out."

Nathan wiggled his eyebrow, grinning. "Soon, my man. I see a basement. We have got to get a good look in there. Maybe we'll find the Necronomicon."

"Lucky for us you can't read."

"It's got pictures, though. Maybe I can trace a few. Get

'em tattooed on." He grinned and opened the door to the basement.

It wasn't the video nasty setting Nathan hoped for. It housed a lounge area, a kitchenette, and a bathroom. Bunkbeds hugged the walls surrounding a large open floor area. Pressed against the opposite wall, a low stage had been raised. If anything, it was pretty much state of the art. Foldback speakers hung from the ceiling, and so did strobe lights.

"Shatters your slasher movie fantasy."

"Yeah, well, when you figure that it's a multi-million dollar recording studio, it's easy to forget the bones and skulls are for aesthetics."

"Trademark Kvlt," Spiros said. "The kind you see on MTV."

"This shit's set up for after-parties. You can bet there's been some debauchery in here."

"And if not, there soon will be. Let's get the guitars. I want to try the speakers. And then we can tell the boys everything is all set."

Nathan opened the basement doors and sunlight filtered down the steps.

A short while later, they had carried their guitars into the upstairs jam-room and plugged in. Spiros palm-muted a few open chords.

Nathan let the chugging notes rattle his eardrums before playing with the dials on his amp. He hit the same rhythm again and nodded. "Yellow Blood of the Red Planet's Slaves?"

Spiros's smile stretched from ear to ear. "Ok, *boooooooyyyyy,*" he growled, mimicking the Tall Man from the *Phantasm* movies, and stomped his effects pedal before fingerpicking a lilting intro that could have been in the original score.

Nathan added his own swirling build-up, taking full advantage of the chorus pedal, before they dove into a huge riff together. The music crunched from the speakers, and Nathan was certain he could feel the air being pushed by the driver cones. He soon dropped into a lower octave version of the original melody and Spiros slipped into a lead over the top.

Forgetting all the shit of the previous few days, Nathan rode the groove, loving the fact this was happening. Of all their new songs, this was the one he was most excited about getting into the live setting. They had taken the main theme from the film and transposed it into a driving outro full of blast beats and blackened death-metal thrashing. Sure, Entombed had already used the melody, but that was years ago, and there was no way modern crowds wouldn't love it to bits. He was pretty sure they wouldn't need to know the movie either. As they moved towards the song's closing movement, a tirade of riffs that came after a false finish, he let the waves of sound reverberate through him and smiled. Everything else: Corey's death, Lisa's bullshit, and Spiros's dramas were nothing but distractions. This band was what mattered; what had always mattered, and after everything, they were going to make it mean something to the rest of the world. Finally.

She waited for Anton to turn away from his table before speaking. She knew why he'd wanted her to come to his apartment. Despite his claims of superiority and spiritual aloofness, he was no different than every other prick who'd tried to use her in the past. When he faced her, she noticed his contemplative expression. She'd made sure not to enter too far into the apartment, standing near the elevator and keeping the lounge between them.

"We need to have a serious conversation," he said.

"I don't think we do. I'm done with you, and as soon as I can get Stephen to see sense, he will be too."

He appeared to mull it over, then inspected his occult toys with curiosity. "I'm afraid things aren't going to work out the way you're thinking, my dearest. You owe me, you see."

The sheer arrogance of the man was appalling. "No, I don't," she said. "For a long time, I thought that I did, but you're no different than any other con-artist. Whatever it is you're doing with your NLP and your pretend rituals, you've got no power over anyone. You take advantage of the weak, and you keep them weak through drugs and your pseudo-religious bullshit, but not me; not anymore."

He grinned. "Is that right?"

On the way here, she'd made sure she kept herself angry, dwelling on the wrongs that she'd endured throughout her life and the things she'd done with Anton since leaving rehab behind. "Yeah, that's right. I'm as good as gone, and I'm going to take that poor man with me. He needs support, not your manipulation."

"Do you remember when he was undergoing his ritual that I told you how clueless you were to what was happening here?"

She narrowed her eyes.

"You can go, you can. You can relapse into oblivion for all it matters. I expected more of you, though. I thought you were ambitious and that you'd be here trying to gain power through my methods. I thought that sooner or later, I'd need to be rid of you. If you're willing to do it yourself, that suits me fine, but let me tell you something for free: when it comes to Stephen, you couldn't be more wrong. He won't be going with you. He is with me until the bitter end, and he'll be the one who helps me get what I want."

"And what is it you want? Money?"

He laughed. "Do you think I'd be so crass as to announce anything to you? I'll put it in perspective. You think that Stephen needs support. Stephen has everything he requires, and he is so locked onto his goals, that he would abandon you in a split-second if he thought you would hinder him in any way."

"You're wrong, and I'm going." She called the lift. "Don't contact me again."

"Stop there and listen. I have something to tell you." He strolled across and sat on the arm of the couch. "I notice you wore jeans tonight. If your body language didn't tell me something, that certainly would. He knows why you befriended him. We had a discussion about it. He didn't take it well. I doubt he'll stick around. Worse, though, did you know someone broke into the heroin stash at Amielle's and that he's the only one who lives with her at the moment?"

"He was clean and sober when I saw him."

"Indubitably. What's interesting, though, is that there's been news online about his band. Have you heard what happened to their new vocalist?"

A cold shiver ran up her spine. "What?"

"An overdose. Apparently, his friends and family are adamant that he wasn't a user. You know what I think?"

She didn't want to know what he thought, but she knew where this was going already. He was trying to plant doubts about Stephen in her mind, trying to make her see him as untrustworthy.

"I think," Anton said, "that he's an ambitious man and he has one singular goal. I think he arranged things so he could rejoin his friends. His goal is to make that band of his huge, and he has *strong motivation* to make that happen. You might say he owes it to himself and to a higher power."

She'd heard enough. She called the lift again. "Fuck you. Don't contact me again."

She stepped into the elevator as his laughter rang out behind her. She had to remember the bastard was a master manipulator and that everything he owned was a result of his skill at persuasion. If he'd told Stephen why she had originally approached him, she would have to talk to him.

She couldn't deny that she'd been put up to it, but she knew the truth: the guy had latched onto her, and her betrayal would crush him. She didn't want that. As she had gotten to know him, she'd realized he wasn't pathetic. He was lost. Only old-fashioned perseverance would help him get better, not the pseudo-religious bullshit Anton offered.

As for the stuff about Polyphemus's new singer, she'd have to check what had happened, but she couldn't believe that Stephen would do anything as malicious as Anton had suggested.

The elevator arrived on the ground floor, and as soon as she had reception, her phone buzzed. There were several group messages to her and Stephen from Anton in her inbox. Each one of them contained a photo of her in compromised positions. BETTER KEEP YOUR MOUTH CLOSED the final message read. WE WOULDN'T WANT THESE GETTING OUT TO YOUR ART GALLERY FRIENDS.

She ignored the messages and called Stephen.

He didn't answer.

Oaks sat with his notepad in front of him and a pen in his hand. He should be writing, he knew that, but the cockroaches scampering under the couch were putting him off. The sound of their wings fluttering made him feel sick to his stomach. He was sure he could hear them clicking, conversing. He had a suspicion that if he listened hard enough, he'd be able to understand them, and that he had the seeming to thank for that.

Things were tense in the house. Amielle clearly wanted to speak to him; wanted to confront him, but it was obvious to Oaks that she wasn't sure how. Lately, he'd been picking up extra feelings from people, something he'd put down to the increasing influence the entity was having on his understanding of the world. Ultimately, though, it was his own guilty conscience that stopped him from breaking the ice. He was fully aware she knew he'd smashed in the bathroom cupboard and taken the smack, but admitting to it could lead to extra questions. He couldn't have that, so instead, he sat in awkward silence, contemplating the vision the presence had given him earlier.

A shadow shifted in his peripherals. Scrawled words on his notepad writhed as something cold slithered down his spine. *It's almost time*, they said. *You'll need to go to your room soon. Make her think you're sleeping.*

He watched the words; made sure they'd settled, then yawned loudly and made a point of going to the kitchen and pouring himself a glass of water. "I'm shagged," he said for Amielle to hear.

She snorted in response, and he went to his room without saying another word.

Once inside, he flopped onto the bed and flicked the notepad onto his messy desk. As he lay there, wondering exactly how he was going to get out of the room unnoticed, the presence in his peripheral vision slipped away and coalesced into shape at the foot of the bed. Again, Oaks felt that strange sense of longing the creature, the demon, he supposed, inspired in him. Whatever it was, it clearly thrived on desire and that manifested in a lustful feeling. Deep down, he knew there was far more going on here, and supposed this was only a side-effect the creature seemed to have, but he couldn't deny that the more the entity wanted from him, the more he wanted it in return.

As he considered this, the thing took his hand and drew him up from the bed. It gestured at the wall, and it seemed to melt, to become translucent. "*Go now,*" it said. "*The time approaches.*" It drew him towards the shimmering view appearing where the internal wall had previously stood, and Oaks realized it was the same park he'd seen in his earlier vision.

He stepped into the wall and seconds later, he was surrounded by low bushes. Wind rustled through them. The fluttering of birds and squabbling of bats filled the canopy. A concrete path appeared ahead of him, and Oaks stalked it, knowing to turn left and head towards the birdwatcher's hideaway overlooking the lake.

The seeming shifted in his peripheral vision. He was growing used to its constant presence and couldn't remember what life was like without it. It was always babbling in his ear, and even when it wasn't directly appearing and confronting him, it was feeding him information and making suggestions. That was how he knew Traine would run past the hide soon.

Apparently, the big vocalist made a point of running through the park every night. Unfortunately, for him, the park's reputation as an unsafe place—thanks largely to several unsavory incidents in the late 90s—kept it free of other runners. Needless to say, that worked in Oaks's favor.

As he sat on the bench in the hide, wondering exactly how he was going to bring the man down, he felt something cold and clammy close around his heart and squeeze. He dropped off the bench, scuffing the palms of his hands and saw the garden bed beside the hide was ringed in rocks the size of a man's head.

The entity loomed over him. *Too much thought,* it said, and was gone. Only one word lingered in his mind: *Act.*

Oaks reached for one of the rocks and noticed that beyond the garden, a small fenced off area had been installed to protect new growth. The temporary fencing was held in place by a ring of star pickets. He neglected the stone and prowled across the garden. He drew the star picket out of the freshly tilled earth and pulled it free of the orange barrier. A full four-foot long, it was heavy enough for bludgeoning and its spiked base would easily crunch through skin and bone.

The pounding of footsteps came up the footpath.

He held the improvised weapon like a sword and waited behind the corrugated iron blind of the hide. Soon, he heard labored breathing and the tinny blare of music playing through someone's mobile phone. Oaks recognized the song as one of Chimaira's: "Left for Dead". He waited a second or two longer, and then, as if the entity had given him a cue, Mark Hunter bellowed lyrics about becoming a monster.

Oaks spun out from behind the structure and swung the picket with all his might, smashing it across Traine's jaw, clotheslining the Violent Dead frontman and shattering bone.

The bastard hit the concrete with a thud. His phone scattered into the distance and as he rolled, he spat teeth to the ground. His jaw had shifted awkwardly to one side, and he moaned in agony. His well-known cookie-monster growl was nowhere in sight. All he could do was whimper and whine.

Oaks paced forward, enjoying the riffage blasting from Traine's mobile, and hefted the star picket up like a javelin. So this was Hank Traine brought low. He was pathetic. All that posturing on stage and the hard man image he adopted for promotional videos and photos was nothing when measured against him now.

Traine had no awareness of what was happening. And, in fairness, that shouldn't be a surprise. That blow would easily have knocked the sense out of anyone's head. "Hey," Oaks said to the bleeding vocalist, "You know who I am."

Traine whimpered and laid his eyes on Oaks.

Oaks saw the recognition in them. "Yeah, it's me. I want you to know it's nothing personal. You're just *in the way*." He slammed the star picket down into the man's throat, striking a glancing blow that tore skin free in a massive flap, ripping the aorta and jugular open.

Traine's ruined throat rasped and gurgled as his body thrashed.

Oaks struck again, this time spearing the implement into the man's guts.

Hank clawed at his wounded throat, grasped the picket that protruded from his stomach, and moaned wordlessly into the night. Above them, the bats squabbled. A short distance up the path, Chimaira blasted their way through riff after tasty riff. The night-time scents of the forest had disappeared beneath the coppery odor of blood and the stench of shit and half-digested protein emanating from Traine's intestines.

Oaks thrust the picket down one last time. This final thrust was the most brutal of them all. It splintered the side of Traine's skull, entering at the temple and pushing through brain as it sparked on the concrete pathway beneath him.

His job done, Oaks yanked the picket free. He threw the weapon like a javelin. It splashed into the lake below their vantage point. He made his way towards Traine's phone. It still blasted out Chimaira. Oaks grabbed it and hurled it into the water, cutting Hunter's words short. He took Traine's wallet and stared at his corpse. This needed to appear like a mugging gone wrong. He hefted the dead man by the ankles and dragged him off the path, leaving a trail of blood in his wake. He tossed him behind a tree before covering him with deadfall.

In the hideaway, a shimmering portal had opened. Through it, Oaks could see his bed. With this done, the Violent Dead should no longer be a threat to his destiny.

CHAPTER FOURTEEN
THIS GODLESS ENDEAVOUR

When Chops pulled into the Symbolic car park, Ricky and Scott were already smoking cones at the patio table outside. He waved to them and parked next to the dock. He slid open the van door and began to pull his drums out.

Scotty wandered over and handed him a bong with a freshly packed cone. "Here, man, you're playing catch-up." He beamed from ear to ear and slapped Chops on the back. "This shit hits like a bitch." He grabbed the bass drum and took it up the stairs to the studio.

Chops pulled on the bong as Ricky came over and grabbed more equipment. He coughed thick grey smoke. "Did you thumbscrew that or what?"

"Told you, man, you're playing catch-up."

They all laughed. Chops handed the billy to the bass player. "Where's Hank. Dude's usually the first one here."

"Only us today," Ricky said. "He had to go see his Mum. It's her birthday or something."

"Not like we need him to jam, though," Scott said. "So it'll be good to work on some of the cues without that loudmouth bastard cracking jokes and acting like the know-it-all he is."

More laughter. If there was one thing that had been abundantly clear through their jam sessions over the last few weeks, it was that aside from being a kickass vocalist, Traine could play every instrument in the room and plenty that weren't. An education at the conservatorium of music would do that, Chops supposed.

He snatched up his double-kick and drumstick bag. After he was set up, he tapped out a quick rhythm and nodded to the other two guys.

"All right, hit "Providence"," Ricky said.

Chops counted them in and together they were off. As usual, the shit was tight and heavy, leaving no doubt in Chops's mind which of the two bands he was currently associated with was in better shape. These guys were on top of their game and musically, they pissed on Polyphemus.

They blasted through another half-dozen songs, and Chops ripped his shirt off, throwing it in the corner. He knew the stereotypes about drummers, but when you hit the kit like he did, it was impossible not to work up a sweat. He mopped his brow, and they were straight back into it. One thing he had to get used to was the fact that The Violent Dead's setlist was of main stage headliner length: they had to play for twice as long as most bands, and deliver the energy along with it. They were the band people were paying to see.

Finally, when they came to another smoke-break and threw in their buds, he asked how often they jammed without Traine.

"Not often," Scott said. "Prick's hard to get rid of. Surprised we haven't heard from him."

Ricky checked his phone. "Yeah, he'd usually text. Hope his mum's okay."

"He'll be sweet," Maddox said. "He knows we've got a damned good drummer keeping us in line."

Chops nodded appreciatively. "I have to say you guys are the best I've jammed with. It's an honor."

"Come on, let's not go sucking each other's dicks quite so soon." Ricky added some tobacco to the bowl and stirred it in. "You talk to the Polyphemus boys?"

Chops stared into the distance. "Been waiting for the right moment."

"Well, everything's all good on our end. The only thing

it depends on is whether you're recording with them or coming on tour with us."

"I'll record with them. I have to, they've practically begged me."

"Fair enough," Scotty said. "I feel that. I always liked their tunes anyway, man. That last album was killer. Shame about Oaks. He's a good vocalist."

Ricky agreed. "True that," he said. "How's he doing?"

Chops honestly didn't like these conversations. He was always worried he was going to say something that would upset the Violent Dead guys, especially as they knew Corey too, but he had to be honest. "It was tense at first, but he was on fire the other night. If he stays sober, it's going to be a killer album. They've brought Rusty in and Nathan's slid to second guitar. You guys know Rusty?"

"Yeah, man, good musician," Maddox said.

"Yeah, well, with two guitars, we…they…sound fat live. Spiros is a weapon. The songs are good too."

"You sound excited," Ricky said as he passed him the bong.

Chops chewed his lip. "If everything didn't feel so tragic I would be." He meant it. If things were different, he'd feel like the band had a chance of blowing minds with the new material. It was progressive, it was complex, and it was dark. Somehow, though, it felt doomed.

"How's everyone handling the Corey thing? You guys are getting plenty of bad press at the moment."

Chops had seen it. It was impossible not to. The band might be small fry in the great scheme of things, but bad publicity was always going to make the news, and social media only brought everyone further into each other's business. They'd all shared the requisite heartfelt messages online, but the industry-related websites and message boards were all talking about Polyphemus's drug addictions. "It's what you'd expect. Everyone's bummed as hell, but they're over a barrel. The label's pressing hard for the album. If I didn't know better, I'd say they want to capitalize on it all."

The silence was punctuated by the bubbling of Maddox's bong. "Come on," he said. "Let's go jam some more. This shit's depressing as fuck."

"Well, are you going to say anything," India asked, breaking the silence. "Are you going to invite me in so we can talk, or are you gonna leave me hanging here?" Her face was a painting of regret, but she had used him; had treated him like a dumbass because she had been put up to it by Anton. How could he trust her after that?

He felt the presence slither into the inner reaches of his psyche and stepped aside, gesturing to the couch. He didn't know whether to be angrier at her or Anton. They both deserved his rage, but he could barely muster up the necessary feeling to show that anger. If anything, the only response he could generate was dejection. "You had me fooled," he said. "You're certainly good at your job."

She sobbed. "That's because I wasn't pretending! I can't lie to you; yes, I was initially asked to make you feel loved and welcome, but I wasn't pimped out. I did those things because I wanted to, not because I was put up to it."

If only he could believe that. He knew who she was before she'd come out of the facility, and he knew that he'd happily return to the junk if he didn't have the seeming to keep him on the straight and narrow. "People don't change, though, do they?"

"Yes," she said. "They do! I told him I was done, and I want you to be free with me. Walk away from him. Walk away from it all and come with me. He's bad news."

He snorted. "And where are we gonna go? I've got commitments. Don't you have art shows to promote?"

"Metaphorically." She approached him. "But none of that shit matters. What do you want out of life?"

He stepped away. Felt a shadowy tendril in the corner of his awareness. "I want what I've always wanted. I want to make my band huge. I want to travel the world, and that's no place for a relationship, especially with someone as untrustworthy as you."

"Is that why you broke into Amielle's cupboard?"

"Who told you about that?"

"Anton, of course. You think I'm the only one he's stitched up here? He's manipulating you, and I'm the collateral. I don't know what he wants from you; I don't know what he's got on you, but it's bullshit." She stepped closer to him again, reaching out a hand to touch his arm. A smudge of grey began to materialize behind her. She wasn't aware of it.

He shook his head. "No," he said. She might be right about Anton. After all, the prick certainly had his own agenda, and Oaks had never been let in on what exactly that was, but the fact was that she couldn't be trusted. "I told you. I can't be swayed. I've got commitments."

She grabbed both his arms, imploring him. A wisp of smoke began to crawl around her throat. "You can have your commitments but come away from Anton. I don't know what he wants with you, but things are not right."

This time, the entity spoke in his mind before he could respond. *Remember that you owe us the fealty of four others. Remember that you all must succumb to our will and deliver us what is ours.*

He pushed her away. "I can't. There are things I must do."

"Then tell me what you did with the drugs. I know you didn't take them, and I know about the band's new singer."

That stopped him. What did she know exactly? "What are you talking about?" he asked. If she knew exactly what had happened, then things were about to get real bad.

"I know he died, and I know that Anton suspects you

played a part in it. Do you trust him not to use that against you?"

The humanoid smoke swirl behind her didn't have a face in the traditional sense, but it eyeballed him nonetheless.

"And do you think I would do something like that?"

She sobbed again; grabbed him and pulled him close. "Of course not. I know you. I know you think I don't, but ever since I met you, I've known you're a sweet person who needs something to latch onto. Some way to know you're loved and needed."

He felt the tears in his own eyes begin to well. He thought about Corey, about bringing that syringe full of venom down; about the brutal murder he'd committed last night. This girl didn't know that, but she was right.

Do not give in, the seeming said. *Do not be drawn from your path. You owe.*

He pushed her away again. "You have to go," he said. "I can't do this with you today. I have shit to do, and I need time to think about it. With you here, I'll jump headlong into something when I don't know what I want. I can't do that when I'm on the verge of something so amazing."

Tears streamed down her face. "This could be amazing." She practically moaned it at him, speaking through a contorted expression. "I'm so sorry for hurting you, but I really think this—no matter how it started—is what is meant to be.

Remember your visions. You have to make them come true. Your choices have repercussions. "No, I've dreamed what's meant to be, and it's with the band. I can't sacrifice that."

A huge sob racked her shoulders. "And if I gave you an ultimatum, would you sacrifice me? Is that what you're saying?"

"You've made your own bed. I would have taken you with me, but you can't be trusted. It's a shame, but something better will come along. I'm going to the top."

She spun on her heel and left, slamming the door behind her.

He heard her car start, and then he flopped onto the couch, holding his head in his hands and letting the tears run.

It's for the best. The entity sat beside him on the couch. *I can give you everything she can.* It morphed into her, nuzzled his neck with her nose and ran a clawed finger along his collarbone. It nibbled his ear and he faced it, desperate for another of its visions.

He kissed it full on the lips, on her lips, and he felt its clawed finger penetrate his stomach once again. As he lay on the couch, visions of himself on a huge stage, surrounded by his bandmates from Polyphemus, and a blood-red sky overtook him. As he felt his body undulating, Chops blasted the drum-kit. The gyrating sea of adoring fans pulsed in ecstatic movement.

Soon it would all be his.

When he had come home to an empty apartment last night, Nathan couldn't help but feel relieved. With everything that had been going on, his home-life had deteriorated thanks to Lisa's continued presence. He was over walking on eggshells in his own home and was sick of trying to avoid her, so he'd loved the peace and quiet that having the house to himself had provided. In her absence, he cranked up the volume on the television, cracked a couple of beers, and smoked a fat bowl while he watched *The Thing*. When that had finished and she *still* wasn't home, he sent her a text message to let her know he was going to lock up. If she had found somewhere else, he wanted to know so he could have his own bed.

He watched a few cartoons before falling asleep on the

couch. When he came to a couple of hours later and she hadn't returned his text, he wondered if she was okay. He dialed her number and left a message. He told himself that he didn't care whether she was okay or not, but he knew it was bullshit. As much as she was a massive pain in the ass, he didn't wish her any bodily harm, and she was still a pregnant woman – whether the baby was his or not. That done, he fired off another text and crawled into the spare bed.

When he woke and the house was still empty, he logged onto his socials and saw that she hadn't been active all night. Fuck it. He couldn't spend all day worrying. If she wanted him to know what was going on, she could tell him. Moving on, he popped two slices of toast into the toaster and rolled his morning joint. That was when someone thumped on the front door.

He checked the time and called out. "Who's there?"

"Friends of Lisa's," a voice answered. He pinched out the spliff and opened the door to find a hipster-looking dude with a bright red beard and a guy in a hi-visibility shirt hanging by the letterbox. There was a van in the driveway.

"What's up?" Nathan said. "She okay? I couldn't get hold of her last night."

"Like you care," the bearded dude said.

"We've come to grab some of her things," said the other bloke.

"Who are you?"

"I'm her brother," Hi-Vis said. "Now, we don't need any trouble, but she's done here. Are you going to let us in or do we need to call the police?"

Nathan didn't know what to say. He'd been pushing for it, but with the truth smacking him in the face, he wasn't sure how to respond. "You can come in," he said, "but tell me what the fuck's going on."

"You've chosen not to be a part of anything. She's taken that on-board, and after a big night, we're grabbing some of her things. She's coming to stay with us for a while. She'll talk to you about it later," Hi-Vis said, his tone easing.

Nathan stepped aside and gestured them in.

"Where's her room?" Hipster beard asked.

Nathan sipped his beer and rubbed his forehead. "It's through here, but is she okay? What sort of big night?"

The burly dude in the work shirt sighed. "Man, it's not our place to tell you, but there's no reason for her to be here. You're a toxic son-of-a-bitch and she deserves better. With the reason gone…" he took a deep breath and the bearded guy put an arm around him.

"You never wanted this shit," the bearded guy said, "and there's no need for you to worry. The baby's gone. She lost it. Now will you let us through? She needs people who love her."

Nathan's stomach dropped and he fell to his knees. The horrible things he'd said came to his mind. The scare the other night. The fact he'd wanted not to have this extra helping of chaos in his life. "Shit, I'm so sorry," he said.

Hi-Vis leaned on him. "You don't have to say sorry to us. You've stuffed her up big-time, though. You owe her the world and you hurt her, man."

"On any other day, I'd kick the shit out of you," Hipster Beard said, "but I'm needed elsewhere."

"No, do it," Nathan said. "I deserve it."

"Get out my way," Hi-Vis said. "Keep drinking; keep poisoning yourself and everyone around you. Your whole world is falling apart, and you do nothing but keep drinking. Do you think we don't know; that she doesn't tell us? You're a piece of shit and you never deserved her." He shoved Nathan to the floor and they made their way down the corridor.

Hipster beard stepped past him, leaving him a crumpled mess.

What had he done? In his stress to make the band work, he'd hurt this girl. He'd never meant to, not consciously, but that shit couldn't be changed. He'd wanted her gone. He'd gotten his wish in the most painful way possible. He skulled the remnants of his beer and grabbed his phone; tried to call her. No answer.

In his head, it had been so simple. He was so sure the kid wasn't his, that he'd pictured her bouncing the baby on her knee while she calmly told him that yeah, it was all a mistake and she was sorry for the inconvenience she'd caused him.

He'd imagined telling her that it was all okay, and that accidents happened, and that if she ever wanted to get a babysitter and hang, she would be more than welcome. She was a great screw, after all.

What a jackass he was.

He stayed on the couch, waiting for the two guys to load the van with her suitcases and bags full of perfumes and clothes then got on the phone to the hospital.

"Hello," he asked, "Can you put me through to the post-natal wing?"

They questioned him and told him that yes, Lisa was there but that she'd asked not to be seen by him at this point. They took a message, and he finished his bowl of weed before putting his shoes on. He needed to get out of the house and drink some more beer.

CHAPTER FIFTEEN
AS THE PALACES BURN

Spiros saw the missed call from Nathan, but he'd have to worry about it later. With Pandora nowhere to be seen, he'd had to pick up some of the extra slack on the business side of the family greengrocery. He sent a text, promising he'd call in a bit. He had several more invoices to pay and a shit-ton of orders to place. Usually, he and Pandora shared these duties throughout the week, but with his recent schedule, and the fact he had Corey's funeral coming up, he didn't know if she'd be around to take care of it.

Across the room from him, Calliope's highchair was empty. He'd drowned out the endless silence of his massive property with plenty of music. Nevermore's *Godless Endeavour* album was currently ripping out of his surround sound system. He loved the leads on this one, and it didn't often leave his rotation, but it wasn't doing it for him today.

He paused it and saw that a message had appeared on his lock screen. For a moment, he let himself believe that it was Dora, but yet again, his hopes were diminished. This time it was his brother wanting to know if there was any word.

He dialed Pandora's number and waited for the phone to ring out before leaving what must have been the fifteenth message in the last forty-eight hours: *"Baby, I love you and I want to talk to you and Calliope. Call me. Please."*

He thought about returning Nathan's call, but he couldn't deal with more of the dude's melodramas. His own life was complicated enough, and he was done with the *Jerry*

Springer shit-show that his old friend was making of his own.

He went into Calliope's room and pushed her rocking horse so it swung backwards and forwards. Her pillow was gone from her cot. God, he missed her. He missed them both so much.

Someone knocked at the door. "Spiros, bro, you home. It's me, Oaks."

What the hell? It wasn't like Oaks to show up here unannounced. It was far more likely that he would go to Nathan's, and for that reason, Spiros thought the two of them might be together. It was weird that Oaks hadn't said so, but whatever. He was a weird dude.

The vocalist was on his own. He too seemed downtrodden. Misery was going around like the plague lately. "Come in, man. I wasn't expecting to see you until after the funeral tomorrow."

"Yeah, well, I realized it's been years since I paid you a visit. How's the family?"

"They're good," he said. He didn't know if Nathan and Oaks had spoken, but he couldn't be bothered going through it all. "In their own way."

Oaks raised an eyebrow. His previously clean-shaven head had given way to stubble, making him look like something of a hard ass. Spiros knew nothing was further from the truth, but he smiled to himself.

"You good, man?" Oaks asked.

"Yeah, I'm fine."

"You seemed a bit odd when I mentioned the missus then."

"It's nothing. They are off with relatives."

"You didn't go with them?"

What the hell was this? The dude was acting like the Spanish inquisition. "Enough questions, man. If you've spoken to Nate, you know things are shit. If you haven't, things are shit. You want a drink?" He watched the vocalist suspiciously. The prick was up to something. He passed him a tin of beer. "So why are you here?"

Oaks's eyes shifted. He grinned. "I can't pay you a visit anymore?"

Spiros laughed. "Don't give me that. You know you are always welcome. Ever since we were little and you had to visit me in my parents' home, you have been welcome." He waggled his finger in front of his old friend. "But you don't do it often anymore. I cannot remember the last time."

Oaks cracked the beer and drank deeply. "You were always straight to the point."

"If it's about the band, you know you are already recording with us and I, personally, can do no more than that."

"I think we should go straight on the road."

Spiros stretched his arm behind his head, pulled the black hairband on his ponytail tight against his scalp and sighed. "You are a relentless son of a bitch. I said—"

"I know what you said, but you know as well as I do that the best time to promote an album is when it's hot off the press."

Spiros poured himself a glass of water. "Dude, you don't think this is a conversation to have when everyone's with us? We don't know if Chops will be in the band. My wife is probably leaving me, and God knows what's going on with Nate. That doesn't even bring the Corey thing into the equation."

Oaks made as if to speak, but Spiros cut him off.

"Please, my friend, I do not mean to be rude to you, but things are up in the air. I am being, as I always am, honest. And this is not something you have to convince me about."

Oaks nodded in contemplation. "And if all those things work out?"

"Then you know that I love you. I don't know if you know, but I was always happy to have you in the band. Things were hard after your overdose, there's no denying it.

We are reaping the consequences of that. Get online and read what's being said about us now that Corey has died because of drugs and you can see that we are suffering as a result of everything that's happened. I can only assume record sales are down. Our welcome from concert promoters is yet to be known. But I love you, and if I know that Polyphemus is good for your wellbeing—and it still tours—I want you to be part of it. First and foremost, we are friends you and I."

Oaks held out a hand for Spiros to shake. "I love you, brother."

"Piss off with your handshake," Spiros said. He grabbed Oaks and pulled him in close for a big bear-hug, patting him on the shoulder and squeezing him tight. "The feeling is mutual, but as you know my wife is not here. You keep saying things like that and I might think you are coming onto me." He let Oaks take his seat on the stool by the breakfast bar and laughed with him. "Does this make sense to you?"

"I can promise you something, Spiros. You're going to get the best vocals I ever put on tape on this album, and there's something else. Having something to do, something to keep my mind on, something I love; that's better for my wellbeing than anything else has ever been. If we hit the road—and I've gotta say that I've got a good feeling that once we start recording Chops will come around—I'll be better than ever."

"I don't doubt it, but let's worry about that when it matters. In the meantime, what do you say we go for a jam?"

That strange glint reappeared in Oaks's eyes. He nodded.

Spiros grabbed a beer. "Lead the way," he said. "You know where the jam room is." On the way, he checked his phone. Still nothing from Pandora.

He couldn't believe what he'd heard, what Ricky had confirmed for him. The body they'd found at the wetlands belonged to Hank. Someone had murdered him on his run. It was mental, first Corey and now this. As the news headlines flashed again, showing a snippet of police tape around the entrance to the park, he couldn't believe that a man he'd come to call his friend had been brutalized and bashed to death in that very location.

He hadn't had a chance to speak to Ricky or Scott yet, and he didn't count on doing so anytime soon. The three of them were tighter than nun's nasties and they would be seriously grieving, but by all reports, the attack on Hank had been particularly savage. He was only recognizable because he'd been reported missing by his girlfriend not long before they found a corpse wearing his clothes, a Psycroptic tee and an old pair of running shorts.

Chops blew his nose and wiped his tears away. What was wrong with the world? First Corey, and now Hank. No doubt conspiracy theorists everywhere would be cooking up stories about whatever they thought was going on, but the facts were simple: sometimes life sucked. At the moment, it did, and not in ways that always seemed so obvious.

Yeah, sure, Chops wouldn't be touring with The Violent Dead, but the way he saw it, that shit didn't matter at all. Both Corey and Hank were good people. Hank had a girlfriend and a young kid; Corey was a top bloke. Both had been taken way before their time.

He watched the news headlines cycle around again. On screen was a glimpse of the body-bag forensics had stuffed Hank into. Chops was disgusted the news would show that footage. Hank's family would see that. The shit was wrong on every level. He sent a message to Scotty and Ricky, telling them that he was here for whatever they needed; that all they had to do was message, but other than that, he'd be out of their hair until they wanted him.

The way things were going, he wasn't sure he even

wanted to make more music at the moment. He'd see his commitments with Polyphemus through, but other than that, he was done with the whole touring thing for a while. He muted the television and scrolled to a flight-finder. He'd been keen as hell to see Europe. Maybe if he could talk to Nathan and Spiros, they could get into the studio earlier. Maybe he could get his tracks down and get the fuck out of here.

"Yo, another one of those Kaiju black ales, my man." Nathan paid the bartender and sauntered across to the arcade machine next to a table full of young people. It might have been early, but in this part of the town, the bars were never quiet. The familiar main riff of Helmet's "In The Meantime" chugged through the sound system and he nodded his head as he pumped coins into the machine. There'd be bands playing later. Before they started, he wanted to enjoy the serious buzz he had going. The only thing that was going to improve that was something cathartic. The Helmet track was good, but *House of the Dead*, a classic arcade shooter from his youth, would double his pleasure. Blasting zombies into little pieces was precisely the sort of thing that could help him with his frustration.

He was halfway through the first stage when a Violent Dead track, "Providence in the Fall of an Angel", fired up. That was why he loved this place. They had great beer, great arcade machines, and a great selection of metal tunes. And that was when he heard the young group beside him start talking about Hank.

"Did you see the news? He was murdered last night."

A vivid red bite-mark flashed up on the screen as Nathan paid attention to what they were saying. He focused his attention on the machine and blew the zombie's head off. Blood fountained out of the stump of its neck, and it fell. A timber barrel came flying through the air and he splintered that with several shots before the next voice spoke.

"The singer? How?"

"Mugged," the first voice said.

Another bite-mark flashed up and the INSERT COIN command followed. He fired the time down to zero and spoke to the group. "Excuse me," he said. "I couldn't help, but…"

"Holy shit," one of the youngsters said. He had a sharp fade and a Slayer t-shirt on. "You're Nathan March."

It had been a long time since he'd been recognized, but if he was honest, that was half the reason he came here. A few months ago, this place was a meat market for musicians like himself. He held his hand out and eyed the ladies. One of them blushed and whispered something to her friend. "I am," he said.

The kid shook his hand and asked for a selfie.

"Sure," Nathan said, "but what are you saying about Hank?"

"Holy shit," the first girl said, "you don't know?"

He had a sick feeling in his stomach. "Don't know what exactly?"

"I thought you guys were friends. I thought all you metal dudes were friends."

"Yeah, we are; we know each other well."

"Wait," a second dude said. "Weren't you on tour with them when—"

Nathan knew where this was going. "Yeah, we were, but can you tell me what it is I don't know?" His guts were roiling, the beer sour in his mouth.

"Hank's dead, dude. It's all over the news."

A cold shiver ran down his spine and he dropped to his knees, clutching his hands to his open mouth. This couldn't be. This had to be a mistake.

The group stared at him. The second dude pulled out his phone and started filming. Nathan immediately held a palm out to obscure the camera's view.

The girl who'd blushed pulled the phone away. "Stop being a dick, Bradley."

He dropped the phone and shook his head. "He was mugged. Beaten to death on a run last night. Didn't do it to himself like your lot."

Silence broke out around the table. Nathan, reeling from the news, took a moment to register what had been said. When it hit, he felt the anger rise like a bubbling volcano. He hurled his beer at the kid, screaming "Fuck you!" The glass hit him in the face, and the half-pint of ale washed over the dude and splashed the others around him.

Nathan leapt, swinging an overhand punch at the kid's face, connecting hard. Half-sprawled across the table, he was unable to get out of the way when the first dude—the one who'd been polite—thumped him in the side of the head.

He rolled away from the blow, but the kid he'd punched had joined in too. The girls scrambled and the two kids rained down blows, pummeling Nathan in the head, arms and shoulders as he curled into a ball.

Security scrambled towards them and wrenched the two boys free as the epic closing riff and Traine roared over the powerful wall of guitars: "We defy! We defy augury! It is not! It is not…to come! It is not to come!"

Nathan pulled himself to his feet and spat blood. "Throw these dicks out," he said.

Security pointed to him, raised a thumb to the bartender and twisted it up and down, waiting for the final approval.

There was a moment where Nathan thought they were going to throw him out too, but instead, the guy shook his head. "The two young ones," he said to security. "This guy's cool. We know him."

As security walked the two kids to the door and shoved them aggressively outside, all but one of the girls followed.

The other girls asked her if she was coming.

She shook her head. "I'll call you."

They rolled their eyes and left. The two dudes hurled insults at Nathan, telling him they were gonna fuck him up.

Nathan gave them the finger, then touched a hand to his already bruising cheek. "You want a beer?" he asked the girl.

"Let's get you cleaned up," she said.

She took him into the bathroom and washed his face. Her touch was tender. Gentle.

Nathan hadn't felt a touch like it in a long time, and he let the sensation of friendly hands, not sexual but kind, brush against his swollen face. When she wiped a wet paper towel over the blood and cleaned him up, she inspected his wounds, curious, and he stared into her eyes.

"Don't look at me like that," she said. "It's creepy. You're too old, and I'm not interested."

He didn't get it. "So what?" he asked her, unsure why anyone would be so kind and abandon their friends to clean him up. "Why are you here then?"

"It's the right thing to do. No one's asked you if you're okay lately, have they?"

He snorted.

"So, are you okay?" she asked. She stared into his eyes again.

If he didn't know better, he'd say she was trying to read his thoughts. He considered giving her a smart-ass answer but resisted. Here was, for the first time in a long time, a real kindness, right when he needed it most. "No, I'm not okay. I will be, but that news about Hank, holy shit, I don't know what to say."

"You lost another friend earlier this week too, is that right?"

He nodded. "And this morning I got some other news. It's not been a good week."

"You want to talk about it? No pressure," she said, "no judgement."

He laughed then, bemused. "You're some sort of angel, right? Is that what this is, you find people, do them kindness when they need it?"

She giggled. "Nope, just your lucky day, I guess. I could see you were hurting, and I was taught that compassion is king. I was taught that when we see opportunities to do right, we should do them. Kindness is everything."

"Well, Miss Kindness, I'm Nathan, and I don't think I'm ready to talk yet. I will buy you a beer if you want, and I'm not hitting on you either. I could just do with some company."

"I'm Arabella," she said, "and even if you were hitting on me, it wouldn't change things. As I said, you're too old, and I'm not interested."

She was confident and strong. He liked her. She was also right. To her, he must be a crusty old mess. Worn out, stinking like alcohol, bruised, beaten. He was kidding himself, and he had to realize that he didn't need to ruin the life of this charming young lady. Best just to enjoy the attentions of the angel and move on with his life.

After a beer and some laughter, as well as a chat about the good times he'd shared with The Violent Dead, before everything went to shit, he bid his farewells and she left. Another couple of rounds of *House of the Dead* later, he stepped outside to find a cab home.

The two kids were waiting for him.

They lunged into him with the ferocity of animals, knocking him to the ground and kicking him in the guts until security pulled them away for a second time.

When they were done, he was left on his own, nursing his wounds and crying into his own drunken arms while he waited for his taxi to arrive.

CHAPTER SIXTEEN
THE FUNERAL GARDEN

The morning of the funeral, he woke with a sore head and sorer ribs. Vicious pain crawled through his chest when he inhaled or laughed. Fortunately, he hadn't laughed much. Corey's funeral was sad and somber, and he couldn't imagine the wake and impending after-party being much different, not that he'd be attending that part of the affair. Already, he felt like everyone was staring at him and the other members of Polyphemus as if they were personally responsible for Corey's death.

Members of bands from across the scene milled around in black suits and black ties, their eyes like needles prodding him when they thought he couldn't see them. Face-to-face, when he was speaking with people he'd played music with, toured with, gotten drunk with, he could see the judgement hiding behind their façade; knew that the band's reputation was central to the discussion going on out of earshot.

And then there was the news about Hank. The Violent Dead's members hadn't attended. They'd sent their apologies through Chops, who was smoking a joint with Rusty over by the entry to the central chapel. Nathan, who'd walked in with Spiros and Oaks, patted the Greek on the back and headed in their direction. For once, Nathan didn't have a beer in his hand. Spiros had talked him out of it and bought him a Powerade and some paracetamol on the drive in. He fumbled in his pocket for those. He'd already crunched two, but his head was throbbing from the blows it had taken and the beers he'd drunk yesterday. He needed to numb that.

As he approached, Rusty made space and held out the spliff for Nathan. He accepted it gratefully, took a hit, and passed it to Spiros, who then passed it onto Oaks. The five of them bumped shoulders. Nathan winced with each connection. "Ain't this some shit?" he asked.

"You see the way everyone's staring at us?" Chops asked.

"Who cares?" Spiros asked. "Did we do anything wrong? We can argue and explain that we didn't, but people are hurting. They need to feel the way they feel until they are done with their grief."

"Speaking of which," Nathan said, "how're you holding up, Chops?"

The drummer pressed the knuckle of his right index finger to his lips. Wiped a tear from his eye. "I'm broken, man. I just...obviously, there's this shit, and we'll be back here for Hank in no time."

Spiros pulled him into a bro-hug. Nathan stood, awkward, wanting to get in on it, but too sore to act. Instead, he stood close to Oaks, who was tight-lipped.

After a while, Chops pulled himself clear. "It's fine. I'm fine," he said. He gestured to the celebrant who'd made his way to the chapel entry. He was an older gentleman, professionally dressed, and he nodded politely as Chops made eye contact with him.

Rusty excused himself and intercepted an older couple on their way in. He hugged them and they met him with a warm welcome.

"Corey's folks," Chops said.

Rusty continued to speak with them before the celebrant announced that the ceremony would begin in ten minutes.

"I've been asked by a few people if we'll be hanging around for the wake," Chops said.

Nathan watched the other guests meandering towards the chapel. In a way, it was funny seeing a gathering of death metal musicians walking into what was, really, a miniature church together. "No longer than is polite," he said. "I got some shit to sort out this afternoon."

"What happened to you anyway?" Chops asked as Rusty returned.

Nathan drank a deep swig of his Powerade. "It's a long story." He didn't need to go into detail. They didn't need to know all about the bullshit with Lisa when they had so much other death on their plates, but while he had, ultimately, gotten what he wanted, there was something pyrrhic about the way it had finished and he couldn't leave it alone.

He needed to talk to her. What he thought had happened hurt way more than the ass-kicking he'd taken, and he needed to try to absolve himself from guilt; wash himself clean in the waters of forgiveness he hoped he could squeeze out of Lisa's tears. He knew he was a real asshole, but historically, he'd always been able to eke out that forgiveness through conversation. He needed it to happen again.

If he was feeling like this, then she must be feeling a thousand times worse. He wasn't sure how to handle that, but appearances were everything. He had to create the impression that he was there for her. Make her see *he* wasn't the bad guy.

"In short, Nathan, you were drinking too much. Today is not the day to have this discussion, because I think you are aware of it."

"I always drink too much," Nathan said.

There was a moment of awkward silence. Spiros put a stop to it. "Yes, well, when we're emotional, our constitution can be weak. We should head into the chapel, though. The celebrant is trying to give us polite hints."

After the ceremony, when Corey's flower-adorned coffin was wheeled behind a curtain, Chops asked them to wait in the foyer.

Nathan trudged slowly, already feeling like he needed a

real drink and a couple more paracetamol to start feeling somewhat human again. With his chat with Lisa still to come, he knew he'd be putting the beers off for a little longer yet, but the urge remained, especially when he could already smell alcohol in the air.

Once they were all gathered, Chops, an expression of pensive apprehension on his face, opened up. "As you guys know,' he said, "I was supposed to go on tour with the Violent Dead boys before we started recording."

"Shit, man, I'm sorry," Nathan said.

"Just listen." Chops bit his knuckle again. "That's obviously not gonna happen. What you don't know is that they asked me to tour Europe with them right after I was done recording with you guys."

"Holy shit," Spiros said. "That would have been amazing."

Nathan's stomach lurched. He felt Oaks tense as the drummer unveiled his secrets.

"Clearly, that's not happening either. I'm at a bit of a crossroad. I don't know what I want to do. Part of me is thinking I can go to Europe by myself, see castles, backpack, that sort of shit."

"But?" Spiros asked.

Nathan noticed that Rusty was hanging on Chops's every word. He'd initially suspected that the bass-player would already be privy to this when Chops started, but that didn't seem to be the case. Personally, Nathan thought that meant this was probably bad news; that Chops was about to pull the plug on it all.

"I'm getting there," Chops said. "I originally thought I could go tomorrow, but I think we should get in touch with Cormac and get in the studio early. Those pics you guys took were radical, and I think it'd be a great way to get our minds off everything and lose ourselves in the process."

Nathan observed everyone's reactions. He was stoked. He thought it was exactly what they needed. The only look that confused him belonged to Oaks. There was something shifty in his response. Outwardly, he was grinning, but there was something dark in his eye.

"So what do you think?" Chops asked. "I know I've gotta get my head clear, and I think this is the perfect way to do that before I head overseas."

"I'm in," Rusty said.

Spiros agreed.

"I'm there," Oaks said. "I can't fucking wait! Nathan?"

"You know I'm in, you dipshits. I'll call Cormac. We'll be able to make it happen, no sweat." The shifting glimmer in Oaks's eye was gone and he was grinning like a loon, but Nathan couldn't forget what he'd seen. If he didn't know any better, he'd say it was fear. Of what, he couldn't be sure.

By the time Spiros was driving home from the wake, Nathan riding shotgun and Oaks chilling in the back seat, the studio had been arranged. Cormac had agreed to move the dates forward in an instant, and Polyphemus would be in the studio tomorrow. Only a few weeks ago, the pressure the label had placed on them had felt impossible to live up to, but somehow they had made it work.

He was about to ask Nathan to crank up the Meshuggah when Oaks spoke. "What do you make of Chops wanting to go to Europe?" he asked.

Spiros bit his response, wanting to see where the vocalist was going with this. He had a feeling he already knew, but it never hurt to gauge the situation before speaking. Fortunately for him, Nathan was more than willing to speak. "It's pretty understandable," he said. "I've been speaking to him a bit lately, and although he's not shown all his cards before, he'll be gutted. Right on the verge of the biggest move of his career, he sees that shattered, and loses a mate in fucked-up circumstances."

Spiros was impressed. Nathan was capable of the odd surprise when he wasn't sinking piss. He had no doubt that his friend would be on the beers as soon as he was home, but hopefully today had done him good. Hopefully, he'd wait till later in the afternoon more often in the days ahead.

"It doesn't bother you that he kept it all secret?" Oaks asked.

"He didn't really. He told us from day one that he was jamming with them and filling in for Howie. He's a gun drummer and as soon as Howie made it plain that he couldn't return, they were gonna poach him. It's the way of the world," Nathan said.

Oaks grunted. "We need to keep him," he said. "We should book a Euro tour as soon after recording as possible."

And there it was, as predicted. Spiros met Oaks's eyes in the rear-view mirror. "Don't get ahead of yourself. That's not what Chops wants from his trip."

"I know that." He shuffled in his seat, staring into the rear-view mirror intently. "But like I said yesterday, I've a feeling he'll come around once we start recording."

Spiros was sure Oaks's eyes were different.

"Wait, what happened yesterday?" Nathan asked.

Spiros sighed. "Stephen paid me a visit. We had a jam and a conversation. I was going to talk to you about it after we dropped him home."

"Talk about it while I'm here," Oaks said.

"Shit-yeah, go for it," Nathan added, pausing the track, "Suffer in Truth". It hurt his ribs, but he leaned around to make eye-contact with Oaks anyway. "You sneaking around like a sly bastard?" He grinned and stuck his tongue out. "I don't think it's the worst idea."

Spiros, agitated, drummed his fingers on the steering wheel. "Steve came around and brought up the idea of going on tour as soon as the album is done. I told him the truth:

everyone is hurting and I couldn't make that decision alone."
He had harbored no doubts that Nathan would be willing to
plunge ahead. He was always the kind of guy who'd dive
headfirst into murky water without checking the depth, and
here he was, doing exactly that. "You know I love you
Stephen, but this needs to be a conversation we *all* have—
and that includes Chops and Rusty—but you, in particular,
need the all-clear from your case-manager."

"I'm not an imbecile," the vocalist said.

"Yo, he didn't mean it like that, but this would be huge,"
Nathan said. "Man, I'll champion the hell out of it, but your
health is important. I know the album's going to kick the shit
out of people, but we have to get everything right."

"We will," Oaks said. "I will, I can promise you that."

"Then let's have the conversation when we get there and
we've begun tracking," Spiros said. "Don't get me wrong, I
want this, but I have to think about my wife first. I told you
things are shit, but if I leave to go on tour to Europe then
there will be no recovery for my marriage." He became
aware of Oaks's eyes again. They had become distant, like
he was mulling over a particularly difficult decision. "I have
to smooth things over first, and the simple fact we are
recording early is not going to make that easy."

"You need to let us know how that conversation goes,"
Oaks said.

Nathan seemed surprised by this. Spiros let the comment,
as weird as it was, settle for a second. He considered ignoring
it, but he couldn't. "I don't know what the fuck I would have
to report for, but my business is my business. You know how
committed I am. It's why I'm in this position, but like I said
before, don't get ahead of yourself. You are contracted only
until we are done recording, so calling the shots on whether
or not we tour, and on how I deal with my fucked-up
marriage is way out of your schedule."

"And I told you that you'll come around once we're
recording," Oaks said. "Just you wait and see."

Spiros shut his mouth and stared ahead. Thankfully, he'd be dropping the prick home in a few minutes. It had been a long day—a huge day—and the last thing he needed was to pick a fight. "I think we need to park the conversation until we all have our bearings a bit more. Everything's shit right now, but maybe in a couple of weeks it won't be. Maybe we all need the clarity that only the studio can give us."

"Fuck!" Oaks said. "We need to realize there's a gap at the top of the food chain. This album could blow us up. It *will* blow us up. We need to capitalize and tour everywhere The Violent Dead isn't. We need to take this album across the world. I guarantee that we'll be the biggest band on the planet by the time we're done! Can't you see that?"

Spiros skidded into Amielle's driveway. "You're home. Get some sleep. Nathan will pick you up tomorrow."

"Suit yourself," Oaks said, "but remember what I've told you. We *have* to capitalize."

Once Oaks had entered the house, Spiros planted his foot and veered onto the road. "Can you believe that prick? What is wrong with him?"

Nathan took a deep breath. "I need a beer, man."

"Do you hear me? What was that?" Spiros knew he had lost his cool, but if Nathan wasn't going to consider the bullshit he'd just heard, the total lack of compassion for everyone involved, maybe they were all fucked. "You telling me you are okay with what you heard?"

Nathan shook his head. "No, man, I'm not…"

"Then what? Why no reaction?"

Nathan held his hands up and gestured for Spiros to chill. "Like you said, it's been a big day. Everyone's on edge. You and I, we've both got our own problems to deal with and we're not properly in the box; probably won't be until tomorrow. You ask me, that prick has his own shit going on. He's upset too, he feels out of place, he knows he's got to make it work and apart from us, he's got nothing. He sees this disappear, what does it leave him?"

Spiros inhaled. Exhaled. "You're right," he said. "We'll worry about it when the time comes. Tell me, though, before I drop you off, did the other guy come off better or worse than you?"

Nathan laughed. "Better, but I got him first. Lost my shit in pretty much the same way you just did. Douchebag kids talking shit about stuff they don't know. I threw the first one and got taken down. I've had worse."

"Well, you're home. You can have that beer soon."

Nathan picked at a hangnail. "I will, man, don't worry about that. I gotta talk to Lisa too."

Spiros raised an eyebrow.

"Not what you think. She's gone. So is the baby. Her brother came by and got her stuff yesterday. Didn't say much but said enough. I need to talk to her. Give her my condolences."

Nathan's black eye and sore body made a lot more sense all of a sudden. Given everything, he was taking it well. Too well, to be honest. "You let me know if you need me," was all he said. He knew when it was time to talk and when it was time not to.

They drove the last of the journey in silence, and after dropping Nathan home, Spiros made it to his own place in a few minutes. Pandora had been there.

He could smell her perfume and that hurt, but mostly, he was gutted he'd missed Calliope. He missed her smiling little face, and the two front teeth she had developed lately.

He fought back tears and read the note.

Spiros,

I have been reflecting and I know that your band is important to you. I understand it is something you have worked hard on for a long time and that it is your dream to make that work. It is, however, not my dream.

I understand you need to meet your legal obligations with the record label. For me, that has to be the final thing you do with Polyphemus. From there, you need to hang up your guitars. You have a family and a wife, and touring the country, the world, with your mates is not acceptable for me or for Calliope.

I am sorry for your recent losses. I know they have been hard on you. Maybe, though, there is a silver lining. Maybe it makes you realize which things you do not want to lose.

You are scheduled to record at some stage in the next few weeks.

Once you have done that, call me. We will decide together what it is we do next. Until then, know that your daughter misses you very much, but that she is safe.

I will send you pictures tomorrow, but for now, I do not wish to talk and will not answer your phone calls. It makes it too hard to stick to my convictions.

With love,
Dora.

He folded the note and stuck it in his pocket. It wasn't the letter he wanted, but it made it easier to make any decisions he needed to about touring Europe. If that was something everyone else wanted, then they could go with his blessing. He couldn't lose his daughter.

He had thought that Pandora would relent and he would get his way again—as he usually did—but it seemed that this time, he was going to have to think like a family man.

He tried to call her, but the number wouldn't connect. She must have him blocked. That was frustrating, but considering the thought she'd signed off with, he had no choice but to respect her wishes.

He poured himself a couple of fingers of scotch and went to pack his things for tomorrow's trip to the studio.

Oaks had gotten in touch with Anton as soon as he'd arrived at Amielle's halfway house, and the life coach had picked him up from there shortly after.

Classical music—some sort of opera from the sound of it—throbbed from speakers in the ceiling. Beyond the wrap-around windows, the black water of the coastline sparkled beneath the moon, and headlights of cars travelling along the esplanade.

Anton unfolded a black cloth and poured several powders onto it. "Do you remember our conversation about servitude?"

Oaks nodded. The shifting presence in his periphery came forward, and for the first time he knew, properly knew, that Anton harbored something similar in his own mind. "I do."

"The time to repay them is close."

Oaks eyed the man. "You know what I've been offered, why don't you tell me what's in it for you."

Anton laughed, smug as ever. "Still inquisitive. I suppose that's good. It's hard to say for sure, but what do people always want? For you, the answer is obvious: fame and fortune. For me, it's not so simple, but you're not going to get a monologue if that's what you're hoping for. You want what you want, and I have my own interests. Mostly, that amounts to knowledge. For my service, there are things I want to know. I shall have them when it's done, and you fulfilling your obligations is a part of that. We've all had to bring in others. Me included."

"And what is it that we're providing this service for?" Oaks felt the seeming bristle at this, almost as if it was laughing at him. He already knew something of this through sheer osmosis, and knew that this wasn't some sort of Christian devil. It wouldn't be stopped with crucifixes and holy water, that was for sure.

Anton shrugged. "Who can tell? Something ancient. Something powerful. Something that cares not an iota for us."

"So what does it get out of our service?"

He began mixing powders. "Honestly, I don't know and I don't care. There's a selfishness to it all that appeals to me. I get what I want. You get what you want. Ultimately, they get what they want. I daresay they want souls. I couldn't tell you why, and I don't care. It's not my concern. Let's get on with what we came here for."

Oaks cycled his fingers, wanting Anton to hurry things up. He talked too much.

"Obviously, you know that the entity wants you to bring the rest of your band into its service. You won't be able to use the same ritual we held for you."

Oaks already knew that didn't matter. Everyone in Anton's little cult had been initiated that way, and while it had a certain appeal, it was a pretty messy way to make things happen. He had a sense, though, that the powders the life coach was playing with were the real key. "The ritual's only for show, right?"

"Kind of. It's more than that, but essentially, the ceremony itself doesn't matter. It only prepares the mind. Rituals have power, that's why churches and organizations across the world are full of them. Go into any house of prayer, and when all the little lambs are raising their hands in the air and channeling their thoughts towards the figurehead at the pulpit, you'll feel an energy in the room. That's not an accident. The same principle applies here. You'll need some way to create that, but most important is this." He scooped the prepared powder into a vial and gave it to Oaks. "You don't need to know what's in it, but that's what'll open the right portal in their minds. Give them that before you perform the ritual and you're golden. You'll be the biggest band in the world."

The entity shifted and something like a sensual touch slithered through Oaks's mind, running down his spine. "The kinda shit that's in LaVey's book will do the trick?"

Anton grinned. "Exactly. And yes, bodily fluids, blood...semen, they work wonders. It's why we use the goat here. Just make sure you give them the powder. I'm sure that won't be difficult for you."

"What happens if I don't succeed?" The thing inside him bristled again.

"I wouldn't advise failure. They want what they want. One way or another, they'll take it." Anton folded his black cloth and stood. "Now, let's get you home. I've got other things to do here."

Surprisingly, Lisa had come to the door. Given what he knew, as little as it was, he hadn't expected that to happen. Even if he hadn't treated her like a piece of shit, she'd be well within her rights to never speak to him again, but she'd forced herself to the door. Her brother pottered around in the background, listening as she leaned painfully on a side-table by the entrance and spoke to him through the locked screen. "There's nothing you can say that makes this all right." She stared at him with eyes as cold as the grave.

She knew him too well. All he'd wanted to do was talk to her and absolve himself from the guilt he felt, but she'd barely let him get his words in. "I want you to know—"

"There's nothing. I don't want to know what you have to say. You've done what you've done, and you've chosen what you wanted. This is the bed you've made, and I hope you die in it. Like our baby did. And pay attention when I say *our* baby, because it is. It *was*. It was no one else's, it was yours and you abandoned it like you abandoned me."

"If you can let me speak."

"No." Tears welled in her eyes, threatening to spill, and she sniffed a runnel of snot into her leaking nostril. "You twist things. You lie. You make it seem all right, but this time, you're wrong. It was ours. You didn't fucking want it, and you got your wish. Just fuck off. Just get out of here. Get out of my life. Live in pain. Live in fucking agony. Fuck off."

"Lisa…"

"You heard her," her brother called from inside the house. He came to the door. "Get the fuck out of here before I jump on your fucking head," he said through clenched teeth. He wrapped an arm around his sister and closed the door.

The door closed before Nathan could respond. He staggered to the car and slumped into the driver's seat. He pressed his head against the wheel, feeling the throbbing desire for a beer pounding in his alcohol-deprived bloodstream and twisted the key. If she didn't want to accept his apology, that'd have to be her problem. There was no way that kid could have been his. The timing didn't add up. Couldn't add up, because if he thought about it and realized he'd been wrong the whole time, he'd never drink enough to wash away the guilt he was feeling.

He pulled onto the road, hoping that from tomorrow, Polyphemus would give him more than enough to focus on and stop him from thinking about what he'd done here and how it might bite him in the ass.

CHAPTER SEVENTEEN
FORMSHIFTER

If there was one thing you learned from bunking with a bunch of blokes in an enclosed space, it was that as much as your inner child told you to take the top bunk, you had to ignore the urge. Hot air—and farts—never stayed low for long. With everyone drinking beer, eating shit food, and taking whatever else they were going to take while they were here, there might be more farts in the room than riffs.

Nathan unrolled his sleeping bag and spread it across one of the low bunks. He checked his phone and made his way upstairs where Spiros and Oaks were setting up their laptops and, if he knew Spiros, having a grand old chat about last night's terse conversation. The dude was never one to let a grudge simmer, and he would have called Oaks on it as soon as they were alone. It was how he operated.

Nathan groaned as he made his way up the small steps. He was feeling a lot better than he had yesterday, but he was still sore as hell. To be expected, really. Hopefully, he'd catch those pricks one on one once things settled. He stopped by the fridge. "Either of you want a beer?"

"Nah," Spiros said. "I'll wait for the others."

"Oaks?"

"Nah, I'll let it sit. Gotta be on top of my game. Don't wanna get messed up too early."

Nathan shrugged, grabbed himself one, and sat with the others.

Spiros dialed up the volume on his Marshall. The hum of

distortion swelled and he chugged a palm-muted open chord three times in quick succession. The sound was beefier than a buffalo's ballsack. When he ripped out a quick lick, the tone was warm and sharp. He grinned, stomped the pedal to drop the distortion, and began to fingerpick his way through a chord progression. That too resonated crisply. "You going to set yours up? Wouldn't mind having a run-through before Chops and Rusty get here."

Nathan grabbed his axe and held it like a gun, pointing the headstock at his two friends, pretending to fire. He plugged it in and exchanged open chords with Spiros until they had comparable levels. He let the electric hum run through him and closed his eyes. "There's a feel to this place. We've gotta capture it in the sound. It's dangerous. It's..." He searched for the right word, then gave up. "It's fucking heavy. I dunno if it's the cemetery, the cabin in the woods vibe, or the air, but it's that blackened mood, man. I bet you those Norwegian church-burners felt the same sort of shit."

"Bullshit," Spiros said. "Their whole vibe came from busted amps and Satan's hairy cock." He laughed. "I get what you mean, though. There's something *spiritual* here."

Oaks clutched his knob and thrust his hips forward. "I'll give you something spiritual!" He laughed. "You boys smoked too much of the green shit on the way out here."

"You don't feel it?" Nathan asked, bewildered.

"Yeah, sure," the vocalist answered, "but wait till later. Wait till we're really cooking and then we'll get right into the vibe here. I got us some pharmaceuticals that'll tune us right into a parallel dimension..." He stopped when he noticed the two guitarists regard each other. "Relax, it's not what you think," he said.

"Man, first time I saw you after you got out you were reluctant to smoke a bowl with me. Why the change?"

Spiros watched as Oaks took the comment in stride.

"Easy," the singer said, "I know I'm right as rain. This shit ain't gonna trigger anything except a damn good buzz, some fucked-up visuals, and a killer jam session."

Nathan shrugged. "Well, he's honest. What do you reckon, we gonna allow it?"

Spiros nodded. "He says there's enough to go around – and if it helps us get Zen with the spooky cemetery and the fearful forest, then I say we smash the shit."

"It'll be good," Oaks said, sitting on an amp. "Tons of bullshit has happened lately. It'll be awesome to lose ourselves in the thing that matters most: following the dream we had when we were kids."

Nathan found himself nodding; noticed Spiros doing the same.

"Deadset," the vocalist continued, "everything is ripe for us to kick ass this time. These songs, they're killer. All the bullshit that's happened, as shit as it is, is going to put eyes on us. When the album drops, when the gigs land, people are going to pay attention. People will flock to us, trust me."

"Amen, dude." Nathan swept through a few scales. "Let's play some Death."

In response, Spiros ripped straight into "Crystal Mountain".

"No! One of ours, dudes. This place is about *our* fucking songs. We're gonna make history. Going straight to the top here and touring the fucking world."

Nathan pretended not to notice the way Spiros peered wistfully out the window and broke out of the riff with a couple of muffled chords. "Something new?"

"Shit yeah, man. "A Million Life Forms on a Million Planets". Do it."

After they had played it through, Nathan went for another beer. This time he grabbed one for each of his two friends. "You remember sitting in McDane's math class and writing tabs on the calculator?"

"Hell yes! Of course," Spiros said. "That guy was weird. He never cared."

"What got you thinking about that?" Oaks asked,

cracking the beer on the lip of the amp.

"What you said before. We've been working on this a long time, man. What happens if it flunks?"

Spiros swigged.

"It won't," Oaks said. "Trust me. Once we hit the shit I brought, I'm gonna show you pricks a ritual I learned."

Spiros shook his head. "What the fuck happened to you? *Ritual*? You gonna tell us you've been born again? Gonna stop wearing shoes and buy a shack in a commune with that douchebag Paleo Pete?"

"No way. Been learning some shit about focus and inner power. It's all mind tricks. It's like when we used to play with a Ouija board."

"Ghosts?" Nathan asked disdainfully.

"No, man, nothing like that. Just getting into your own consciousness. Getting lucid."

Nathan realized the nervousness he typically associated with Oaks these days was gone.

The sound of a car entering the grounds, its tires crunching gravel, came from outside. Nathan listened to the thumping punk and distorted basslines of Raised Fist's "Tribute" thud their way through the closed windows of Chops's vehicle and smiled. "They've timed things right."

Oaks nodded. "Tonight, boys, we're gonna have a blast."

Chops honked the horn and called out from the sliding door of his van. "Come and help carry some shit, you lazy fucks."

"Drummers," Spiros said. "Always subtle."

Nathan shook his head and finished off his beer.

Chops waited by the van with a joint hanging from his lips and his dreads pulled up like a pineapple's crown. Beside him, stacked in after the drum-kit, were three giant blue coolers. As Nathan, Spiros, and Oaks made their way across, Spiros spinning shit like usual, Nathan without a beer for once, and Oaks strutting confidently towards the vehicle, he patted the first cooler. "Three big strong boys for three big boxes of grog. Perfect!" He slammed the first one into Spiros's eager arms and followed straight up with Nathan. "Don't drink it all at once, Dr Pisstank," he said.

"What have we got? Plenty of lager, I hope."

"Dude, there's everything: ale, stout, lager, some cider. The VD boys gave it to me. They knew we were recording and wanted to wish us all the best."

"It sucks so much, what happened to Hank," Oaks said.

Nathan agreed, lifting the lid on his cooler to see what he could spot, but Chops watched the vocalist with interest. Deep down, he knew it wasn't that strange for him to say something like that—he was always awkward; selfish as well—but it felt forced. Nevertheless, he let it slide. It wasn't long ago that Oaks had been a greyed-out junkie, and with the turn of events leaving him to return to the fold, it was perversely serendipitous for him. In the end, Chops didn't bother responding. He simply held out the final cooler. "And the last one for the man of the hour," he added.

Rusty returned from the bushes where he'd drained the lizard. "Got a cemetery over there." He pointed to it. "We ought to get some photos for the liner notes of the album. We'll get some sick imagery."

"Yeah, why not," Chops said. He wasn't sure he wanted to be in a cemetery again yet. He'd had enough of them lately and couldn't help but think of Hank and Corey beneath the ground. It didn't matter that Corey had gone up the chimney of the local crematorium, the meaning was the same.

"I'm gonna go walk through it later," Oaks said in a flat voice. "I always liked that. Kinda gives you peace of mind. Read the headstones, contemplate the lives of everyone below."

Rusty hefted two solid bass guitar cases out of the van, regarded the singer and laughed. "Come on, you tripper," he said. "It's drinking time."

Chops grabbed an armful of cymbals and stands. He took a moment to contemplate the specter of the massive goat skull adorning the entry to the studio, trying to shut out the sound of noodling guitars coming from within the building. Birds, crows mostly, capered in the trees and. Bugs and insects clicked and buzzed around the low bushes.

Hopefully, the recording would go smoothly and Oaks could keep his weird bullshit to a minimum. No one he'd ever known in the industry had been the same after going through what Oaks had, and he wasn't sure how this would all turn out, but so long as everyone was good and professional, shit should be fine.

By the time he made it inside the door, the others were already returning for more of the kit. Having only seen the photos Nathan and Spiros had taken of the joint, he had to stop and inspect the impressive premises. Cormac had outdone himself. Despite the isolated nature of the place and the fact they wouldn't exactly be getting pizzas delivered, he had to admit that it was a pretty nice studio.

Voices approached as he made his way downstairs to check out the bunking area. Like the rest of the joint, it was impeccable. Sure, there were sleeping bags, shoes and an assortment of other random objects lying around, but when they weren't recording, it was going to make a rad place to hang.

Nathan was at the top of the stairs preparing to pass down his suitcase. "What you got in here, man? Fucking rocks?"

He took the suitcase, making a joke and plonked it on the bunk that stood farthest away from the rest. He did not want to be trapped in the mist of the beer farts that would no doubt steam the room up later. He went across to a small sliding window in the rear wall and opened it. There were holes in the flyscreen, but it was more than serviceable. Inspecting the courtyard beyond the window, he could see the quality of the digs extended to that area too. There was a massive fire-pit for bonfires, complete with a rack of pokers, axes, saws and bellows for getting it started. Around that, several barbecues were spread out across the green grass, a pond glistened in the afternoon sunlight, and, in the distance, the cemetery stretched across the land. It was bigger than he expected. In the past, the area had been home to a thriving community of gold miners. In those days, life had been cheap—and short—and the cemetery attested to the period of twenty to thirty years of prosperity the town had enjoyed.

"Yo, Chops, stop playing with your dick and come and have a shot, man!"

Nathan never wasted any time when it came to drinking. "I'm coming, dude. Pour me one – and don't drink it, you fucking degenerate!" He eyed his suitcase. He needed to get his toiletries and shit sorted before heading up there. If he wanted the prime real estate in the shower, he needed to secure it before anyone else did.

And that's when he noticed Oaks's bag rested open on his bed. He didn't trust that the guy's turnaround could be so complete, so successful without some sort of substitute, and last he'd heard, they hadn't bothered to prescribe methadone. Come to think of it, he'd thought the guy should be reporting to the halfway house. And then it clicked, no wonder he wanted to go for a 'walk'. He was probably using in the cemetery like some weird goth poser.

He checked to make sure no one was watching and opened the bag. He didn't have to look hard to find the vials of white powder. He didn't know what exactly it was, but it didn't matter. The one thing they'd made clear was that he had to be off the smack. If things like this were being kept secret, could they be sure that was happening?

After everything, the last thing Chops wanted was more drug drama.

"Chops, man, we're waiting."

He snapped a photo of the vials. "Coming, dude, fuck!"

The other four blokes had set up on a counter near the kitchenette. The bottle of whiskey stood like a totem among five worshippers, the brimming shot glasses. Nathan, clearly the maestro of this early step on the way to their inevitable inebriation grinned at him like a loon.

"You're maniacs. You in particular, Nate."

Nathan lifted his shot. "Today is for celebration, scumbags." He waited for everyone else to lift theirs. "Fucking cheers, bitches!" In unison, they clinked their glasses and necked the whiskey.

It burned as it slid down Chops's throat and into his stomach. He slammed his glass down onto the table. "If today is for celebration and jamming, I demand you hit me again," he said.

There were raucous shouts and laughter. Nathan handed him the bottle. "Pour then, you filthy animal!"

He held the bottle like Rafiki holding the baby Simba high above the Serengeti, then spun the lid off with a practiced flick of his thumb. It rattled to the floor and he rapidly filled the five shot glasses with the brown liquid. "This time, we say *salut*!"

"Salut!" Rusty called.

"I hope you're not that premature with your girlfriends!" Chops shot at him.

"Only your mother!"

There was more laughter and then the drummer placed the shot glass down. "In preparation for the ceremonies we will hold here, I will count you in like a true drummer."

"You have enough fingers to count that high?" Spiros asked.

More laughter erupted around them and the drummer clapped his hands four times.

The shots went down, and this time Spiros took the bottle. "This time we say *Ya mas!*"

With the third round swallowed, they dissipated around

the room and the speakers erupted with the unmistakable explosion of Cannibal Corpse's "Hammer Smashed Face". The staccato riffs pounded and then the bassline sent the room into raptures.

Beers were clinked and joints were sparked, and from somewhere, a deck of cards—complete with naked women inserting numerous objects into numerous orifices—found its way into use. The songs cycled through the playlist, covering luminaries as diverse and different as Refused, Sleep, Decapitated, and Revocation before Chops noticed Oaks had disappeared, presumably for his walk through the cemetery.

He weighed up the odds of starting a difficult conversation, but given that no one was drunk—tipsy yes, drunk no—he reckoned he was safe. "What do you guys know about Oaks's habits?"

Nathan and Spiros locked eyes across the table. Rusty watched them, bemused.

"I-and I know how this will sound—his bag was open, and-"

"Dude!" Spiros said.

"No, it's not what you think." This was already going pear-shaped. He couldn't be starting shit before they'd recorded a note. "I knocked it and I saw he had some powder in there."

Nathan sighed. "Don't try to defend it. Shit. We get it, you don't trust him, but you can't be going through people's bags. We need at least a pretense of trust here."

The drummer tried a different tactic. "I'm worried. I looked, okay, and I know it's wrong, but it all seems too good to be true." He paused. "Besides, you're telling me he's not a bit weird lately?"

Spiros snorted. "Dude, don't worry. I agree. Nate will tell you that Steve and I had a fight in the car after the funeral, and he is weird, but he's all we've got."

"We don't think the powder's anything to worry about

anyway," Nathan said. "He's already told us about it. It's some sort of psychobabble spiritual powder. We've agreed to have a little ceremony later, some shit he's picked up from some self-help group he's been involved with."

Chops couldn't help but laugh. "What kind of self-help group does drugs?"

"That's why we think it's not anything bad. What's that leafy stuff they sell at markets and conventions, Salvia? We think it's that kinda shit."

Chops felt the early markers of guilt settling into his thoughts. "Okay, I shouldn't have looked. You think I should apologize?"

For the first time, Rusty spoke up. "I think you need to let it drop. We know about it. The last thing we need is tension. Let's get through the night, start recording, and try to enjoy ourselves."

Spiros raised an eyebrow. "He's right. Let it drop. Enjoy the process. We're doing what we can to do the same."

Nathan collected up the cards and shuffled them. "Yeah, man, he's been through a lot, and he's convinced himself that this album will break us big. Thinks we can use the vacuum left behind by the Violent Dead tragedy to take advantage. He's gonna bring up the prospect of touring; already broached it with us."

Rusty whistled.

Chops massaged his temples. "I'm getting another drink. I know you want one, Nate. Anyone else?"

Spiros raised his hand. "Of course. But listen, we will humor him until we have the recording done. The rest we can address later, through the label and the proper channels if that's the case."

Chops waved a hand dismissively. "Easy."

There was no way he was touring with Oaks.

With the cemetery stretching out in front of him, Oaks welcomed the feel of the seeming shifting and moving in his peripheral vision. At first, it had been a weird and uncomfortable sensation, but it had become a part of himself he wanted to embrace. As he thought about it, he couldn't believe how close things were to coming together. After the unravelling spools of his life had led to the collapse of the last tour and his own personal nadir, he'd thought he was done for. He'd thought there'd be no chance of the band letting him join again, and that if he wanted to do anything, he'd need to break out on his own. Fortunately, though, the seeming had helped him take control of his life. With he and it practically one, he knew tonight was the night he'd be able to repay the entity with what it wanted: the service of his friends. Together, they'd become the biggest band since The Beatles. It didn't matter that their own brand of death metal was as hard-hitting as a sledgehammer, once people heard their songs, they wouldn't be able to help themselves from giving in to the power the music held.

It is good to fantasize, to visualize, but remember that you must complete your half of the bargain.

He only needed to come up with a ritual they couldn't resist. Getting them to take the drug wouldn't be a problem. Shit, the way they'd started partying already, the bigger problem would be keeping them off it. He'd rack it up and pass it around like coke. Fuck, he'd mix it with coke if anyone had brought some, and they probably had.

He felt a clawed finger caress his neck and he realized the entity had taken shape again. This time, it appeared as that swirl of humanoid smoke he thought of as its natural form. It didn't need to take the shape of anyone else to convince him any longer. Not even India. In this shape, it was everything he needed, and he could already feel his arousal swelling in his pants.

The entity caressed him again, and this time its claw trailed down his spine, drifted across the ticklish flesh of his belly and clutched his cock. It jerked it twice. Its cold tongue licked his earlobe and despite the fangs he knew were in its maw—which was crazy considering it appeared only as smoke—it nibbled the nape of his neck and whispered to him. *Your arousal is all-important. There is nothing to sacrifice here, but you have the seed of life within you.*

The entity drifted away from him and squatted on an ancient grave. It reached a hand into the soil, through the soil, and then brought it up, holding a skull out like a gift. *This and four others. Daub them in your blood. Make a pentagram with them as the points.*

"Once I've done that?"

In the moment, you'll need only to follow my lead, Say the words I say. You'll have no drumbeat. No goat. Ejaculate in the center of the circle. A token offering of life.

He took the skull and inspected it. Once it had belonged to someone. Had represented the most important part of a person. Their freedom, their life, their thoughts and their autonomy. Now, though, it was nothing. An object; a tool to be used in bringing others into a way of thinking. "In case you didn't notice, I don't have anything I can use to dig into the other graves.

But you do.

He inspected his feet and noticed the crowbar. Where had that come from? The entity, squatting in front of him, gestured deeper into the cemetery. It hadn't seemed this big when he'd first entered, and he certainly couldn't recall seeing any crypts, but nevertheless, he was in front of one. If he didn't know any better, he'd assume he was in one of the great cemeteries housed by a major city, not the kind of country cemetery filled with the families of hicks, travelling salesmen and farmers he'd ventured into moments earlier.

He clutched the crowbar and checked over his shoulder. The shifting smoke-shape wavered in his vision, standing as it urged him towards the crypt. "What's your name anyway?"

"*I noticed you have been thinking of my appearance as a thing that seems and that will do. I am you. You am I. We are one. Complete your work. You will need to return before they come searching for you.*"

The gate to the crypt was locked, but it mattered not. The stone blocks the hinges were bolted into were old. The cement keeping them in place cracked with only a few blows from the crowbar. Once he levered the tool into place and heaved, the hinges tumbled loose. The wrought-iron gate opened without much hassle.

Inside, several tombs, presumably housing members of one family, lined the walls. Whoever they were, they'd had money to set themselves up like this in their afterlife. Everyone in Oaks's own life had gone up a chimney in a budget coffin once their state funerals were completed. He spat on the floor and drove the crowbar into the lip of the first tomb. Heaving and levering the tool, the lid groaned as he pried it open.

It slipped and the crowbar fell to the floor with a metallic clang, but the lid partly opened. With sweat beading on his forehead, he drove the tool into the gap and pressed all his weight on it. The lid slipped and parted. Inside rested the skeletal remains of a child, only eight or nine from the size of the carcass. He grabbed the skull as if it was worthless rock and dropped it to the floor before starting on the next tomb.

This one came more easily. The remains inside were clearly bigger and more mature. Several teeth were missing and beneath the funeral clothing, it was clear the person they'd once been was a crooked and crippled individual. He plucked the skull and moved on.

When he was done, the entity waited for him at the broken

gate. When he exited, he found he was on the outskirts of the cemetery by the studio. Music blared from the building. Laughter, raucous and drunk, barreled out of the open doors, and guitars were already chugging.

The thing inside him disappeared as he got his bearings, but despite his better judgement, he didn't drop the skulls into the bushes as he approached the studio. He would fulfil his part of the bargain and make Polyphemus the biggest band on the planet. He arced around to the rear of the building, towards the fire-pit.

Unnoticed by the others, he lay the skulls out like the five points of a pentagram and drew intersecting lines between them. At the center of his work, the fire-pit sat devoid of heat and empty of flame, a receptacle in waiting. This was where he would make it happen. This was where he would offer the others up to the entity and its brethren.

CHAPTER EIGHTEEN
LEVIATHAN

Nathan was about to piss in the bushes when he saw Oaks coming around the side of the building. He waved the horns at him and undid his fly as he approached a tree opposite Spiros's car. "Yo, hold up. I'll be done in a minute."

"You want me to watch you piss?"

"You make it sound so perverted." Nathan laughed at his own joke. "Hold up." He finished his business. Oaks was there, leaning on the wall.

"Had a few already, I see."

Nathan, aware of the buzz he was riding held out a fist for the vocalist to bump. "Fuck yeah, bro. We all have. You gotta catch up."

"Soon. Where's Spiros?"

Nathan cocked an ear. The bass and the drums were rolling through "Fur, Fangs, and Flayed Flesh", another new track, but he couldn't hear any guitars. "Dunno. Maybe talking to the missus. His shit's all screwed-up too. It's all of us, man."

Recognition passed across Oaks's face and Nathan let his old friend pull him in until he had an arm around his shoulders. He slumped into the embrace and drunkenly rubbed the vocalist's bald head. "That's why we need this to work."

"It will, but tell me what's up," Oaks said.

"With Spiros? Shit with his wife. She left him."

"No. With you."

Nathan sniffed. Spat a loogie onto the dusty car-park gravel. "Long story."

"That Lisa chick?"

"Yeah, man, she lost the kid." He couldn't bring himself to regard the kid as his own, not verbally anyway. He'd done what he could to stop himself from thinking about it, but he needed to keep moving through the evening and get the band playing, jamming, recording even; without that, he didn't know how long he'd keep the thoughts at bay.

Oaks squeezed his shoulders. "Don't worry about it. We'll make it not matter."

It did matter, though. Once the band blew up, he'd make sure she had whatever she needed from him. It wouldn't fix anything, and it would probably be seen like his usual grandiose gestures of regret and apology, but he hoped he remembered when he sobered. He'd been thinking about that Arabella chick who'd blown him off before he got his ass properly kicked. She'd said something about compassion being king, and although he'd fucked up massively, he might be able to build on that idea. Of course, they needed to make the band work first.

"You hear me?" Oaks asked. "We've got this. We're gonna kill it with this album. Movie soundtracks, festival headline slots, commercial radio, we'll open it all up with this one, and we won't need to sell out to do it."

"You think we can manage that without making a soft-cock album?"

"I know it."

Nathan was thirsty. "C'mon, let's grab a beer."

"I'll get it," Oaks said. "Wait here. I wanna show you something."

"Bullshit," Nathan said. "You're up to something."

"Doesn't matter. Just wait here."

Nathan spat on the ground again. "Whatever, dude. Hurry up, though. I'm thirsty."

He waited until Oaks reappeared with a couple of beers.

He cracked the first one on the banister of the low steps leading into the studio and passed it to Nathan before cracking the second for himself. "It's around back. Let's go."

Once he stepped around the corner, Nathan wasn't sure he was *actually* seeing what was in front of him. The eye sockets on the bulbous bone-white stone had to be tricks of the shadow. The thing itself had to be a joke. It couldn't be a skull because that would be mental.

He let Oaks guide him forward, and as he approached it, he saw the others. *What the fuck?* He crouched. Reached out a tentative hand and picked it up. It was light. Far too light to be stone. Instead, it had to be some sort of resin.

He twisted it around, examining it. "It's realistic. Where'd you get it?"

"Where do you think I got it?"

Nathan knew this had to be a set-up and he wasn't going to give Oaks the satisfaction of getting one over him. "No idea. Internet. Some creepy site of the macabre; eBay or some shit."

Oaks laughed, low and throaty. "Come on, man, they don't sell skulls online. Least not to people like me."

From Nathan's squatting position, the sun was behind Oaks and his face was pitted in shadow. He seemed to be leering down. Around him, there seemed to be some sort of blur. "Go on then, tell me. I give up."

Oaks pointed into the cemetery. "Well, okay, not there exactly, but the principle's the same."

"Bullshit."

The singer grinned again. "Yeah, nah, it's bullshit," he said. "I got 'em from an old science and biology warehouse. Apparently, they used to use 'em in science labs. Forensics classes and shit."

If he didn't know better, Nathan would have thought Oaks was lying. He always got this weird look in his eye when he was spinning shit, and it was there again. There couldn't be another explanation for the skulls, though. "All right, I'll bite. What's with the theatrics?"

Oaks squatted beside him. "We're a metal band, right? Let's embrace it; get a little kitsch and have a proper ritual. We do that in combination with the shit I brought, and I guarantee, man, you *will* trip balls."

Nathan stood, holding out a hand to help Oaks to his feet. "You're insane, you know that, right?"

"Hell yeah! Let's get some drinks into us."

Spiros had managed to get himself away from the revelry when he felt his phone vibrating in his pocket. Hoping beyond hope it would be Pandora, he had checked it immediately and seen it to be an unlisted and private number. His first inclination had been to brush it off, but then he realized she might be calling him unlisted.

He hustled out the door and outside to where things were quieter. "Hello?"

"Where is she, asshole?"

Whoever was on the other line was drunk. Inebriated, even. "I think you got the wrong number, dude. Have a glass of water. Get some sleep."

He hung up and slipped inside, stopping by the kitchen for another beer. His phone rang again before he made his way to the table.

"I told you," he said. "Wrong number."

"Pandora, you jerk. What have you done with her? Where have you taken her? She's not answering my calls. Not in touch at all."

"Who is this?"

The man on the other end coughed. "Doesn't matter. Just assume that your wife knows who it is, and you can't keep us apart."

Spiros went outside, shoving past Oaks and Nathan as they came in the front door.

The voice continued drawling as he put the phone on speaker and sat in the driver's seat of his car. "Did you find out? Did you have to put a stop to it? Couldn't you deal with what your neglect had wrought?"

The voice was familiar, but he couldn't pinpoint it. "Who the fuck is this?"

"The man who's been fucking your wife. Who loves her."

His stomach went cold. The blood in his face drained. "No. She wouldn't."

"She wouldn't?" The man laughed, and it clicked.

"Seb?"

"You're so fucking clever, aren't you? So fucking smart. So fucking rich. Fuck you. She loves *me*."

Spiros let the rage pass. Connors was a creep. He was married. Pandora would never lower herself to his standards.

"If she wouldn't," Connors said, "Then ask me how I know about that cute little birthmark beside her twat."

Spiros hung up the phone. Threw it at the floor of the car with all his might. Punched the horn. Punched it so hard the plastic framework popped off and the horn stayed on, blaring anger into the bushland and across the cemetery.

The other dudes started pouring out of the studio, wondering what had happened.

The horn blared. A long, angry moan in the darkening light of dusk.

Spiros stared at the others as they approached. He snatched his phone up and popped the bonnet. He stepped out of the car, unable to hear what they were saying as he moved around to the engine bay. He yanked the wires connected to the horn. They didn't come. His hand slipped off and he caught it on the bonnet latch. He swore, shook his hand and tugged the wires again.

By this time, Nathan was beside him. "Everything okay?"

Spiros grunted. "Yeah, it's fucking dandy." He wanted to

scream. Wanted to shout. To punch someone. To vent all his frustration and to destroy something beautiful.

He went into the car, popped the boot and pulled pliers out of a toolkit. He snipped the wires.

Nathan went to say something but stopped when Spiros glared at him.

The others watched on, amused.

"Let's get a drink and play some fucking metal."

He stormed past the others and snatched his beer off the card table. Skulled it. He couldn't believe it. They'd only had each other since their wedding day. Through all the tours, all the festivals, all the gigs, he'd always remained faithful; had always remained true, and for her to fuck that douchebag Seb. What the *fuck?*

Worse, he couldn't call her. His phone was in pieces. The screen was shattered.

He poured himself a shot of whiskey and nailed it.

The others were slowly milling into the room. Oaks was approaching, but it was Chops he was interested in. The drummer had made his way to the kit. For a moment, the Greek thought Chops was going to take a seat, but instead he reached into the bass drum and pulled out a little bum-bag. Inside was a packet of white drugs. He poured some of the contents onto the snare, racked a line, and motioned for Spiros to come over.

Spiros hit it and pounded his chest. He felt like Superman as the coke hit his bloodstream. He spun and grabbed his guitar as Chops racked up everyone else. Without wondering what everyone else wanted to play, he started working his way through the opening riff of Slayer's "Angel of Death". If anything was going to work out some frustration, that would.

Chops sat at the kit. He had a huge grin plastered across his face. "Start again."

When he did, Chops joined in at the appropriate moment. The others picked up their instruments. By the time they were approaching the first breakdown, the groove was locked in. The anger was slipping away.

Once he'd ripped through the solo and the song had finished, they took another round of shots and racked another couple of lines before blasting through some more of their own tracks, old and new.

Whatever Pandora had done, he could worry about it later, when the album was recorded and they'd spent some time on the road where he could get his revenge and act like the rock god he was. Calliope would be there when he was done. She was going to live a long life and so was he. With his role as the lead guitarist in what would easily be one of the world's biggest bands once they got this album recorded, he'd be more than able to support her for the rest of her life and give her everything she'd ever want.

He didn't need Pandora for that.

With the booze and the coke charging through his bloodstream, Oaks took control of the practice space like a vocalist performing for television cameras. He stomped between Spiros, Nathan and Rusty with the menacing gait of an apex predator. During breakdowns, he beat the cymbals with his microphone. The wall of noise was an emotionally charged, drug-fueled being, almost sentient with power, pulsing with the rhythms and buzzing with leads that wasped their way around the studio.

The entity inside him, the seeming, reveled in it and gave his vocals demonic qualities he had never before tapped into. His cookie monster growls had always been good, but here and now, they were powerful and imposing. When he moved into shrieking, he sounded like a cacophony of imps calling for blood. When all of that had support from the gang vocals that occasionally interspersed the band's chaotic grooves, the sound was immense.

He knew why. He had made the seeming a promise, and it was time to pay up. In between his vocal lines, the entity had been egging him on, caressing him, grabbing him by the throat and cajoling him to make this the most powerful performance of his life so far. *"Imagine your sound when they all feel the same force within them. Imagine your destiny,"* it said as the final bars of another new song, "Flyblown Extremities", came to a crashing stop.

As the band took a breather and Chops racked up several more lines, Oaks realized night had cradled the cabin in its black embrace. The entity whispered to him, and he held out a hand. "Wait up, Chops. I've got something to add to that."

The others looked around at each other, and Chops shrugged his shoulders. "Go and get it." His eyes blazed. Runnels of sweat ran down his reddened cheeks and his skin glistened as he beamed a grin at the others. "Hell yes! These songs are good, man!"

Spiros agreed. He whooped and threw the horns. "We're going big-time, baby!" His pupils were dilated to the max. He punched his chest rhythmically.

Chops pounded the double-kick in response and Rusty was off, walking a distorted bassline across the ominous beat.

Oaks couldn't help but recall the pounding beat from the night of his initiation. He could smell the goat's hot piss, its animal fear, its shit. He could feel its blood as it was daubed onto his forehead and the entity sliding inside him for the first time, inserting its proboscis and taking him for its own.

By the time he returned with his own vials of powder, Rusty was slapping and popping his way through a funked-up riff and sumo-walking across the space as the others laughed at him. He hadn't realized, but he'd hitched his shorts up so high, his bollocks dangled out the left leg and his cock flopped around like a dead rat.

Oaks joined the laughter and emptied the contents of the vial right on top of Chops's pile of coke. "Get some of this shit into you." He divided a line for Chops, and it went straight up the drummer's nose. Spiros followed, then Rusty.

Nathan approached. "What is it?"

"Who cares?" Spiros said. "Snort it!"

Nathan did.

Oaks then hit his own line, and the entity inside of him cooed. He walked to the door, opened it with a grandiose gesture, and pointed out to the fire-pit. "Come, let us prepare the ritual!" He waved them through, slapping asses as they passed.

Chops was the last through. Oaks had watched him shrug his shoulders at Rusty, but knew the guy was in deep. "Don't worry," he whispered into Chops's ear. "It's all going to be worth it. Just have your mind open and be ready to get fucking metal!"

As the others stood around, ogling the skulls and asking him how he'd come up with this shit, he waved them off, laughing and telling them it was gonna be worth it. "Think of it like a séance," he said. "We're gonna tap into some shit before we start recording."

He poured petrol into the fire pit, encouraging the others to throw timber in on top. As he produced a lighter from his pocket, he pulled a stick from the pyre and dipped it in the fuel canister. He touched the flame to the flammable end of the stick, lit it, and cried, "We're on fire and we're gonna burn the world with our righteous flames!"

He dropped the torch into the pit, and it ignited with a rush. Fire ran up the lowest depths of the pyre, engulfing the petrol-doused branches in the conflagration. The fire sizzled and crackled. Smoke poured forth. The others punched the air and whooped.

Inside Oaks, the entity seemed to swell and stretch. This was it: the moment that would secure his position as the lead singer in the biggest band on the planet; the moment his dreams would come true.

Follow my lead, the seeming said in his mind.

He didn't need to be told. He knew that he needed to be normal and when guidance was necessary, it would come. "More booze!" he shouted.

Nathan raised a bottle of Jaeger he'd brought out to the fire-pit and bellowed. He took a hit and passed it to Rusty who did the same before passing it on again. The bottle went around until it was gone.

Spiros ran inside and returned with two more bottles. While he did that, the flames in the fire-pit grew and grew. They licked and clawed. Smoke curled.

Oaks produced another vial of the powder and snorted another pinch. He passed it around and, again, the others followed suit.

Once they had all taken swigs of the bourbon Spiros had brought out with him, Oaks grabbed the skull closest to them. "This," he said, "is only the structure around which and inside which life can grow. It is nothing. It is inconsequential. It is a framework."

Their shouts were somewhat confused this time, but he continued, levelling it like Hamlet holding Yorick eye to eye. "What it can hold, though, and what it can support can be immense. Especially if we invite the right powers in."

He held the skull out to Rusty. "Hold this level."

Rusty, grinning and side-eyeing the others awkwardly, took the skull and held it in place.

Oaks pulled a folding knife from his pocket and before anyone could stop him, he slashed a huge cut across the palm of his hand. He clenched his fist, squeezing until blood sluiced down his wrist, vermillion water from a wrung sponge, and then planted his hand firmly on the skull's forehead. He dragged the palm of his hand down the skeletal face, leaving a smear of blood running down the deathly visage. When he was done, he repeated the action on Rusty, marking him with blood. He chanted as he did so. "This is the mark of the willing. This is the mark of the destined. This is the mark of the inviting flesh."

Inside him, the entity mouthed the words with him, once again driving his actions with maniac enthusiasm. *Mark them all,* it said. *Mark them all!*

He plucked the skull from Rusty's hands and planted it at the pinnacle of the point where it had come from.

The flames grew higher. The fire-pit had been engulfed by a raging bonfire.

Oaks plucked the next skull and held it aloft. "Who's next?"

Spiros stepped forward and Oaks welcomed him. He held the skull as Rusty had done. "This is the mark of the willing!" Oaks chanted.

Rusty joined in. "This is the mark of the inviting flesh!"

Nathan and Spiros joined in, and although he did so less enthusiastically, so did Chops.

"This is the mark of the destined." Oaks said and planted his bloodied palm on Spiros's face. The guitarist grinned, loving the whole process. When Oaks pulled his palm away, the guitarist whooped again, throwing the horns at the sky.

Chops snorted another pinch of coke, and Oaks was aware that the drummer was somewhat resistant to events. He was participating, but he was hesitant. Despite that, he knew that the skinsman would be feeling as much of a buzz as he and the others surely were. He could feel the blur of the drugs he'd felt that night in Anton's club, and that was the clincher. They would be opening Chops's mind as much as they had opened his own, and when things started to happen, Chops would go with the group.

He made a come-hither gesture to the drummer. "Come forth, my friend!"

Chops scrutinized the others. Rusty and Spiros, already slathered in Oaks's blood, mimicked the vocalist.

Chops took the skull Oaks offered and held it out like a ceremonial goblet. Firelight flickered over him, casting his face in various shades of red and orange. His dilated eyes danced from left to right and a bead of sweat trickled down his forehead.

Oaks clenched his fist again, wringing more blood from the palm of his hand. "This is the mark of the willing!" He planted his open palm on the skull, smearing sanguine fluids on the brow.

"This is the mark of the destined," Rusty said.

Oaks stared into Chops's eyes, searching for weakness. "This is the mark of the inviting flesh!" He pressed his hand on the drummer's face, leaving a bloodied palm-print behind. In the glow of the bonfire, the blood appeared to bulge and move.

He gestured for the drummer to place the skull at the vertex of the triangle where it belonged and grinned at Nathan. His old friend stepped forward eagerly. He was clearly as drunk as he'd been in a long time, but the focus in his eyes revealed that he was more than ready for his part in the ritual to begin.

Nathan picked up the fourth skull and raised it high. "This is the mark of the willing!" he said along with Oaks, who painted the object as he had the others. "This is the mark of the destined. This is the mark of the inviting flesh!" He pushed his forehead into Oaks's bleeding palm and made sure he was anointed.

After returning his daubed skull to its rightful position, he presented the fifth one to Oaks. The others closed in and joined the chant. Oaks smeared blood on the skull, and passed it to Nathan, who held it reverently. Then, with a final flourish, he once again drew his knife and cut a deep line across his forehead. Blood welled and spilled down the creases of his face, gathering in his crow's feet and trickling down his cheeks like tears.

Oaks took the skull from Nathan and placed it in position so all five of the skulls sat at the sharp points of the pentagram. He gestured for each of his bandmates to stand above the skulls. When they did, he beat his hands together in a slow clap. Blood sprayed from his wounded palm, splattering his shirt and torso, and the others joined him, clapping slowly.

After four beats, Oaks let loose with an 'Om!' After four more, he did it again, and after four more, the others joined in. As they chanted, he once again lifted the petrol canister. Walking the lines of the pentagram around his bandmates, he tipped the petrol onto the ground. It glistened in the flickering firelight. As he completed tracing the angles with the liquid, he once again joined his bandmates in their clapping and chanting before gesturing for them to stay as he walked away from the fire, towards the front of the studio.

A small part of him could hardly believe he was standing next to a skull daubed in Oaks's blood, clapping and chanting, but Nathan couldn't stop. This was nuts. Somehow, though, he knew it was only going to get crazier.

When Oaks reappeared, naked and wearing the goat skull that adorned the front of the studio, Chops looked at Nathan with a confused expression.

Nathan shrugged his shoulders in response.

Spiros, though, had to say something. As Oaks approached, he chanted in time with his rhythmic clapping, "We. Can. See. OM. Your. Pee. Pee. OM."

The other boys laughed, but Oaks didn't miss a beat. He slapped the skull in time with the beat. As he chanted his "Om," the voice seemed to come out of the goat's bone maw, giving it a deeper baritone. Nathan couldn't help but join in, not stopping even when he realized that Oaks had a boner. The vocalist's cock stuck out like a stubby branch. But that wasn't the weirdest thing. No, what Oaks did next only escalated the strange tension filling the air.

He reached into the flames, not flinching when they licked his flesh, and plucked a burning torch. He touched it to the petrol he'd poured on the ground and the pentagram lit up, enclosing them inside its burning perimeter.

Nathan—and the others—continued to clap and chant, caught in the moment.

Oaks began to chant a new litany. "We are the willing!" he called. "We are the destined. We are the inviting flesh that calls to you and offers its use. We are the willing. We are the destined. We are the inviting flesh! We grant you access!"

Rusty joined him. "We are the willing! We are the destined..."

Spiros.

Himself.

Chops.

Oaks removed the goat skull from his head. Blood covered his face, his throat, his shoulders. He could have been dipped in a bucket of it.

The goat's horns mimicked his penis, pointing towards the sky.

Oaks stood above it.

He pointed at them all and wrung blood from his hand, lubricating himself. As he chanted, his hand worked.

Nathan continued chanting the new litany that Oaks had offered them, watching in disgust as his old friend debased himself in front of them all. He cast his eyes around the scene. Rusty, Spiros, and Chops appeared as shocked as he was, but all of them chanted.

Oaks, offered up a new chant, syncopating with theirs. "We offer you this token of life! We offer you this seed. Come forth! Come forth! Come forth!"

He continued repeating the mantra until his body shook and he fell to his knees. Jizz sprayed onto the goat's skull. Oaks raised his arms like he'd done something miraculous.

Nathan was about to laugh when the bonfire's towering

flames became green. Something inside them moved. Cavorted. Convulsed.

Oaks once again took up the previous chant. "We are the willing! We are the destined. We are the inviting flesh that calls to you and offers its use. We are the willing. We are the destined. We are the inviting flesh! We grant you access!" He clapped his hands.

An explosion of green smoke burst out from around him and when it cleared, Oaks's form had doubled in a strange blur. For a brief second, Nathan thought he was drunk, but the shape was too similar to one he'd seen before; huge, hulking, barrel-shouldered. From its head, gigantic horns pointed like the top of Baphomet's sigil. Then it was gone. Oaks was the only thing visible. The shape reappeared and quickly vanished again, leaving only a smudge around Oaks in the general shape of that monstrous being. It was like an aura that was only a void.

Just chill, man, you've done a ton of drugs. You're drunk. Just roll with it. Just roll with it. The shape continued to glitch into existence, to manifest as Oaks surveyed everyone in the band.

"The power is within us!" he said. "The power is ours! We only have to accept it. To promise to bring others to it!" He clapped his hands again and the shape, a bigger, stronger, more supreme shadow of Oaks cast by the flickering green firelight, mirrored his movements.

The singer beat his chest, bellowing. "I have promised to bring in all of you. To deliver music to millions and, in turn, to offer them."

Nathan regarded the others. They were clearly seeing the same thing, but he didn't know what else he could do. At least not until Oaks clapped his hands four times, and boomed, "OM!"

Nathan immediately, with everyone else, repeated the process.

Beat. Beat. Beat. OM! Beat. Beat. Beat. OM!

The green flames licked up, and as Nathan followed them, he saw the sky had turned red. Somehow, he knew he stood at the gate of a momentous decision and that if he wanted it, he and everyone else in the band could have that red sky and everything else that surrounded him. He was no longer in the courtyard of Tomb Studios. He was watching Polyphemus dominate a stage from the midst of a festival crowd. It was like watching something from the Moscow Monsters of Rock festival. The audience was going apeshit. Oaks was leading them in a frenzy of rapturous moshing. He, Rusty, and Spiros windmilled maniacally as they whipped through the final riff of "The Morass", an ominous death-prog piece. Lightning forked across the sky, and in the flashing light, he saw that, in this vision at least, all of them were shadowed by the hulking shapes.

The Oaks on the stage stared directly at him, making eye contact through the crowd, and then he spoke directly into the mic as the song's familiar closing riff ploughed furrows through his mind. "The power is within us. The power is ours. Accept it. The power is within us. The power is ours. The power is within us. The power is ours. Accept it!"

The song finished and Chops counted in the next. After four clicks of his sticks, Nathan heard the phrase, "Om!" and snapped back to reality.

From inside the studio, feedback screeched. It hummed and curled and spiked through the night air, loud and oppressive. Before him, Nathan saw verdant green flames lick the sky like tongues, and as well as the hulking shape that had previously shadowed Oaks, four more cavorted and convulsed around him. They moved in time with the feedback and the repetitive beating Om that the other band members were still—that *he* was still—chanting.

Oaks exploded in fire. The green flames swallowed him, becoming blue and green where they burned on his left hand. He lifted it and pointed directly at Rusty. "Commit!"

Nathan wasn't sure he wanted whatever Oaks was

offering, but this was some wild trip and if it could give them the credibility, the respect they'd always striven for as a band, then he would accept. When his turn came, he would commit without question.

"What do I do?" the bass-player asked.

"Step forth. Kneel. Let it inside you."

He stepped forward.

Oaks laid a hand on Rusty's head, a faith-healer curing a desperate leper of his illness. Flames erupted from his hand and engulfed Rusty, who screamed in agony. Oaks helped him to his feet. "Go. Enter the ritual fire and embrace your future!"

Nathan watched in awe. Rusty entered the flames and disappeared.

Chops shook his head, desperate to get the vision from his mind. He'd already told them he wasn't touring. Recording the album, partaking in a night of drunken, drug-fueled debauchery; he was down for that, but whatever was going on here, he wanted no part of it. He was done with being a touring musician, and everything that the vision had pointed to was related to that. If he wanted success, the vision promised it to him; Oaks promised it to him, but he didn't want it. He wanted to run for the hills.

As he watched Nathan step closer to Oaks—and whatever those shapes were—he realized he hated the vocalist. That was who had brought him to this point where he wanted to run from music. He didn't trust the prick, and watching this, everything fell into place. It was too convenient. Too slick.

He realized Nathan was about to kneel and offer himself. "Nate! Move back, fuck it. This isn't right!"

Oaks had got himself caught up in some bullshit, and it

was going to end in tragedy. For Chops, there were no two ways about that. As a studio musician and veteran of the circuit, he'd recorded for church-burners and satanists, refusing only to hit the skins for Nazi punk bands and skinheads who'd tried to hire his services from time to time.

Now, though, he was going to add any band Oaks worked with ever again to that list. He slapped his face and focused on what was going on. Nathan was still clumsily staggering towards the vocalist. No wonder, the guy's mind was a mess. Spiros had dropped to his knees; was clutching his face, screaming into the void.

The black shapes, huge and evil, rollicked in the flames. Oaks's fucking hand was on fire, and yet, despite his complete lack of interest in being a part of this, Chops couldn't help but feel compelled to run into the circle and put an end to the madness. Fuck Oaks and fuck this.

Oaks—or whatever the thing inside him was—levelled eyes of fire on him. It raised a hand. A bone hand. The fire had eaten through the flesh and sinew. Nothing remained but skeletal bones, like the one they'd had on early merch.

Chops pulled free again and cast his eyes to the tools on the rack near the fire. A splitting maul rested against it. He stepped through the flames still, somehow, burning behind him – that petrol should have burned out ages ago – and yanked the tool free from its hook. "Nate! Move out of the way you dumb bastard!" He hefted the tool and ran at Oaks. As soon as he stepped into the pentagram, Oaks, as naked as the day he was born, eyes glowing like burning coals, roared. Chops jabbed the butt of the axe into Oak's chest, nudging him back, and stepped forward aggressively, feinting with the weapon.

Oaks dodged, but Chops came again. He had lost sight of Nathan and Rusty was still nowhere, but he couldn't worry about that now. He swung the maul, cracking Oaks hard in the temple.

Oaks stumbled. He shook his head and then, as if

expanding, he swelled into a hulking horned shape and threw a bone fist. It crashed into Chops's chest, sending him flying. Ribs cracked as he landed with a thud.

The drummer landed heavily and rolled, heels overhead. His lungs emptied with a whoosh. He wheezed. His sternum rattled. He wondered if he'd punctured a lung.

The monstrous thing that had enveloped Oaks plodded towards him. The other things continued to cavort in the flames. If he didn't know better, he'd swear they were laughing, observing this whole catastrophe unfold with malicious glee.

Aware of the others watching on, he scrambled painfully in the dirt. Rusty was now visible, standing amidst the flames and chanting, but recognition glimmered in Nathan's eyes as he looked at Chops and turned to face the monster.

That motherfucker.

It hurt to move, but Chops reached for the axe.

Spiros was climbing to his feet, eyeballing Rusty.

The bass player had stepped out of the fire and was closing in on the guitarist.

Chops was torn. Something was seriously wrong with Rusty, but Spiros would have to handle it for now. The Oaks monster was the bigger danger, and Nathan was taking a knee before it.

He ran towards the demon again and swung the axe with all his might as the beast reached its bone hand out to grasp Nathan's forehead.

The maul only struck a glancing blow, but it was enough to distract the thing from taking Nathan. The monster roared and spun towards the drummer.

Nathan bellowed his frustration.

Chops backed away, pivoting so he could sprint if he had to, but Rusty was dragging the screaming Spiros towards the green flames. Inside the firepit, another of the shapes had disappeared and Rusty seemed to be shifting, growing. Chops knew what he had to do.

He whipped the maul wildly through the air, aiming for the bass player's crown. It connected with a crack and a squelch. The heavy axe-head smashed through Rusty's skull and sent his teeth spiraling to the floor in an explosion of gore and viscera. Rusty dropped to his knees. A black shape that seemed to be smoke rushed out of him and into the green flame where it disappeared.

The drummer yanked the axe free. A scrap of Rusty's cheek, momentarily stuck to the blade, flapped in the air as he swung it over his shoulder and pointed it at the monster. Only it wasn't the monster, it was Oaks. He screamed incoherently, outraged at what Chops had done.

"Stay away from me," Chops bellowed. "We're done. We're done!"

The monster briefly became Oaks again. The vocalist, apoplectic, bellowed at him. "You've fucked it. You've fucked it all! We could have had the world. We could have had the whole...fucking...world."

"Bullshit! You can't keep blaming everyone else. We're fucked because of you!"

The monster erupted out of Oaks. It clutched Chops by the throat with its one good hand; lifted him from the ground and shook him like a rag doll. The drummer kicked, desperate. His vertebrae were cracking beneath the pressure, and then he couldn't kick any more. He could only swing, limp, as the monster thrashed him around. He thought about Corey. About Traine. Everything fell into place.

Nathan approached, both hands raised. "Put him down!" he called as he approached. "We can work this out."

Oaks, or at least the thing he'd become, laughed.

Chops saw blurring movement as the creature lifted him high into the sky. For a split second, he saw the monster smile, and in that smile, he would have sworn he saw Oaks screaming for the thing to stop what it was doing. For the split second after, he saw the ground rushing closer to his face. Then he hit it. Hard.

Nathan saw Chops's head hit the ground. The whole moment, which could only have lasted for an instant, played out in slow motion. The drummer's legs folded over him. His back snapped and crumpled at an awkward angle, but his head took the worst damage. Blood and brains pushed out of his ears, his face imploded into a crater, and blood oozed across the grass, black and terrible in the flickering light of the green bonfire.

Nathan's stomach lurched and a lifetime of beer and whiskey and drugs threatened to spew out of him. Somehow, he held it down.

The monster prowled towards him, its face softening. The horns disappeared and it shrank. Its face shifted into Oaks's familiar visage. "It doesn't have to end here. Offer yourself to them." He pointed at the fire, where only two shapes convulsed. "They have Rusty now. They have Chops. Give yourself to them and tour the world with us."

The monster came out of him like smoke again. "*Give yourself to us and we can bring them back. Can give you the world.*"

Nathan heard footsteps behind him.

Spiros, pale with terror and shock, had the maul. "Go to the van, Nathan."

"No, wait. This can work out. This is what we want!"

The Oaks monster snarled.

Spiros hefted the splitting maul over his shoulder.

"*Do you want the world, Spiros. It's yours for the taking.*"

"Listen to him, Spiros." They were so close! They could *have* the world. They could have *anything*, but Spiros had to listen; had to give himself to Oaks.

Oaks became himself again. He raised his arms as if seeking to embrace the Greek.

Spiros swung the axe.

Nathan screamed in rage.

As the weighted tool hurtled towards Oaks, the vocalist dropped an arm to try and stop it. The weapon hit the skeletal hand below the wrist, shearing it free from the forearm and continued its journey towards Oaks's midsection where it bit into flesh and came to a stop. The bone hand crashed to the ground, grasped at nothing, and fell still.

Smoke oozed from the wound in wisps as Oaks spun away. It grew over him, and he swelled in size before limping into the distance and disappearing into the cemetery.

"What have you done?" Nathan screamed, still on his knees.

Spiros held out a hand, offering to help Nathan to his feet. "That was our chance!"

Spiros shook his head. "No, it wasn't. When you sober up, you'll see sense." He grasped Nathan's hand, dragging him to his feet and around to the front of the studio. Inside, something exploded. Feedback screeched. Bolts of electricity arced. Smoke billowed out of the windows.

He cast a wary eye towards the green flame, hoping Oaks—or whatever he'd become—wasn't lurking nearby, and pulled open the driver-side door to Chops's van. The keys were in the ignition. He knew he'd drunk too much to drive, but if he couldn't count himself sober after the rush of the last few minutes, he never would again. He sparked the engine and Raised Fist boomed out of the speakers. He killed the stereo immediately, listening only to the whirring engine, the crackle of stone under the tires, and the calls of night-time insects.

"We have to see if Oaks is alive," Nathan said. "You need to think about this."

Spiros reversed out of the driveway, veered onto the road with a screech of tires, and left Tomb studios behind. "If you mention it again before we get back to town, I guarantee that I will walk away from Polyphemus for good." He turned the stereo on and twisted the volume dial as high as it would go.

Inside the cemetery, Oaks moaned in agony. The seeming shifted and writhed, slipping in and out of him as it flickered and coalesced. Tendrils of its smoky presence pressed into the wounded stump of his wrist and blanketed the torn flesh. As the blood continued to piss, the supernatural layer of skin swelled and coagulated, catching the fluid and redirecting it into a more solid shape. Black, veinous fingers grew and stretched from the wound.

Oaks watched this with an expression approaching sheer bewilderment. With his good hand, he explored the gaping cut in his side. The maul had cut him deep, smashing its way into his intestines and leaving shit-stinking fluid to trickle down his side in black runnels.

There too, the seeming's smoky essence began to work. It coated the hole and pressed into it, mending torn organs and binding flesh. When it was done, the seeming crept into Oaks. He was aware of it inside him, and it felt good. He had begun to crave its presence and rely on it. A wash of warm endorphins filtered through him as he mentally embraced the demon.

And then it drove a spike straight through his mind, bringing on the worst headache he'd ever felt. His days of withdrawal in Maverson had nothing on this. Sweat broke out on his forehead. He clutched his face, aware of the black mutant hand and its strange, groping fingers.

As he doubled over, the seeming appeared before him. It stood over him, a school bully taunting a weak and pathetic loser. *You have failed.*

Oaks whimpered.

The seeming was no longer smoke. It appeared to him as it had to the others when embodying him. Huge and seething, its shoulders rolled with hulking power as it showed its anger. Its horns reached to the sky like lightning rods. Its barbaric snout was reminiscent of the demonic presences drawn by a hundred cultures over a hundred millennia. Piss ran down his leg.

"I tried. I did everything you asked."

"You fucked up. You took the path, but you could not bring the others and they have escaped, surely to scatter into the wind like displaced seeds."

"I'm sorry."

"Sorry is not enough. One way or the other, we need them. You must hunt them down."

"No, they don't want this."

"They have no choice."

Oaks racked his brain. Surely, with the others dead there was no way the band could work.

"You don't need to worry about that. When we took the others, we took them with us. They can easily be reborn from blood and fire."

"Nate," Oaks said.

The seeming glared.

"Nathan was with us until Chops prevented him. He wants this. Let me talk to him. Let me find him."

The demon slipped inside him and a vision swept over Oaks. Tomb Studios was a wreck. Rusty's and Chops's ruined corpses littered the ground and fire billowed out of the structure. The goat skull too lay where it had been left.

The green flames of the bonfire smoldered on coals. Within them, he saw himself. Whole, despite possessing a black hand that wasn't his own. He lurched over Rusty, picked something off the ground, and stuffed them into his pockets: teeth.

When he had them all, he hefted the dead man to the bonfire and, with mounting disbelief, he cast the teeth into the flames, which exploded to their previous roaring height. He stood Rusty on two feet, and as a cavorting shape appeared in the flame, the corpse took a shaky step towards the raging fire and into the licking flames. The shape grabbed the dead man and disappeared inside him.

A shambling noise sounded behind Oaks. Chops's corpse had started twitching and clawing its way across the ground towards him. The drummer's head was a pancaked mess, but within the mincemeat of brains and bone that made up his brow, a single eye was levelled on him. *"Into the fire."*

He grasped the drummer by his beefy shoulder and dragged him towards the flames. A second cavorting shape appeared. It stood waiting over Rusty's burning body and tilted its head curiously as Oaks lifted the drummer's prone form and dropped it into the flames. Instead of letting it fall, the shape caught the body and melted into it.

Then, dreamlike, Chops started to melt, sloughing goopy skin to the base of the fire. This time, though, the fire didn't reduce the flesh to nothing. Beneath the waxy slime of the man's skin, a new form emerged: the drummer reborn. At the same time, the crumpled and charred bones of Rusty began stirring. From beneath them, a hand punched through the ashes and the bass player climbed out of the coals and stood beside Chops. "Get the others," he said.

"Bring us back," Chops added. "Get the others. Bring us back. Take the world. Let us regain our lives. Fulfil our destinies as rock stars."

The vision disappeared and Oaks saw the real world manifest around him. The seeming was gone. He was alone in the cemetery with his thoughts. *It's not actually them, is it? I saw them die. It can't be.*

"*Have you not seen enough to know that our power is absolute. Enough of them remains to be reanimated, to fulfil your purpose and take what you want from this life. Is that not enough?*"

It was. The wind blew, carrying the faint scent of acrid smoke with it, and Oaks climbed to his feet. He stepped through the cemetery gates and walked towards the studio. Hopefully, his bag would be unscathed and he could get dressed. There was no way he could walk home naked. When he got there, he found the basement doors unlocked. His bag lay where he had left it. His phone sat on top, half-charged.

He threw a black shirt and jeans on, then noticed the missed call on his phone. India.

Once he was clear of this place, he would call her.

CHAPTER NINETEEN
DEATHLESS

At Nathan's place, Spiros was quiet. He was distant and as far as Nathan knew, pressing him to see how he was feeling could only be a bad thing. If the roles were reversed and he'd lost his shit before laying into Oaks with an axe, he'd want space to collect his thoughts before having a deep and meaningful conversation about it.

The Greek rolled a spliff and sprawled on the couch. He sparked up and exhaled a plume of smoke.

Nathan fished a couple of beers from the fridge and popped the caps with his lighter. The second flew to the kitchen floor and he watched it roll under the oven, uncaring. It could stay there. He handed Spiros his beer and hit the joint. Wordlessly, they smoked it and drank their beers before Nathan spoke. "You ready to figure this shit out?" he asked.

Spiros bit his nails and sat forward with a jerk. "What's to talk about, man? Call the cops. I gotta get to my girls, so call the cops and we can forget it ever happened."

Nathan sloshed the last mouthful of his beer, necked it, and fetched another. "We can't."

"Yes we can. He fucking killed people. He turned into a—"

"No one's gonna believe that!"

"Doesn't matter. DNA. Forensics. They'll figure it out."

Nathan cracked the beer. "You forget…" He pictured the maul smashing through Rusty's skull like a baseball bat through a raw egg. Heard the sound. Felt the spray of the viscera. Saw the teeth and brain fragments flying through the air. "My...our fingerprints are everywhere. Drugs. The ritual."

Spiros jerked his thumb out of his mouth, ripping the corner of a nail free.

Nathan thought his chest was going to explode. His hands were shaking. His breath hitched. He swigged the beer. "Chops killed Rusty."

"It *wasn't* Rusty. It was one of those *things*, man. He was dragging me to that green fucking fire. He *saved* me."

Nathan fumbled with his bag of weed. "Gimme those papers, man. We've gotta calm down. We've gotta figure this out."

"He saved me and Oaks killed him for it." Spiros fumbled with the papers before tearing one out. It ripped in his hands, catching on the packaging.

Nathan snatched it off him. "Calm down, dude. Jesus. We've gotta do something and we can't do it all panicked and shit." He rolled another joint. He fired up a fat cherry on the blunt and passed it to Spiros. "Smoke that," he said before immediately rolling another for himself. "Way I see it is this: We can't run. Sooner or later, someone's gonna go out there, probably once Cormac can't get hold of us and sends the pigs. We've gotta beat them to that and call first. No other way around it."

Spiros chewed his lip as he tapped ash into his palm. "And the bodies?"

"Wasn't us. We were attacked. There was a fight. We ran."

"Bullshit. There's no way that flies. Forensics, man. You saw what happened to Rusty. To Chops. To Oaks. We'll go to jail."

"No we won't. While they figure it out, we get outta here and report Oaks to the authorities. He's the man we pin it on."

"Dude…"

"Don't fucking 'dude' me. It's his fault." He met Spiros's pensive face with his own. "That way, while the cops go looking for him, lock him up, we get outta Dodge. Go to Europe, Mexico, fucking anywhere. Wait till it blows over and channel it into music."

Spiros shook his head. "You are as obsessed as he is. You're a monster too."

Nathan raised his hands. "What, we're supposed to give up our dreams?"

"My dreams are dead. For God's sake, man. Not only my dreams. My friends are dead. Can you see that or are you too selfish?"

Nathan hesitated. Began to speak. Choked back his words and sipped his beer instead. "You know I didn't mean it like that, but this is all so mental." He tried to suppress a blast of rage, but he couldn't hold onto it. "And fuck you, man, you're as involved. You've got blood daubed on your face too. I see it. It's not all me. The only one who said no was Chops. You wanted it as bad as Oaks. You wanted it as bad—"

"As bad as you?" Spiros leapt to his feet and prodded his old friend in the chest. "Is that what you're going to say? As bad as you? Because fuck you, no one—not even Oaks—wants this all as bad as you do. You enabled him. You were still begging him to—"

Nathan hit him. He stepped into the blow, walking forward and sending Spiros into the couch. He dove on him, but Spiros kicked out. Nathan fell into the coffee table and beer splashed on the floor. The guitarist was on him before he could scramble to his feet. He held Nathan's wrists tight.

"Stop it, you idiot. We can't fight. We can't fight."

Nathan thrashed wildly, trying to break free of Spiros's grip, but couldn't get the leverage he needed.

"Listen to me, fuckhead. You do what you want to do. You call the cops. You get Oaks arrested and you come up with whatever story you think is going to work for you, but I'm going and I'm not coming back. I'm out of here. I'm finding my wife. I'm finding my family, and I'm taking it all. Polyphemus is dead."

The words sank in and Nathan stilled. His breath hitched. "No," he said. "You can't." He pulled away from Spiros's grip and moved to a sitting position against the couch. He pulled his knees up. "You don't mean it."

"I do."

It was funny that he'd used those words. The band had felt like a marriage for most of his life, but what Spiros meant was *I don't* and that was what hurt. They'd been through everything. "But we gave everything," he said, knowing it was a feeble argument.

"And it didn't work. This cost us all we had, or close to it. I'm going to try to pick up the pieces before they are nothing but dust."

He stood. "I have no phone, Nathan. And we have Chops's van, not my car. If you mean to call the police, do it, and I will keep you in my thoughts. This is goodbye, my friend." The guitarist moved towards the door, wiping his eyes.

Nathan sobbed openly. "Don't…we can…"

"No, Nathan, we can't. My family is all that I have left. *If* I have them left. Try to find something that you can cling onto."

As he left, Nathan bawled. He truly had nothing. Chops, Rusty, his child…all dead, and there was no way Lisa would let him anywhere near her. He had only the band. And his beer.

India was in there, Oaks knew that. The seeming had made

finding her easy. Plucking up the courage to knock on her door, though, that was something he had to do all by himself. He knocked with his unmarked hand and waited. He hid his burned hand in his pocket.

When India came to the door, she shielded her eyes from the early morning light, appraising him. Her expression was not the one he expected. When he'd run this through, she'd brought him into the house with open arms, desperate to see him again, eager to forgive whatever had happened before, but in real life, her distaste was obvious. "You're using again. It's the only reason you could be here at this time of the morning."

"No," he said. "I need to talk to you."

"Go home."

A pang of black bitterness rose in his gorge. So did a momentary vision of himself in the fetal position, screaming. "Just, please, hear me out. I need help," he said, clutching his bald pate.

India gasped. "Your hand!"

He slammed the wounded extremity beneath his armpit. "It's not what you think." To her, it must seem gangrenous or frostbitten. She probably figured he'd been injecting into the webbing of his fingers, trying to hide the track-marks.

"Then what is it?"

"Please, let me in. I need your help. I can explain. About Anton. About this. About..." The seeming shifted in his mind again. "About other things."

She bit her lip and shook her head. "I'm calling you a cab. You've got until it...wait, how did you get here?"

He wondered if the road from the studio that had somehow become her road was still visible. "I walked."

She clearly didn't believe him, and he didn't blame her. He wasn't exactly a trustworthy man anymore. She disappeared inside before returning with her phone, swiping through the pages of an app. "You've got about fifteen minutes. Come in. And start talking."

Inside her house, everything was as he'd last seen it on the night he'd killed Corey. The television was dusty and unused, but in the middle of the room, a huge canvas, mostly swirled in black, took center-stage. Globules that could have been red morning stars or blood splatter dotted the darkness, and a silver streak tore across the scene. Beside it, shadowy scarecrows twisted and convulsed on a reddened shore. He'd forgotten the poem the scene was from.

"It's impressive," he said.

She grunted; pointed at a seat. "Start talking."

In the half-light, she seemed like something from a noir film. Her face melting into the darkness. She was passing out of his life. Unless... "Anton's worse than you ever expected."

She rolled her eyes. "No shit. I told you he's only a dealer with a taste for the dramatic. All that shit with the rituals and the goat's blood, it's performance art, a way to get people to buy into his product. He's selling dreams, and the theatrics are a key part of that."

"You're wrong." He felt the seeming shift.

She rubbed her forehead. "He got you hooked again, didn't he? Let me see your hand."

He pushed it into his pocket. "It's worse. He did something to me. Put something in me. He's onto something. He..." *how to say it without sounding like he was high?* "The rituals...they're real. Ever since that night with the goat, I've...had a presence in me."

"It's the drugs. You need to get clean."

He was out of his seat and in her face before he'd thought about it. "It's not drugs! Will you listen?" He grabbed her by the face. "I tried to shoot up. The thing inside me rejected it. It fucking pushed it out of my arm. I took Amielle's stash and I tried to shoot it all. Tried to end it all. The thing. The thing—"

She grabbed his blackened hand. It writhed beneath her grip. "What happened to you?"

The hand pulsed. Tendrils like wisps of smoke slithered around her fingers as he stared into her eyes. "The thing he put in me—I call it the seeming—it wanted everyone in the band to join it—or its masters—or whatever, and Anton told me how to make it happen. Told me to give it what it wanted. He sold me out to this thing, this fucking *demon*." Its presence in his mind began to lessen. As it released its grip, his abdomen started to hurt. His hand began to ooze. Smoke poured off him. "Do you see what's happening? It's coming out!"

India hesitated. "What's happening? What do you mean?"

"It's coming out. It can do that. It can control me, but it can manifest too. It can."

The familiar hulking, horned shape loomed over him, laughing. It was a blurring of reality; an erasure of physics, and then it was gone again. So was his pain. The wound from the maul had healed. His blackened hand was once again solid and comfortable.

"Now do you believe me?"

"No! You are tripping serious balls. What do you want me to do about it?"

He didn't know. It felt right. "I wanted...I wanted to apologize. If things were different. If things were...I don't know. If I hadn't fucked up again, we could have been good."

"I'm not your fallback. I'll talk to Anton. Get him to help you, get him to stop giving you this whatever it is, but that's it. Once it's out of you. Once it's gone. You're on your own. Take your band. Take your filthy soul and get out of my life. I can't have you here."

Oaks dropped to his knees. "I'm sorry. I just..."

A vehicle pulled into the driveway. "Wait here." She went outside and spoke to the taxi driver. When she returned, she put a hand on his shoulder. "I'll make you a bed, but you don't touch me. You don't talk to me. Get some rest. You need to sleep off whatever it is you've been taking. I'm going to see Anton."

If there was one thing India had hoped she'd never have to do again, it was drive to Anton's house and see the slimy bastard in the flesh. In a way, she couldn't believe she was doing it. She should have sent Oaks packing, but she knew he was a victim, whether he saw it that way or not. Anton had recognized a mark as soon as he'd laid eyes on Oaks and had used him in some horrible way.

The shit coming out of the vocalist's mouth tonight was like nothing she'd ever heard. Tall tales of rituals and possessions were one thing, but claiming he'd been healed by some sort of supernatural presence meant he'd slipped into psychosis. Whatever Anton had him on was dangerous. The shit needed to stop.

She parked her car and made her way to the elevator, checking her phone to ensure she had the voice-recorder app running. She'd considered going straight to the cops, but Anton was a smart bastard with money. She'd need hard evidence if she was going to make anything stick. As soon as he saw her face on the video intercom, he grinned and buzzed her up. When the elevator came to a stop on the penthouse level and the doors dinged open, he was standing with arms wide, grinning.

"What *has* the cat dragged in?" His grin and his tone made it sound like a throwaway comment made to an old friend, but that wasn't his style. "Will it be the usual?"

"Don't get excited." She gave him as wide a berth as she could, staying within reach of the elevator. Weird music, Gregorian chants or something, played from the speakers in the ceiling. He loved his weird stuff, that was for sure. "I came about Stephen."

"I should think he's done with you."

"He's at my place, sleeping off whatever you gave him."

"He's recording with his band."

Interesting. He'd known about that, and it surely broke the terms of Oaks's release from rehab. "No, the drugs you gave him caused some sort of psychotic episode. They had a fight or something. It all went tits-up. What did you give him?"

The life-coach laughed. "I didn't give him anything. He's his own man. Mostly."

"Cut the shit." She stepped forward, forgetting herself. "You're going to leave him alone. He's a good man, and he doesn't need to be taken advantage of."

"People keep telling me that about him. Funnily enough, I never noticed. Between the drugs, the booze, the break-ins, the other vocalists in his proximity dying strange deaths, I had him pegged as the *opposite* of a good person."

"I know what you're doing."

"Do you?"

"I told you to stay away from him once already, and I mean it. You get him high again, you sell him drugs again, you talk to him again, and—"

"And you'll what?" He shot out a hand and grabbed her pointing finger in a powerful grip. "You'll make threats? You'll talk tough?" He laughed, shaking his head then wrenched her arm down, bending her finger so hard, she thought it was sure to dislocate.

"You're hurting me!"

"Good." Something in his eyes shifted briefly.

India was certain they flashed a different color, but she was too busy trying to pull her hand free from his to be certain. When she got it free, she stepped closer to the elevator. "Stay away from him. I mean it."

When his hand shot out a second time, he clutched her by the throat and pulled her into the room. She squealed, but he didn't let go.

"Let's be clear on who calls the shots around here, because it's not you." He led her away from the elevator, deeper into the penthouse. She scratched his forearms, tried to kick and scream, but he held her with the relentless grip of a bird of prey dragging a rodent to its lair. "Now, because the fool can do nothing right, tell me what you know about his latest clusterfuck." He tossed her to the ground and stood over her.

"Fuck you!"

He booted her hard in the ribs. Bone cracked. The wind rushed from her, and she collapsed. "There are things in motion that you would do best not to fuck with. He had a job to do, and you will tell me what you know about his failure."

She scrambled away, crawling deeper into the penthouse. A hand closed on her left ankle and pulled her closer to him. He clutched her hair and lifted her head so she was face to face with him. She spat, aiming for his eye.

He smashed a fist into her face. "You need to think, India. What you don't tell me, he will, and trust me when I say he will. So if you want to save your own life, speak up and tell me what he has told you."

"No fucking way. Let me out of here. We'll go. You'll never see us again."

"That," he said, closing his hands around her throat, "is not an option."

The pressure became immense. She couldn't breathe. Her lungs started to burn. She writhed, desperate to escape, but his hands only closed tighter, crushing her windpipe.

CHAPTER TWENTY
UPON DESOLATE SANDS

He had missed four calls from Cormac before he'd crawled out of bed, but there was no way he was calling back yet. Groggy, seedy, and feeling like he'd been hit by a runaway freight train, Nathan chewed two paracetamol tablets and finished the half-bottle of warm beer resting by his bed. Once he'd brushed his teeth, he stared at his phone again.

Deep down, he knew he should be calling Cormac first, but he needed to speak to the cops. Needed to get an early alibi in there and explain what had happened. All night, he'd dreamed of the maul powering into Oaks's abdomen. In those vivid nightmares, he'd seen his friend dying, bleeding out on the ground of the cemetery, only to get up and continue stalking him, pleading with him to record one last song. In the cold light of day, he knew that despite his fears, Oaks could be alive.

The thing possessing Oaks had changed him. Nathan doubted a wound like that would be enough to kill the hulking beast that had grown inside the vocalist. It was vast and powerful, undoubtedly keeping Oaks focused on harvesting the rest of the band. Whether they came willingly or not wouldn't matter to it.

On top of that, if Oaks was alive, there were the others to think about. Someone had to get Rusty and Chops. They had families, friends. They couldn't be left to rot. It wasn't fair. He couldn't do that to them. He needed to talk to Spiros again too, needed to find out if things were over. Find out if he'd have to strike out on his own. After all that, then he could talk to Cormac.

Someone hammered on his front door, rapping it with the determination of a seventh day Adventist. A voice boomed through the timber. "Hello, Nathan, you in there?"

"Cormac?" Nathan opened the front door to the liaison from the label. The dude was sweating and stressed. "What are you doing here?"

"What the fuck am *I* doing here? Jesus Christ, let me in. You idiots are supposed to be recording at Tomb. I've been out there and found no one. What the hell is going on? If there were more dramas, the label's gonna pull the pin, man. Talk to me."

Nathan ushered the dude inside. "I need coffee. You want one?"

"No fucking way. I've already had four. I'm having fucking palpitations. Tell me why you're not recording. Tell me why you're here."

"Wait, you've been out there?"

"I'm the only one who's been out there. The place is pristine. Not even a beer can lying around. I thought you'd all collectively overdosed or died in some kind of ritual suicide, but nope, you've been here drunk off your ass."

Nathan pulled a mug off the dishrack. "That's not true."

"What?"

"You can't have been there."

"What do you mean 'I can't have been there?' I *was* there."

Nathan pictured the scene. His head was foggy, but inside that circle, daubed in blood, everything had been real. Was he going crazy? Could they have imagined it? A group hallucination brought on by Oaks's ritual? What about Rusty? Chops? Oaks? The fact the studio was on fire? He sat down. Sighed. "Cormac, you gotta understand, something fucked-up happened. If you're telling me you were there and not pulling my leg, something seriously weird has

POLYPHEMUS | 252

happened."

"Well spill the fucking beans, man, because I'm gonna have to explain this today. I'm supposed to report on it all, and you've got nothing."

"I can't tell you, man." He couldn't believe he was so calm. It might have been the comedown or the hangover, but he suspected it might be shock.

"Why don't you start by telling me about the others?" Cormac was pointing. Leaning forward in his seat. Spittle flew from his mouth as his anger escalated. "Spiros. That fucking junkie, Stephen. Chops. Your new bass-player, whatever the fuck his name is."

Dimly, Nathan was aware he could burst into tears at any moment. The sound the splitting maul made as it splintered Rusty's skull—that wet crack—replayed in his ears again and again. "Rusty. You don't even know his name. It was Rusty, so shut up and I'll tell you what happened."

But Cormac didn't shut up. He was out of his seat. "It doesn't matter what his name is, was, or will ever be, because your band is dead. You're dead. You'll never work in the industry again. When you reform and reconcile and start a Bandcamp website to sell your shitty merch, no one's gonna touch you with a ten-foot-pole. You're finished."

Nathan let the storm of words pass. "You done?"

"I told you who's done. You and your shitty band of self-obsessed junkies and alcoholics."

"I can get you the album. I only need time."

"Time to what? I bet you've already had your first beer. While you pretend it's all about the music, it's not. It's all about you and your idea of what it means to be a rock star. To drink beer. To cruise through life like a piece of shit floating down a sewer pipe."

Nathan fished out his phone. Found a video of the band playing in the studio and played it. "I can get you the songs. I can get studio musicians. I can record them. Give me time."

"You've had all the time in the world, and you've pissed

it away. You're done, Nathan. You're done." The liaison strode to the front door. "Don't contact me, Nathan. I put my ass on the line for you, and you fucked me. I'll send an official letter this afternoon. Your contract's cancelled; the label will want their day in court."

Nathan watched the door swing shut and threw his coffee mug into it. "Fuck you, then, man. Fuck you." He picked up the nearest acoustic, strummed through it, screamed. He smashed it into the kitchen bench, shattering it with a dull twang and a hollow crunch. When he caught his breath, he went to the fridge. At least he had his beer.

After leaving Nathan's, Spiros had gone straight home and parked Chops's van in the garage. With no phone, he'd been living in the hope that Pandora and Calliope would be there when he arrived. They weren't. Knowing it was too late to do anything else about it, and not wanting to scare her by calling from the home phone, he'd opted for sleep. Awakened and terrified of the cops closing in, he lifted the cordless from its cradle.

He'd wanted to get rid of it months ago, but Dora had insisted they keep a landline for business purposes. He speed-dialed her number, and for the first time in a while, he heard the welcome ringing of her cell phone.

His conversation with Seb replayed. It was clear his wife had stayed away from her lover in what amounted to their trial separation, but he couldn't help but fear the smug prick would answer the phone and gloat.

"Spiros?" Her voice was silk. It had been too long since he'd heard it and a cocktail of emotions bubbled in his gut; threatened to spill from his eyes.

"Where are you, baby? Is Calliope with you? Can I hear

her voice too?"

There was a pause. "Of course she is. Why are you home, though? You should be recording. You should be with the band."

He couldn't tell whether she was angry or shocked. "We are finished." That cocktail of emotion thickened. The death and destruction of last night's chaos sat heavily in his conscience. The easy answer was that there'd been a drug-induced hallucination and Nathan was a murderer, but his upbringing, his learning at St Quirinus, told him otherwise. That was a *real* demon, and it was inside Oaks.

"So soon? Usually you take weeks to record albums."

"No, the band is done. Polyphemus is done."

"What happened this time?"

He pictured the hulking monster, the cavorting shapes, Oaks wearing the goat skull, slicing his hand open with the knife. "It's too much to tell briefly, but where are you? I'll come to you and stay with you. I don't want to be home right now."

She hesitated. "What aren't you telling me? No secrets. If we are done with this, we are moving forward with nothing but complete honesty."

He pressed his forehead against his fist. "I'm processing it. But I promise I'll tell you when I see you. There are other things we need to discuss as well."

This time, there was more tension in the pause. "What else is there? If the band is truly done, then you know where things stand."

"No. I don't. I heard from Sebastian. We'll discuss that in person. In calm. Not like this."

"I'll text you the address."

"My phone is broken. Let me grab a pen."

CHAPTER TWENTY-ONE
THE DECAYING LIGHT

Nathan sauntered into the bar with a six-pack already under his belt. He hadn't forgotten the last time he'd come here, and he scanned the venue for sight of the kids who'd given him his beating the other day. It felt like it could've been years ago, but for everything that had happened since, it was only a few days. The bruises of that particular fracas were raw and tender. If the shits were here, he'd avoid them, but there was no way he was going to show weakness in a place he considered a second home. That wasn't his style. When he hit the bar, one of the regular bartenders nodded in his direction.

"A pint of the El Jefe, dude," Nathan said.

"On your own today?"

"Yeah, man. Just killing time. Needed to get out of the house, you know. Cabin fever." He didn't mention that he was hoping Miss Kindness, the chick he'd met the other day might be here, but that was certainly part of it. He took his beer and headed across to the *House of the Dead* machine. He pumped in a couple of bucks and started blasting.

As bits of zombie skull and blood flew across the screen and he reloaded, he blinked away the images of his friends being butchered. When the big bastard with the barrels appeared, he saw the hulking monster that had possessed Oaks effortlessly lifting Chops and driving him headfirst into the ground. He blasted a hailstorm of bullets into the prick and moved on past the leeches and dogs. After he died fighting the boss, he skulled his beer and went for another. He downed it while inspecting the rows of albums on the shelf.

Polyphemus's self-titled debut and their second album, *Served Your Own Destruction*, were both there on the shelves. One of the reasons he loved this bar was that it always championed local bands. He knew that The Violent Dead would have albums on here too. Even Bone Totem, Chops's old band, was here. He finished his beer and thought about Cormac's final words before leaving. They were bullshit. It wasn't like Nathan was done playing, and plenty of bands had recovered from controversies before. Cormac might be pissed-off, but he was only a bit-player in a massive industry.

As for there being no sign of a drama at the studio, he couldn't believe that. By rights, the place should be a mess, but if Cormac had gone out there and found nothing, it would explain why the police hadn't come for Nathan and Spiros. It also meant that Oaks was out there somewhere. And if he was, maybe Nathan could revisit the conversation. If Spiros wanted out, fuck him. It had been Oaks and Nathan to start with. Spiros hadn't come until he'd heard the two of them jamming Deftones songs in Oaks's garage. The story from there was history, but if Oaks could do what he'd promised then so be it. There was nothing else tying Nathan to his shitty life as a no-hoper. Why shouldn't he go through with the ritual? He'd meant to before Chops had intervened and ruined everything. Why wouldn't he pick up the pieces, reform a new version of Polyphemus and record the songs they'd already written? It was a no-brainer. Their music was too good to forget, and the opportunity to make them the biggest band on the planet was too close to walk away from.

He checked his phone to see when Oaks had last seen his messages. He hadn't been on for hours, but his phone could have been broken in the chaos of the night. Spiros had broken his. On a whim, Nathan tried Spiros's home number.

It rang out. He wondered if Oaks might be at Amielle's. If he was, he might be able to talk sense to him there.

A familiar drumbeat and riff crept out of the bar's sound-system, gradually growing in volume before the opening track to The Haunted's *rEVOLVEr* album, "No Compromise" hit full speed. Too right. Nathan was done with compromise, and if he couldn't convince Spiros or Cormac to make this work, he knew that Oaks held the only solution. The only solution. He snatched up his keys and ordered a ride on his phone. The singer would have to go by Amielle's sooner or later. May as well do it now.

When Oaks woke, it was already past lunchtime. The sounds of construction machinery hammered from the renovation happening across the road. Cars droned by on the nearby highway, and two dogs barked in the neighbor's yard. He inspected his hand. The black substance had coagulated into a scaly flesh that was warm to the touch. The wound in his abdomen was the same. He sauntered into the kitchen, expecting to see India working on her canvas in the front room, but everything was quiet.

As he approached the fridge, hunger overcame him, and he ransacked it for anything edible. Finding leftover pasta, he considered the microwave but then scarfed it down cold. With that gone, he guzzled a bottle of juice and boiled the kettle. He needed coffee.

The seeming shifted, and familiar wisps of smoke coalesced at the foot of the table. Pain ebbed in his hand and abdomen as tendrils of the black substance writhed away from the wounds, stretching towards the entity like spirit fingers.

"You not going to let me wake up before you start with

your bullshit?"

It shot out an incorporeal hand and plunged it into Oaks's ribcage. It grasped his heart in an icy grip and clenched. Oaks gasped as he lunged forward, trying to wrestle the arm free. When his hands slipped through the swirling black smudge that marked the being's existence he groaned. "I'm sorry," he said, "I'm sorry!"

The creature let go and swelled to its full, imposing height. "*You have work to do. You know this.*"

Oaks scanned the room for any sign of India. "You know I want to complete the work as well. You know that. If I'm going to do it for you, understand there are things I need in my life."

The seeming chuckled.

"I need to know where she is. You know, don't you?"

"*Of course.*"

Oaks slapped the table. "Then tell me."

"*You should know. You told her everything and she went to fix it for you like a good mother.*"

"Anton's? She went to Anton's?"

"*It's time you went there anyway. He has outlived his usefulness.*"

How could that be? Anton was the one who'd started this and given him the gift of the seeming to begin with. Surely he was at the top of the food chain?

"*No. He was, like you, only a pawn who'd been told what he needed to hear to make him act. It was you we wanted all along. After all, what good is one conman who can persuade one or two at a time when a band as mighty as Polyphemus can bring thousands to us in one concert.*" A vision of concertgoers scrambling towards the stage to be converted like Evangelists at a tent revival filled Oaks's mind.

"What's he done with her?"

The entity laughed again. This time, when it faded out of sight, Oaks felt it filling him again. The doorway leading out of the kitchen became a portal that opened on Anton's lounge-room. There, lying sprawled on his couch was India's limp form. He didn't need an expert to tell him she was dead. The black bruises on her throat and the swollen shiner on her eye gave him all the information he needed.

Oaks didn't step through the portal, he ran. As he burst through, he felt the seeming assume control of him. His arms ballooned with muscle. The black flesh of his hand fell away, revealing the skeletal bone beneath. That erupted in green flame. His teeth pushed into fangs. His chest rippled with musculature and he leapt to India's corpse.

He cradled her, brushing her hair from her face. Rage swirled inside him like the smoke that had signaled the first presence of the seeming. Anger became him. He was fire-eyed fury.

"Isn't this a surprise?"

He jerked his head in the direction of the voice. Anton stood in the hallway of his penthouse. He held a steaming mug of coffee. His dressing grown was tied casually around his waist, but otherwise he was as calm and carefree as a man on holiday.

Oaks placed India on the couch.

"Come, Stephen. She was *nothing*. A meddler. An interloper. She was getting in the way. She was making threats. She knew too much."

Oaks swung his flaming bone fist. It crashed into Anton's chest with the power of a rampaging gorilla. The man was driven into the wall, cracking the plaster. He slid to the tiles, spilling coffee everywhere.

Somewhere beneath his anger, Oaks wondered if the bastard would transform into a creature like he had. When he saw Anton's bafflement, though, he knew it wasn't going to happen. The seeming whispered to Oaks then. *"I told you, his usefulness has expired."*

Oaks laughed. "They've abandoned you. You're nothing."

Anton screamed as Oaks closed a massive hand around

his face.

Oaks pulled him to his feet and lifted him. He felt the man's jaw grinding beneath his powerful grip, but he didn't care. The man had killed India. If he had let her live, he would have forgiven him everything. It was obvious that Polyphemus were going to be the biggest, most influential band in history. If Anton had let India be, Oaks would have let him live. Instead, he'd chosen to kill her. *In turn, he'd chosen to kill himself.*

Oaks thrust down on Anton's head and watched him sprawl onto his tailbone. Panic filled the man's face and as he sprawled, his feeble penis flopped out the side of his boxer shorts. Oaks laughed.

Anton tried to scramble away. Tears ran down his face. "Don't! Let me serve you. I have knowledge!"

Oaks didn't need his knowledge. He kicked the man in the guts, driving him across the tiled floor.

Anton wheezed. Painfully forced himself into a crouching position; pleaded. "I can serve you in other ways!"

Amused, Oaks grinned at him. "And what will you do for me?"

"I'll let you do whatever."

Oaks laughed. How the tide had turned. He didn't need Anton's sexual favors, though. As the frontman of the world's biggest band, he'd have all the women he could want. He punched the man again, this time driving his flaming skeletal fist into the top of the man's head like a club-hammer.

Anton fell to the tiles with a thud.

Oaks placed a foot between the man's shoulder-blades. He grabbed him by the chin with two hands, leveraging himself a good grip on the back of Anton's head with his thumbs. He pulled. Vertebrae popped. Flesh tore. Anton's spine cracked as it broke in two. The rest of the noises were drowned out by Oaks's own guttural roar and the sound of the seeming laughing in his mind. As his bellowing growl tapered to a low rumble, the last sinews of skin snapped and curled like ribbons. Viscera and ichor spurted onto the expensive tiles and the beheaded corpse slapped to the ground with a meaty thud.

He held Anton's head high. A stub of splintered vertebrae, stretched and misshapen arteries, spinal cord, and half a trachea dangled out of the gaping mess beneath the jaw. Oaks drank the blood and fluids that dripped from the gaping wound. When he was satiated, he tossed the severed head aside like an empty beer can, spat in its general direction, and returned to India. He couldn't leave her here. She deserved much better.

Her limp form was light in his arms as he caressed her hair, staining it with Anton's blood. When he stepped towards the portal, though, it disappeared. *She must stay*, the seeming said.

"No. I've seen you bring the others back. If you want my help, you'll do it with her."

The entity didn't laugh, but he knew it was grinning all the same.

"Since when do you make demands?"

"Since it became apparent how much you need me. Threaten me with an eternity of torture in hell all you want; if she's not brought back, I won't track down the others."

The demon bristled.

"Come on, you're all about freedom of choice and the fact that I have to act. It's my turn to tell you what I want in return."

"Fame is what you get."

"It only goes so far. She didn't deserve this. She was trying to help for no reason other than the fact she thought it was the right thing to do. You're helping me because you

need the band to be huge. You need us to work for you. She died because of selflessness. Or can you not do it? Is it all parlor tricks and bullshit?"

"Very well. Bring her through, but if you cannot deliver the others, she'll endure infinite torment with you. And that's a promise."

The portal opened. By the time he'd carried her home and rested her on her bed, Oaks had become himself again. He laid beside her and wept.

Calliope giggled happily as Spiros bounced her on his knee. "Did you miss me? Did you miss me?" Her smile suggested she had, and the guitarist wouldn't let anyone tell him otherwise. He continued bouncing her and blowing raspberries on her tummy until Pandora entered the room with a warm sippy-cup. "Already?" he asked.

"I'm afraid so. It's time for her to nap and for us to talk."

He sighed and took the bottle from his wife. "I'll put her down. Then we can talk." He didn't *want* to talk. He knew that he had to and that it was not going to be an easy conversation, but if he could put it off for a bit longer that would be great. On top of all the complexities here, he wasn't comfortable with the way he'd left things with Nathan.

He expected the police to turn up at any moment and take this reunion away from him. Them leading him out of the property in handcuffs and questioning him about the deaths of at least two or possibly even three people would be the last straw in this marriage. He had no doubt about that. As it was, he didn't know if it could be saved. Wasn't entirely sure he truly wanted it to be saved. Infidelity was one thing he'd never succumbed to. In all his nights on tour, he'd avoided the traps of the flesh and the power it holds over so many.

For his wife to have given into these same urges was a big issue.

He nestled Calliope into her portable crib and positioned the bottle where she could easily hold it. In moments, she was nursing happily. He wished he had his phone to distract him from the impending conversation and emotional tension he was no doubt in for.

When he went to his wife, she was sitting on the couch watching him. "Before I talk about anything, I want to know why the change of heart. You were so adamant, and then, after all this, after only one day it falls apart and you're here. You got my message. I know that."

He paused to consider his answer, and then changed course. "No, Pandora. First and foremost there is something that trumps that, that trumps any of that."

She squirmed where she sat. "I don't know if this is the right time to talk about that. It's done. It's in the past, and—"

"In all my time on the road, I never betrayed you. Not when we were dating, not when we were engaged, not when we were married, and not when Calliope was born. I don't know whether this is over yet, but you can start by telling me truthfully whether it is done."

Pandora nodded. "Yes."

"No bullshit?"

"No bullshit."

'What is it you want from this conversation? From this marriage?"

She sighed. "What I've always wanted. You to be present. You to live a life you love that includes us."

He shook his head. "Sorry, that's bullshit. I always did that. You have been provided for with so much money and so many possessions that you are undoubtedly the envy of all in your workplace and friendship group."

"Money is not love, Spiros. Love is spending time at home with us doing mundane and boring shit, not time drinking with your high school friends while you try to become career musicians."

It was always the same. She always hated that he had maintained his band. "We were musicians. We *are* musicians. None of that changes the fact you are family; my number one priority. We have always been there for each other through thick and thin. All of that is complicated by the contract situation. And once I know what's happening with everything else, we have to ask ourselves some serious questions about our future."

"You could easily pay out the contract and it would hardly dent our savings, our investments."

The conversation was going sideways. She was deflecting the issue. At the same time, he was already wondering what Nathan was doing, fearing that Oaks had followed them to Nate's place. "For fuck's sake, Dora. That's not the point. If I wanted out, if I truly believed it was done with, then I would have walked long ago."

"So why are you here? You say you don't know what you want, but you're here. I did what I did." She had started to cry. Tears rolled down her cheeks. "I'm sorry. I thought you were always doing it. Thought you were fucking groupies every night, but why are we doing this if you don't know if you're going to forgive me?"

"Because I've walked now! Because there is a baby in the other room that needs to be as far away from home as it possibly can! I need to make sure she's protected!"

"What are you talking about?"

The truth caught in his chest. He didn't want to tell her, to frighten her, but whether he was going to try and convince her they were safe or, more sensibly, uproot them and move them away, he had to. If the demon had somehow kept Oaks alive, it knew where he lived. Whether he and Pandora stayed together or separated, they had to be as far away from it as possible. "I think you'd better get a drink," he said.

Again, that familiar eyebrow of hers. At any other time,

it was sexy as hell. "There's wine in the fridge," she said.

"No. Something stronger. You're not going to believe what I have to tell you."

When the tale was done, she sat there, her face pale. "OK, you did these drugs," she said. "It was a hallucination. If the building was on fire, if people died, the police would have arrested you already."

"And Stephen?"

"It sounds like he's somewhere and he might be badly hurt. Have you called your friends and checked on them?"

"My phone is broken. I told you that."

She handed hers to him without a word. "Log into your account. Message them. Message Nathan on my account. Jesus, why did you wait?"

Nathan's avatar said he was online. He fired off a message and within seconds, one came back. "Fuck."

Pandora touched Spiros's arm. "What did he say? What did you say?"

"He's going to Oaks's halfway house. I asked him if he was fine and if he'd heard anything. Cormac pulled the contract. He went to the studio and we weren't there. Said there was no sign of trouble. He's going to find Oaks and get it recorded. He thinks he can save it."

"He's like you. He's obsessed."

"He's fucked in the head. I walked away." Spiros closed his eyes and pressed a hand to his heart. A moment later, he opened his eyes. "I truly think this is bad. I don't know what happened last night. I think I lost my mind for large parts of it. Nate told me I did, but I think that whatever is going on with Stephen is real and nothing good will come of this." He rapidly typed another message into the phone and handed it to Pandora.

As she read it, the phone dinged. "He says you can either record with them or swivel, but he's going to make it right with Oaks. He says that the two of them can deliver the album if they have to."

Spiros pulled his ponytail until his scalp hurt. "I have to stop him. Whatever that was inside Oaks, it was evil. I'm certain that Chops and Rusty are dead. I think Oaks must have killed Corey, and I also think that maybe he killed Hank. I have to stop this."

Pandora grabbed his arm. "Think of your family. Call the police. Tell them what happened. Tell them what you suspect. They will intervene. Your responsibility is here."

"They won't believe a word of it. They'll think I'm high."

"Spiros, don't go. If it's all as dangerous as you think, then make a plan. If there is a demon in him, what does it want? How can you stop it?"

"I don't know, but I have to try."

"We are hours away from home. Call the police."

He couldn't do it. He knew that if he ever wanted to fix the marriage and keep his self-respect, he had to stick to his values and go to the aid of his friends. He had to stop them from doing something stupid. He could figure out the marriage after, but for now, his priority was clear. "No, Pandora. I love you. I love Calliope, but I love my friends too. I have to do something." He kissed her, pulling away slowly as she tried to hold him. He went into Calliope's room and kissed the sleeping baby on the forehead before giving his wife one more kiss. "When I return, we will talk out our future. We will leave this place and we will make a decision about what we do next."

CHAPTER TWENTY-TWO
REVENANT

When he got to Amielle's place, Nathan was already drying out and wishing he'd grabbed a couple of road-beers from the fridge. Who knew what the nurse would've made of him turning up at the halfway house with a four-pack of beers under his arm, but fuck it, it wasn't like the people inside hadn't seen and done worse. When he knocked, he heard her rustling about inside. She called out, asking if he was Stephen.

Nathan's heart sank. In turn, Amielle's face dropped when she pulled open the interior door and saw it wasn't the vocalist. "Hey, I heard you call out for Steve. He's not here?"

She peered at him through the security screen, her eyes narrow. The house beyond was dark and seedy. Not messy, but unclean, like it had been infected by an unwholesome spirit. "Who are you? Are you with his band?"

Nathan sighed. "Yeah, I was hoping he'd be here. You haven't heard from him? I'm getting a bit worried. He was supposed to catch up with us the other day."

"Shit," the nurse said. "He told me he was on his way to see you. Told me you were recording. He never made it?"

Nathan shook his head.

Amielle rubbed her face. "We'd better call the cops. I'd held off, not wanting to get him in trouble, but come in. I'll tell them when he left, and I suppose you can fill them in with where he was supposed to get to."

"Wait, maybe we can figure it out. Is there anywhere else

he might have gone? He mentioned a girl a couple of times."

Amielle opened the door and gestured him inside to the table. "Coffee?"

Nathan licked his lips. "I'd love a beer if you've got one."

"Thought you might say that," she said. "You've got that look about you. When was your last drink?"

If she had him pegged that quickly, she must be good at her job. "How's he been doing otherwise? Mentally, I mean. He seem fine to you?" He watched her face to gauge what she thought about him avoiding the question. Apart from a little raising of the eyebrow, she barely registered a response. She must be used to it.

"He's been fluctuating," she said. "You didn't come in to talk about that, though. Do you know his girlfriend, India?"

"You think that's where he might be?"

"There, or with Anton."

"Anton?"

"His life-coach."

Life-coach? Was that who'd put Oaks up to his bullshit? He'd always hated the kind of scumbag who wrote books and gave talks on the things you should know about yourself. His own mother had spent thousands on them before giving in and overdosing on oxy. They were every bit as bad as television evangelists. Cult of personality fuckheads was all they could ever be to him. How had Oaks allowed himself to be taken advantage of by one of them?

Amielle waited for him to respond before continuing. "If he's not in either of those places, then we've got issues. I can't think of anywhere else he could be. How about you?"

Nathan shrugged. "You got their numbers? Addresses?"

She grabbed her phone off the bench; watched him thoughtfully. "I'm guessing you've tried contacting him directly."

"He ain't been on for hours. All my messages are left unread. Doesn't mean he's not ignoring them, but…"

"No, I'm getting the same. I thought he might have

blocked me, but it seems like he hasn't."

Interesting. Something had gone down here before Oaks had left for Tomb Studios. The nurse was shaken, and worried. That was clear.

She wrote a couple of numbers on a piece of paper. The first was headed with the name INDIA, the second with ANTON. "Here," she said. "I've gotta tell you that Anton's not responding to texts, and if Stephen's not at India's, I've got no idea. I have to ask, though, you asked me how he's doing; I need to ask you the same. I only see one side of him. One of the things they do at the clinic is ask close friends to fill in paperwork about the patient to see if they're ready for permanent release to the general public." She grew awkward. "You don't think he's a danger to himself, do you?"

Nathan hoped his expression wouldn't reveal anything, but he could feel his face crawling with anxiety as he tried not to picture the events of the night before. "No, ma'am. For everything he's been through, I can't imagine him feeling that way for a second."

She grunted at his response. "And to others?"

He could only lie in response to this one. "So far as I know, he's never hurt a fly." He pictured Chops hurtling towards the ground. Thought about the fact Hank Traine was dead, right when the drummer was going to join the dude's band. Thought about Corey. "It'd take something massive to change that."

"Yeah, that's what I thought."

Nathan had read a story once in school, *The Ones Who Walk Away from Omelas*. In it, people got to have the perfect life if they could deal with the suffering of one innocent person. If he managed to catch up with Oaks and they got this album off the ground, they'd have to call it "Omelas", because it didn't matter who else had to suffer, neither of them could leave it behind. Not for all the money in the world. "You'd better take my number," he said. "In case he comes home. I need to speak to him."

She grabbed a magnetized notepad from the fridge. "Write it on there. I'll make sure I tell him."

He did so, thanked her and left, dialing India's phone before he called another cab. It rang out, as did Anton's. Unsure where to go from there, Nathan took a ride home. If Oaks was alive, he'd know where to find his old friend.

When he'd cried himself dry, Oaks clambered to his feet and wondered whether anyone had found Anton's body. There was nothing on his Facebook feed or the news, so he assumed the bastard's blood was coagulating on his tiled floor. Good. He deserved to be left there to rot before anyone found him.

India, though, most certainly did not. The seeming had fallen silent on that front. It hadn't approved of him dragging her away from the site of her murder, but Oaks wouldn't soften on this. He might have gotten himself in deeper with his threat not to pursue Nathan and Spiros without her resurrection, but he may also have doomed her to infinite horrors beyond the grave if he failed in his mission. He brushed hair off her cold forehead. The skin felt like cold clay. As he stared at her, he realized he'd dragged her so far into this mess that even death couldn't save her from his bullshit. He should have known not to use her as a bargaining tool.

"It's time to work."

Pulled from his reverie, he stared at the coalescing smudge the seeming had so often loved to appear to him as. "We'll go to Nathan's. He'll be there, but I don't want India involved."

"It's too late for that. The deal is done."

Oaks swallowed his frustration. "If I fail, the deal is done. If I do what you want, I don't want her here unless I can speak to her first. I want to know what *she* wants."

"Succeed and then we'll talk." The seeming shifted and the smudge became tinted with hints of color. It shimmered, and in what could have been a blink, it took the shape of Rusty. *"Come then. Take us to Nathan's. Bring us back."* Rusty waved an arm, shifting into Chops's visage and a portal opened. *"Let's get this show on the road."* Through the portal, Oaks could see the outside of Nathan's little house. The sky was blood-red in the late afternoon light. Clouds cut across the sun like razorblades through an eye, and the balmy evening breeze whipped the un-mowed grass back and forth. Inside, the sound of Aborted's "Coffin Upon Coffin" blasted out of Nathan's speakers. "Do we need a ritual?"

The seeming was a smudge again. *"Either kill him or call out to me and have him grant me access to his flesh. That is all that matters. The ritual is for show, and we are done with pretense."*

Oaks didn't think he'd need to kill Nathan. His old friend had been about to give himself over when Chops had intervened last night, and of all the band, Nathan was probably more infatuated with them becoming huge than anyone else. He was the guy who'd gotten into playing music for the chicks, for the fame, for the fortune, and here it was, a temptation ready to grasp.

"And if he has had a change of heart?"

Nathan wouldn't have had anything of the sort. He was not the type for quiet reflection or introspective moments. His life was a series of bad decisions and beer cans. So as far as Oaks saw it, the dude was a shoe-in. Spiros was going to be harder to convince. From what he could remember of the night before, the Greek had hammered the final nail into the original plan's coffin and dragged Nathan away from events before they could be finished. Once he was done here, Oaks would hopefully be able to rely on Nathan to help him bring Spiros around.

"You expect too much. He wounded you. Be prepared to kill him. Remember that your failure will guarantee the girl suffers for all eternity."

Oaks breathed deeply, clenched and unclenched his fists and pounded on Nathan's door. It wasn't long ago that he'd been in this same place, fresh from the clinic, wanting to hang with his friend and show him some lyrics he'd written while locked away from the outside world. Things had changed rapidly, but essentially, the point then had been the same: to ask Nathan—a man he'd known since they were both in primary school together—to play music with him. His only real care, though, was to ensure that India's death didn't lead to a purgatory far darker than anything Dante could have dreamed of.

Nathan came to the door with a beer in his hand. From the smell of him, he'd already downed more than a few. Dense pot smoke floated in the air, "Boiled Over", a Gatecreeper track played in the background, and the guitarist swung away from the open door without a thought. "Come in," he said. "You know I won't turn you away."

Oaks hesitated, half-expecting a trap, before following Nathan down the hall. He stopped only when his host grabbed a beer from the fridge and tossed it at him. "About time you were open with me," he said. "We've been doing this for so long, but you tried to trick me. I don't get it."

Oaks paused. Inspected the can. It was a brand he hadn't seen before. Some seven per cent pale ale that Nathan had been inhaling all afternoon. There were close to a dozen empty cans scattered across the kitchen bench. Nathan's bloodshot eyes watched him with interest while he cracked the top.

"You gonna say anything?"

"You're drunk."

Nathan laughed. "That's who I am, your drunk friend.

And trust me, you're one of the only people who would call me that. Most would say I'm just a drunk asshole they know. Not you, though, you'd say I was your friend."

"I would."

"But you couldn't be real with me. You hid your bullshit like some creep. You think I haven't figured it out? Your deal with the devil? Shit's metal as fuck, dude. We could have called the album something like it; shown those black metal posers they're not the only ones."

"It's not like that."

"Bullshit."

He met Nathan's glare. If there was one thing he'd gathered from the seeming it was that it was far older than any religion he'd known. It was something else. Something from outer space or another dimension, but it wasn't religion that brought it here. Maybe whatever it was, whatever realm it had belonged to had influenced the ancestors of man when they were nothing more than gibbering monkeys, but it was nothing so easy to define as Nathan was suggesting.

A smoky grey tendril wisped its way into existence behind Nathan. "There are things you need to know. This isn't some glorious promise. I thought it was." He thought of India lying in her bed, unmoving. "There's a price to pay and I don't know what it is. I'm indebted. I'm down for the cause because I have no choice, but it's not right for me to—"

That ice-cold grip that had threatened to snuff his life force on so many occasions once again closed around his heart. This time it twisted. He fell to his knees and screamed.

Nathan spun.

Oaks, panting, appraised him. "We're a means to an end, and if you're in, I can make it happen. I don't think it means anything good for the world, though."

"Fuck the world."

"I...was...worried you were going to say that."

Oaks heard laughter. *"Do it. Make him offer the flesh!"*

"Fuck you."

Nathan looked at him like he was mad.

"Not you," he said to his old friend. "The entity. It's talking."

The grip squeezed again. Oaks fell to all fours.

More laughter.

Nathan watched, dumbfounded.

Oaks clutched his head and curled into a fetal position. "Fuck you. We have him, but you can let me explain! If he's going to give everything to you. Going to sacrifice himself, he needs to know the cost. If he changes his mind—"

"If he changes his mind, what?"

"We..."

"Say it!"

"We kill him!" Oaks sobbed the last, and when he faced Nathan, he was surprised to find him already on his knees. He held his hands in supplication, stretching his wrists out to Oaks in complete fealty.

"How do I do it? Do we need blood? Do I need to jerk off?"

His eagerness disgusted Oaks. The guy was a bigger mess than he'd ever thought. "Wait. Wait. You need to know that they're using me. They told Anton he would have power and they killed him; had me kill him. They lie."

"But will they make Polyphemus huge?"

"Yes. Tell him yes. He will play in the biggest band on the planet."

"Yes."

"Then I don't care the cost."

Oaks had a feeling that there mightn't be much left of the planet when all was said and done and that being the biggest band left on what amounted to a dead rock might be something of a let-down. "You need to know why I'm here, though, because if I could, I would turn away. Everyone is dead. Everyone except you and Spiros and..."

"Fuck Spiros."

"No! Not fuck Spiros! He's a good man and I need you to

say…" This time, the ice-cold grip didn't wrench his heart in a vice-like grip, it ripped it so hard, he could have sworn it was bursting through his ribcage. "Stop!" he said. "You have me where you want me. You have him where you want him, let me speak."

The seeming manifested beside him. It was every bit as huge and lumbering as it had been last night. It loomed over Oaks and Nathan like ominous darkness, swelling and growing with each second. Its horns tore the ceiling plaster. Its toothy maw drooled.

Nathan stared in awe.

"Before I killed Anton, he killed India, my India, and I entered into a pact to bring her back."

"You can have me. Bring her back. Take what you want. We'll both take what we've always wanted. We'll rock the fucking world."

"No!" Oaks pounded his fists on Nathan's chest. "She deserves peace. What I did was wrong. I shouldn't have asked in her absence. Don't you see?"

"Fuck her. Leave her there. You'll have all the bitches you want."

"I don't want. I want to die."

"That makes no sense. We could have it *all*."

"He's right. Have it all. Take it all."

"No. It's a lie. I know it now. I see it, but what I know is that if I fail, it won't only be me who burns in purgatory, it'll be her as well and you need to say yes for the right reason. Do you hear me? Not selfishness, not fame, but because you're prepared to deal with the consequences whether you say yes or no!"

Nathan grabbed his wrists and kissed them. "Tell me what to say! Tell me!"

Someone banged on the front door. Spiros called out, "Yo, Nate. You there? We need to talk!"

The seeming melted into smoke and shifted into Oaks. Nathan laughed louder than Oaks had heard him in ages.

Spiros knocked again.

"This couldn't be more perfect. Tell him to offer the flesh. Kill the other."

"Not yet. I need to talk to him first. I have to give him the option."

Nathan pulled harder on Oaks's wrists. "Who are you talking to? Is it him, the devil?"

Oaks yanked his arms free. "It's not the devil. It's something else, but I need you to listen. You need to talk to him before I do. Tell him what's going on. Don't tell him I'm here."

"But you can tell him."

Oaks shook his head. "He's not as stupid as you. He won't throw himself at this. He'll need to be convinced. Tell him we spoke, but don't tell him I'm here." He went down the hallway, entering Nathan's room. "I'll come out at the right moment. If you can't convince him about this, he'll die."

"You wouldn't."

"It won't be me, Nathan. It takes control. Spiros has a family. We can't allow them to be caught up in this as well."

Nathan stared at him, confused, mind addled by beer.

"Tell him everything."

Nathan nodded. Hopefully he'd get it right. Spiros had always been smarter than the others. He'd know what needed to be done.

"Hey, fuckhead!" Spiros thumped the door harder this time. "Open up. I hear you in there!" The easily recognizable riffs of Psycroptic's "Become the Cult" were grooving their way out of speakers, and raised voices, agitated and unclear amongst the wash of sound, cut over them. He couldn't quite make out who the other voice belonged to, but his suspicions were enough to fill him with dread.

He wriggled the doorknob, hoping it would open. When it didn't, he pounded again. "Dude! It's me, Spiros, open the door."

He had no clue what he was going to do if his fears proved correct and Oaks was in there. All he could do at this point was hope that he wasn't too late and that Nathan would listen to reason. Somehow, he didn't hold much hope for that. The dude was probably in the midst of another bender. If Oaks was in there, he could only hope the demonic entity didn't decide on violence again. If it did, the prospect of success was futile.

He pounded again, and eventually Nathan answered. "Hold your horses, dude. Shit." He opened the door, pulled Spiros into an unsteady bearhug and thrust a beer into his hand. "I thought I'd never see you again, man. I'm stoked you're here. This band's too good to abandon."

The dude had lost the plot. As he staggered away from Spiros to usher him through to the lounge-room, all he could do was rant on about how big the new album was going to make them. He hadn't bothered to ask how the girls were, and clearly hadn't understood Cormac's cancellation of the contract as an actual thing of importance.

Spiros felt the weight of the knife in the breast pocket of his jacket and hoped he'd be able to speak sense to his old friend. All the way here, he'd worried that the dude would do something dumb, but he was beginning to understand how far gone Nathan was. They might stop Oaks and cure him of whatever he'd done to himself, but Nathan knew there was a way to make that shit happen, and he'd reopen that box if it meant success for Polyphemus. Spiros couldn't allow that in a world where his daughter was going to live, and dammit, she was going to live.

They stepped into an empty lounge area. "Is anyone else here, bro? Thought I heard you talking to someone."

Nathan waved his hand dismissively. "Probably the

tunes."

"Yeah, probably." Spiros peered down the corridor that led to the bedrooms. "My mistake. Heard the music. Thought there were voices over the top."

A Revocation song had started playing. Wherever Nathan had found the playlist, it was cooking. This was one of the older ones. "Madness Opus" or something like that.

Nathan slid open the drawer in the coffee table and pulled out a bag of weed. "Bucket bong?"

"Roll a spliff." He sat on his favorite corner of the couch. He'd sat there a thousand times, watching horror movies and getting stoned.

Nathan spoke as he rolled the spliff with trembling fingers, not taking his eyes off the paper. "So you decided you wanted to push this thing ahead anyway."

Spiros bit his lip and clasped his hands together. "Nate, man, Cormac spoke to you. He spoke to me too. We're done. There's no label. We're gonna be tied up in court. Polyphemus is dead." And that didn't touch on the fact that they should all be grieving for Chops and Rusty. Cormac had told him on the phone there was no sign of trouble at Tomb, but he knew what he'd personally seen, and the fact no one had heard from those two spoke volumes. Shit was fucked up here, and it was going to fall on him to end it. He couldn't help but think of the old stories he'd loved so much as a kid, like Odysseus blinding the cyclops they'd taken the band's name from. The band had been running blindly into bullshit for too long, and it had to stop.

"We don't need a label, dude. Bandcamp, Patreon, Spotify…we can do it ourselves! Shit, you can't tell me one of the indies wouldn't be stoked to sign us."

Just like Poseidon's son, Nathan didn't know when he was beaten. He was going to rage. He was going to continue sprinting blind into further catastrophe, and there was no telling who would be caught up in the violence if he was able to meet with Oaks again. He'd give himself over faster than anyone could stop it. "I need to know if you've seen Oaks. People are looking for him. Same with Chops and Rusty." Spiros didn't like lying, but he wasn't sure how else to broach the subject. He had heard more than one voice, no matter what Nathan said.

Nathan swilled his beer, upending the can and crushing the empty with one hand. He staggered to the fridge. "Another?"

"Answer the question. Please."

"I spoke to him. On the phone. He said Chops and Rusty are fine. It was a hell of a trip, but we're all ready to record. They're waiting for us, there."

"Stop lying. Cormac told you what he saw. Tomb Studios is as pristine as it ever was. When *we* left the place, *it was on fire* and our friends were dead on the ground."

"That was a hallucination. The boys are there, waiting for us, but I've got to tell you something." He opened his beer and drank, eyes on the posters above the television.

Spiros pulled the hairband holding his ponytail tight, wondering how far down the left-hand path Nathan had gone. "What do you need to tell me?"

The music changed. An Opeth song came on. Again, something old from before they went all progressive. "Serenity Painted Death".

"The ritual he was doing. That part of it's not bullshit. He knows how to strike a bargain."

"No shit. You think I don't know that? That's why we have to stop him. That shit is bad news, and I don't want any part of it. I have a family. I have a future outside of this band, and if you think I'm going to fall prey to some sort of supernatural trick, you are out of your mind. I am done, and you need to be too."

"No, you don't get it. The thing, it's not like Satan. It's more like some sort of cosmic entity. It's not about heaven and hell. It's about ancient power."

"Listen to yourself. Listen to how mental you sound and

then listen to me. Whatever he's playing with, it's dangerous and that shit never goes according to plan. There's *always* a trick. The whole point of those stories is that the demons, the beings, the fucking devils or whatever you call them don't care. They lie. They trick. We mean nothing to them."

"But they'll give us what we want!"

Spiros dropped the last of the joint into an empty beer can and stood. "I need to piss, then I'm calling the cops. We need to report Chops and Rusty missing."

Nathan leapt from his own seat. "I told you already, they're at Tomb. They're waiting for us to come and finish recording!"

"They're dead! They're fucking dead!"

"But they're not. The entity took them. Oaks saw them. He told me. They're waiting! We meet them and Oaks there. We give ourselves to the entities and they give us what we want!"

He shoved Nathan hard and his old friend fell on the carpet. "Tell me, fuckhead, what is it that I want more than anything?"

"Polyphemus! Of course, like always."

"No! I want away from this insanity. I want to go to my family, and I want to leave this all behind. You need to grow up and deal with it. If you can't get there by working, if you've got to sell out to do it, you don't deserve it!"

Nathan was on his feet, wobbly, but upright. "What, you want that controlling, cheating wife to treat you like she always has? You want to walk away from this and live a life of meaningless nothing?" He staggered forward and grabbed Spiros by the collar.

"You've got to listen because there's more riding on this. If we don't agree, Oaks's demon will kill us and take us anyway. There's no escape. It took Oaks's girlfriend and he's trapped now. What do you think it will do to you? To Calliope and Pandora?"

This had gone far enough. Nathan couldn't be reasoned

with. If he couldn't be spoken down, he had to be stopped from striking the deal. Only one thing was going to make that a possibility. Spiros reached inside his breast pocket and pulled the knife. It was a small and simple utility knife he'd taken from the block in his kitchen.

Nathan didn't notice. He was too busy screaming at Spiros. "You've got to say yes, because if you don't, they'll take you anyway and your family will pay the price!" Spittle flew from his mouth as he shook the lead guitarist.

Spiros punched the blade into Nathan's chest.

Nathan's air left him in a whoosh, He fumbled for the blade protruding from his left pectoral muscle, baffled at its sudden appearance. "What the fuck?"

Spiros pulled the knife and drove it into him again, this time bringing it in from the side and sticking Nathan in his abdomen.

"Oaks!" Nathan called, "Help! Help!"

Spiros swung again, aiming for Nathan's heart.

Something crashed down the corridor from the direction of Nathan's room.

Spiros swung the knife again, half-expecting to see the beast coming out of the room, but only screams emanated from that part of the house.

CHAPTER TWENTY-THREE
EVERBLACK

In Nathan's bedroom, Oaks was fighting his own battle. Listening to his two oldest and truest friends arguing, he'd realized that things would be so much simpler if he wasn't here.

He rifled through the drawer in the ensuite room, stopping when he found the tuck of razor blades next to the shaver and brush. He'd doomed India. He'd doomed himself. If he could step into that doom before anyone else got hurt, he could maybe stop the entity from taking what it wanted. He reached for the blades with his blackened hand, but as he closed his grip on them, the black fluid the creature had manifested to replace his flesh disappeared, leaving only the skeletal bones and carpals visible. The pain was beyond any he'd experienced. He snatched the razors with his other hand and the entity's cold grip closed over his heart. The seeming had assumed its full bestial form again. It lifted him from the ground, leaving him flailing and crying.

"Your death will come soon enough, human."

It threw him out of the ensuite and into the bedroom. He crashed into the bed and sprawled to his feet as fast as he could.

He crumpled the paper wrapping from the first razor, clenched his bone hand, raising his arm up so the beast could see, and repeatedly slashed the blade down the length of the radial artery. Blood spewed from the lacerations, and he couldn't help but think of the classic image of the arm with

SLAYER cut into it. He slashed again and again and blood wept freely, sluicing over his elbow and dripping onto the carpet.

He heard India's laughter. The seeming had shifted into her shape. It stood only a few feet from Oaks, laughing with joy. *"Don't you want to save me from an eternity of torment? I thought you loved me. I thought you wanted to dwell in your sorrow and your pain?"*

"You're not her."

The cuts in his arm, some deep and deadly, swelled. The black fluid that had replaced the flesh on his arm filled the wounds, stemming the flow of blood.

"You cannot escape your fate."

Oaks bellowed with rage. He upended the remaining blades, tipping them into his mouth, chewed, and swallowed, grimacing with pain as they cut their way through his throat.

India—the seeming—laughed with joy and shifted into the huge shape of the entity. It grabbed Oaks by the throat, cutting off his windpipe, closing off any hope of the blades finding further passage. *"We can start your torment now."*

The being shook him, and the blades reversed direction. His throat caught, and he realized they were working their way out. The first exploded from somewhere behind his jugular, cutting it as it passed. It spun out of him like a projectile and lodged itself in the plaster of the wall, near the light switch. Blood fountained out of the wound for a second, and then black fluid smothered the damage, preventing Oaks from ending his own life.

The other blades soon followed. One cut through his gums. Another burst out the back of his neck. One more took a chunk of his Adam's apple. The rest clattered into objects around the room.

The seeming dropped him to the floor, where he crumpled into a fetal position. *"We'll let you feel the pain of those. But you will begin your work. Your friends are fighting in the front room. It is time you ended it. Take the one called*

Spiros."

"Fuck you. You do it."

"It has to be your choice. You will act!"

Something Oaks hadn't previously considered popped into his mind. In all the time he'd been under the entity's sway, it had been able to stop him hurting himself, but when it came to others, it had never been the seeming that acted. "Prove you can hurt others like you hurt me."

"Act now or forever suffer with your dead bitch and your guilt."

"You can't do it. You let me think you could, but I'm the only one you can physically hurt. You can stop my heart, but when you possess me, you insist on choice because you can't force me. I'm not doing it anymore. I'd rather die."

The seeming melted into smoke and entered him again. His wounds disappeared beneath the black tar. His body swelled and contorted as the demon took shape inside him. Antlers pushed from his brow. Muscles bulged. His legs elongated and coarse fur burst from his pores. His face stretched into a snout and sharp teeth burst from his mouth.

The door to Nathan's room swung open. Spiros stood in the entry. Blood covered him from head to toe. None of it seemed to be his.

"Kill him!"

Oaks fought the impulse to charge his old friend. "Spiros! Run. It cannot hurt you unless I choose it!"

Spiros hesitated. Stammered. "You...you have to die, my friend."

Oaks roared. The beast wouldn't allow anyone to hurt him. It would safeguard its vessel and fight to the death for it, but if Spiros ran, the creature couldn't hurt him. "Run! Take Nathan and run!"

Spiros glanced to his right.

"Where's Nathan?"

Spiros wiped his face. "Nathan is not going anywhere."

"You killed him?"

"He's alive. I think. I came to see you."

"Do not attack me, Spiros. If you do…"

Spiros lunged.

The creature's giant bone fist crashed into his face with a tremendous crunch, sending him sprawling back into the loungeroom. He shook his head and gripped the knife. "You have to die. This has gone too far."

The creature slapped itself in the face and its monstrous head gave way to Oaks's bald one. The horns were gone. Oaks's familiar eyes stared out at him. "Listen to me. The spirit—the seeming—can only protect me, can only hurt me. All the death. All the murder. It was me. It tricked me into choosing, and I chose!" Tears ran down his face and then the monstrous body disappeared. Oaks was left on all fours, sobbing.

Spiros put his knife in his pocket and stepped forward. "How can I help you? A church?"

Oaks laughed. "No, man. This is something else. Perhaps something that influenced the demons we learned about in school, but not one of them."

Spiros, despite the bizarre situation, chuckled too. "Okay, so it's worse than that. Great." He crouched down over the vocalist. "How do we stop it?"

"I don't think we can. Take your family and run."

"It's not right."

"Promise me you'll never offer it your flesh."

Spiros remembered what they'd all been chanting at the ritual. "That's how it gets in?"

"It's one of the ways. I think you have to speak it. Whether in dreams or in life, you have to speak the words that allow it entry."

"I promise I will never allow it entry."

Despair crawled over Oaks. "Nathan!"

"I told you, he's—"

Something hard and heavy slammed into Spiros. He dropped to his knees.

Nathan stood over him, holding a poker. The hook dripped with gore.

Spiros realized Nathan had hit him with the curved point, drawing blood.

Oaks held pleading hands out to Nathan, but it did no good.

Nathan drove the weapon down like a spear. The greatest pain Spiros had ever experienced ripped through his upper back, his ribcage, and his chest. The hooked black tool punched out of him. He collapsed with a groan. Blood filled the corners of his mouth. His eyes were bloodshot. His shirt was soaked through with his vital fluids, and he smelled like shit.

Nathan fell beside him.

Spiros clawed himself away from his old friend, coughing and wheezing. He was done for, but surely Nathan was dying too. He'd stuck him at least a dozen times; was sure he'd hit vital organs. The Greek climbed to his knees, using the wall to brace himself. The poker impaling him weighed heavily, casting him off-balance. Blood bubbled out of his mouth as he fought the urge to lie down and sleep.

Oaks was convulsing. The monster was reasserting control of its host's body. Nathan had clambered to his knees and had raised his hands in supplication to it. Dimly, he was aware that the stereo was blasting a playlist fit for his last days on Earth. Pig Destroyer's "The Diplomat" was ripping out of the speakers.

"Tell me what to say," Nathan said. "Polyphemus will rule the world."

The horned beast stood huge. It reached its bone hand down to Nathan's chin. Tilted his face upward. "Very well, my friend." It punched itself in the face again.

Oaks's head reappeared in place of the monster's. His internal battle was tearing him apart, but if there was one thing Spiros had to do, it was prevent Nathan from speaking the words that would give the entity—or its kindred spirits—access to him. He fumbled for his knife, wincing as he knocked the poker weighing him down, and pushed himself forward with a desperate thrust.

The knife punched into Nathan's mouth, stabbing right through his gum and dislodging teeth. He collapsed, screaming, trying to pull away from the weapon. Spiros held onto it like a climbing pick, knowing he had to stop Nathan from speaking the words.

He struggled with his old friend, with the man he'd called brother on a million occasions, unsure as to who was more wounded. The poker sent agony through him every time he moved, but he fought on, desperate not to lose. He thrust his hand into Nathan's screaming mouth, grabbing his tongue. It was slippery with blood, but he got enough of a grip on the man's lower jaw to pull himself closer and get purchase. He ripped the utility knife from Nathan's face and plunged it into the pried-open maw. He pressed down with the blade, sawing and tearing, doing whatever he could to sever the man's treacherous tongue.

When he ripped it free and cast it aside, he wondered why the entity hadn't stopped him.

Oaks was once again involved in a battle of his own. This time, though, he was winning. Smoke, something like a shaded smudge on an artist's canvas was boiling out of him like steam. As it exited, wounds previously covered by a black substance appeared all over Oaks. Any normal man would have died already, but he was alive and kicking,

Painfully aware of the blood soaking his clothes and his own weakness, Spiros watched the smudge, which he thought of as some sort of corrupted reality, begin to gather around Nathan. The dude's chest was rising and falling, but from the rattling sound, it was obvious he didn't have long.

"You have to kill me. While you have a chance." Oaks croaked.

"But it's done. Nathan cannot speak," he said weakly. "Please."

Oaks shook his head. "You have to. I will fail the beast, but I've already failed India. She suffers either way. This way, I suffer with her. She won't be alone."

Nathan was dying. He had to be. He could feel air escaping from places it had no right to. His mouth was full of blood and agony, and he'd shit his pants as well. That was the last thing that happened when you died, right? You shat your pants.

That would explain why he was in Hell. Last he knew, he was in his home, dying after driving a poker through Spiros's back. The red sky and the roiling black clouds above a swarming crowd of black-clad metal fans suggested he'd left all that behind. He was before a stage built to resemble a sacrificial altar.

He followed the crowd and joined their thronging mass. He barged through the thick of them and made his way to the moshpit. Others clamored with him, but he was experienced at this. Had done it a thousand times and would do it a thousand more. He pushed through the pit and made his way to the front row. The drummer, Chops, finished his soundcheck and the vocalist came to the stage. He was shocked to see that it was Oaks as he'd known him in the ritual. He'd thought for a second it might be Corey, but Oaks was the naked one wearing the goat's skull. Always had been.

"Before we begin, there's one thing we need to know. Will

you motherfuckers give yourselves to us?"

Around him, the crowd threw the horns and cheered in response.

"Then repeat after me! This is the mark of the willing!"

Nathan repeated the words.

The music had stopped. Pig Destroyer had finished and what should have been the bridge section of Inferi's "Behold the Bearer of Light" had given way to something else. It sounded like a live album. Only the chant was unknown to him. "This is the mark of the willing!" the vocalist called. The audience responded with the same cry.

Nathan flinched beneath the seeming.

Shit.

Nathan's empty fireplace, unused for months, erupted in green flame. A black shape cavorted inside.

Panicking, Oaks screamed at Spiros. "Cut off his fucking head! Cut off his fucking head!"

Spiros, woozy, was resting against the wall. His head drooped. He didn't have long left, but Oaks had to rouse him for one last action. "Get up!"

Spiros stared.

"It's not done. Nate's dreaming. He's saying the words. He's saying the fucking words. You've got to kill him."

"How?"

"The poker. Put it through his skull."

"It hurts too much. I can't."

The green glowing from the fireplace was getting stronger. The music—the concert he thought might have been taking place in Nathan's head—was getting louder on the stereo system. "This is the mark of the destined!" called the vocalist. The audience responded and Nathan flinched again.

Oaks didn't know if Spiros's knife would be enough. He'd seen the entity reanimate Chops and Rusty, but he had to hope that was a trick, something to manipulate him into doing its bidding. He wanted to cut off Nathan's head. That always worked in the movies. No demon could make use of a reanimated corpse if it had no head. He had nothing in here to cut with, though. Spiros's knife wouldn't do the trick. Short of options, he'd have to stomp it in. Things were getting too close.

"This is the mark of the inviting flesh!" Called the vocalist on the stereo. The audience responded.

Oaks ran to Nathan's prone body and stomped his Doc Martens boot down, attempting to kick the guitarist in the face. As soon as the sole met flesh, the seeming swelled, making its presence as a huge beast felt once again. It swatted Oaks away.

"I might not be able to hurt anyone except you here, but you'd better believe I can make her eternity complete hell!" It shifted into India's shape. As if an invisible hand ripped it, a strip of flesh began to detach from her face in a thin ribbon, revealing the musculature and skull beneath. Another strip followed. And another.

Oaks tried to clamber to his feet. The ominous green glow was creeping into the room, and he was certain a black, cavorting shape was getting closer with each moment.

"We are the willing!" the vocalist on the speaker growled. "We are the destined!"

Spiros wrapped both hands around the poker and tugged. The meat of his wounded pectoral muscle squelched as the makeshift weapon ripped through him. He looked to the sky and roared, pulling it clean through. Blood gurgled from the wound. Using the tool as a crutch and pushing himself to his feet, he struggled to Nathan's prone form. His shoulders heaving, he slammed the poker down into his old friend's face, driving it through his eye socket and into his brain.

"You're nobody! Nobody!" He wrenched the iron from side to side and wrenched it out. "You were always nobody!" he gasped, before pressing the makeshift weapon against Nathan's remaining eye and applied pressure. The poker plunged through. A spurt of white fluid burst like pus across Nathan's face. "Your dreams were shit." He stirred the tool, going to town on the brain until Nathan's death rattles stopped. "We were all nobody!" He was crying and screaming, but as he felt the heavy implement crack through the back of Nathan's skull, the green glow began to dissipate.

The seeming roared.

Spiros watched it lift Oaks by the throat and roar in the vocalist's face. *"You will regret this course of action! You will suffer forever."*

"It's worth it, you fuck!" Spiros couldn't believe it, but Oaks started to laugh. "I can't believe I fell for your shit. That Anton fell for your shit. You're nothing." The bald man kicked out, and for the first time the monster physically reacted to the blow, sprawling away from them.

Oaks fell to the floor.

The monster was up again in no time, and it stalked toward him. Oaks wasn't deterred, though. "Take me," he said. "Take me to whatever pit, whatever void, whatever cave you call home and torture me forever, but I promise you this: I will never do your bidding again."

Spiros crawled closer to Oaks, who pulled him to his feet. "How do we stop it?" he asked. He stumbled, but Oaks kept him upright.

"Destroy its vessel."

The monster closed a hand on Oaks's chest, but Oaks kicked it again. This time, it didn't fall, but it was rebuffed, and it tried a different tactic. It shifted shape. Became India again. *"Destroy yourself and she'll suffer forever."*

Spiros spat blood. Pressed his hand to his gaping chest. "Oaks…"

"I deserve it. I killed Corey and Hank and Chops. I killed Anton. It was all me. Never the monster. It could only influence me. It was me who did it and I need to take responsibility."

"Do it in prison."

"I'm weak. I'll give up in there. Relapse. It'll take me again, and who knows what happens then."

In the shape of India, the entity pleaded, wailing as strips of flesh were flayed from her face and her bones cracked into odd shapes.

"It's biding its time now. It lies. It manipulates. That's what it does. Kill me. I have to die." He reached for Spiros's hands and pressed the knife against his own throat. "It can stop me from applying pressure, but not you." He grabbed Spiros's face with both hands. "I always loved you cunts," he said. "I'm sorry. I'm so sorry. I just hope that when I get to where I'm going, she's not there and the seeming lied about her."

Spiros pushed the knife into Oaks's jugular and fell to his haunches, coughing blood and feeling the weight of impending death dragging him down. Arterial blood gushed out in a huge spray and Oaks collapsed onto his knees.

"I'm sorry, Stephen. I'm sorry."

Oaks met his eyes for a brief moment before he crumpled to the carpet. Blood pooled beneath him.

Spiros wondered if the monster had remained here. It hadn't.

He fell to his back and blood poured from his wound. He wished he had a phone or some way to call an ambulance or Pandora or Calliope. It would never happen. He was too weak to get up, let alone crawl. He could only hope they knew he loved them and was sorry he hadn't listened to them sooner. Sorry he hadn't just forgotten about this stupid band. Sorry he hadn't taken them away from here.

His vision was fading. The smell of blood, his own as well as everyone else's was thick in the air and his time was short. As he wondered whether Oaks was in Hell with his girlfriend, he thought about his own eternity. He hadn't had time to get his last rites in order. For him, it didn't matter whether Saint Peter thought he was a good man, but he wanted to be able to judge himself in his last few moments. Given the way he'd let his family down, he wasn't sure he'd done enough. As he wept, the stereo kicked into action again and The Black Dahlia Murder came out of the speaker: "Into the Everblack". It was the last song he ever heard.

His blood ran from his body, spreading beneath him. His last wheezing breaths slowly leaked from his lungs and his pain ebbed away. In moments, the music on the stereo was the only thing that played on.

ZACHARY ASHFORD | 299

A NOTE FROM
DARKLIT PRESS

All of us at DarkLit Press want to thank you for taking the time to read this book. Words cannot describe how grateful we are knowing that you spent your valuable time and hard-earned money on our publication. We appreciate any and all feedback from readers, good or bad. Reviews are extremely helpful for indie authors and small businesses (like us). We hope you'll take a moment to share your thoughts on Amazon, Goodreads and/or BookBub.

You can also find us on all the major social platforms including Facebook, Instagram, and Twitter. Our horror community newsletter comes jam-packed with giveaways, free or deeply discounted books, deals on apparel, writing opportunities, and insights from genre enthusiasts.

VISIT OUR LITTLE-FREE-LIBRARY OF HORRORS!

ACKNOWLEDGMENTS

EASTER EGGS, CHAPTER TITLES, AND WEARING YOUR HEART ON YOUR SLEEVE

Words from the author and some more acknowledgements...

Every time I think I'm finally done with this book, which at this stage of my journey as an author, is the biggest thing I've ever written, something comes up and leaves me thinking I need to say something to avoid an oversight.

So...

First of all, the beta readers who helped me make this book everything it can be, the artists, and those who helped with praise and blurbs: Dan Russell, Steve Stred, Kev Harrison (who I first spoke to about this book over beers in Lisbon), Val T Loughcrewe, Dan Scamell, Joe Ortlieb, and Gav Britton, you all helped make this better.

Jota Cravo and Greg Chapman are the two artists who have changed the way I see this book. When I reached out to Jota, I didn't expect that a bloke who'd done work for some killer bands would want to help. Not only did he jump at the chance, but he knocked it out of the park. That front cover image fills me with joy every time I see it. Thanks, Jota! Greg Chapman contributed the internal illustrations. I gave him some descriptions and told him I wanted something like Berni Wrightson's in The Stand. The artistically inclined among you are probably shaking your heads right now, but Greg's illustrations are phenomenal. The visceral brutality he captured warms my heart. Thanks, brother!

Everyone who helped me pump out the praise section in the front of the book. (And here, I'm not gonna name people because there are still some on the way in before we go to print, and that would be unfair!) You know who you are!

Moving on, I

It's no secret this book is basically a representation of my passions in novel-form. This book is a real labour of love, and for want of a better metaphor, it's the monster I've Frankensteined into existence with equal parts metal music, horror novels, horror films and tragic narratives (yeah, there's a reason it starts with the modern equivalent of 'Who's there?'.

But let's start with the titles of Polyphemus's songs – and even one of The Violent Dead's. These are all little nods to books, plays, and films I love. The astute among you will see references to *Phantasm, The Thing, The Wasp Factory, Hamlet, Macbeth, Romeo and Juliet,* and even a nod to John Langan's incredible work of fiction, *The Fisherman.* Thanks, John. That book is an all-timer for me and you've created something I'll always treasure, so I hope you don't mind me alluding to it with the song title 'On the Shore of the Black Ocean'.

There's more, but I don't want to spoil all the fun for readers. Finding things like that is part of what makes fiction so great. At least for me.

When it comes to chapter titles, though, I definitely have to say a word. One of the things I really wanted to do with this was share my love of metal music. It's been a lifelong journey for me, and although I wouldn't say I was ever a scene kid, and my tastes in metal evolved as I grew older, I still love it with all my heart. As a result, I tried to keep a little bit of everything from the earliest days of my love affair with heavy music to the most recent in this book.

Of course, I won't write a million words about every album mentioned. Music is personal. For me, some of these albums are ones I dig that I think fit the tone of the novel. There are others I love with every fiber of my being. This can be because of special moments in my life, and usually, it is. Music can be like scent with the things it evokes.

When my mother passed away, it was a shock that no one saw coming. I was at a music festival. The band performing was The Black Dahlia Murder. They were touring on *Everblack,* and that album will always hold a special place in my heart, not only because it rips – which it does – but because I can't hear it and not remember the good times with my mother.

Fear Factory's *Demanufacture* is an album that has stayed with me since I was a teenager. I was probably thirteen when it came out. I may have been twelve. I could probably look that up, but it doesn't really matter. Of all the albums I loved as a teen, that's the one that will not be denied by evolving tastes. There are no doubt old photos of me rocking my *Demanufacture* hoodie in the middle of a Queensland summer. On a similar note, the first time I saw the band, we were older, but I remember having a spare fifty bucks. I had a single ticket. On the way, I pulled into my mate Brian's house and told him I had enough to get him a ticket. Together, we had blasted that album on a million occasions. I still love that guy! Brian, this one's for you as much as anyone else.

Anyway, I'm waffling. All I'm going to add is that one of the things that made my day as a young metalhead was checking out the acknowledgements in the back of the CD liner notes and checking out the bands. I'm not sure if kids still do that, but I hope they do. I really hope they do.

In that spirit and without further ado, here's the full list of album references from chapter titles.

Chapter One: Of Rot and Ruin (Hath)
Chapter Two: Demanufacture (Fear Factory)
Chapter Three: The Necrotic Manifesto (Aborted)
Chapter Four: Death is This Communion (High on Fire)
Chapter Five: Ritual (The Black Dahlia Murder)
Chapter Six: Underneath a Melting Sky (Inanimate Existence)

Fortunately, we've created a playlist for you on Spotify. Go forth, listen, and bang your fucking head!

LISTEN HERE

As you can see, some of these are new, some of these are not. There are other albums I could talk about here, but I'm just going to write the list and let you pick and choose what appeals to you. If you want to know what I was listening to when I wrote this book, you can look for the references in the text, because there are some there that aren't mentioned here. Whether you're already a metalhead, or you're a youngster starting out in the genre, there's some gold here. I hope your journey gives you as much joy as mine has – and will continue to.

So, finally, thanks to every band, author, film-maker, screenwriter or director that has enabled me to experience so much joy.

To you, the reader, once you leave here, I hope you can go and create something you're passionate about. It all makes the world a better place.

And if we're not making the world better, what are we doing?

Be kind, be compassionate, and share your love with the world.

-Zachary Ashford.

ABOUT THE AUTHOR

Zachary Ashford is an Australian author, educator, and speaker. His dystopian horror novella *When the Cicadas Stop Singing* was nominated for the Aurealis Award. His other works include the *Sole Survivor* books, *Autotomy Cocktail*, and *Encampment by the Gorge & Blood Memory*. His short fiction has been published by various presses. His love of Ozploitation creature features has seen him called 'a master of bush horror'. When he's not writing stories about the human condition while surrounded by action figures and monstrous memorabilia, he's listening to death metal, hanging with his amazing wife, chilling with his son, or playing with his cat.

CONTENT WARNINGS

I remember when talk of content warnings first became a big deal on the internet. It was an interesting time when many voiced concerns about the idea that horror shouldn't need triggers. I can't say that tracks with me. I love horror. I love violent fiction. I love a good scare and severe tension, but in—and out—of horror, I've chosen not to finish books because elements of what was happening didn't sit right with me. That doesn't mean I'm right or wrong. It just means that I like having the right to choose what I read, should I so desire. The same stands for everyone.

I've scoured the internet for content warnings when I've felt like a book might be taking a path I didn't fancy. I've also been confronted by things that I don't typically want to read in a book with no warning whatsoever.

It's not nice.

That said, I understand how some people don't need content warnings and don't want them. They like the shock. That's also fine, and that's why I like the idea of putting them in the back of the book. You can easily check them, and you can easily avoid them. Everyone wins. And at the end of the day, caring for each other is easy.

So, because Polyphemus is a work of horror, it contains themes and plot-points that some may like to be warned about. I've tried to be comprehensive. If I've missed anything, please forgive me. Inside this book, you will find:

Intravenous drug-use and references

Gore

Sudden violence

Demonic sex

Demonic rituals

Demonic possession

Animal sacrifice

Fart jokes

Alcohol abuse

Toxic relationships

Misogynistic attitudes

Pissweak men who fuck everything up

Sexual references

Murder

The loss of a baby (off-screen)

Frequent bro-ing down

DARKLIT
PRESS

Printed in the USA
CPSIA information can be obtained
at www.ICGtesting.com
LVHW040714271023
762259LV00009B/83

9 781738 705474